LYNN VIEHL

THE CLOCKWORK WOLF

BOOK 2 OF THE DISENCHANTED & CO. SERIES

Pocket Books

New York London Toronto Sydney New Delhi

Pocket Books
A Division of Simon & Schuster, Inc.
1230 Avenue of the Americas
New York, NY 10020

This book is a work of fiction. Any references to historical events, real people, or real places are used fictitiously. Other names, characters, places, and events are products of the author's imagination, and any resemblance to actual events or places or persons, living or dead, is entirely coincidental.

Copyright © 2014 by Sheila Kelly

All rights reserved, including the right to reproduce this book or portions thereof in any form whatsoever. For information, address Pocket Books Subsidiary Rights Department, 1230 Avenue of the Americas, New York, NY 10020.

First Pocket Books paperback edition March 2014

POCKET and colophon are registered trademarks of Simon & Schuster, Inc.

For information about special discounts for bulk purchases, please contact Simon & Schuster Special Sales at 1-866-506-1949 or business@simonandschuster.com.

The Simon & Schuster Speakers Bureau can bring authors to your live event. For more information or to book an event, contact the Simon & Schuster Speakers Bureau at 1-866-248-3049 or visit our website at www.simonspeakers.com.

Cover illustration by Gordon Crabb

Manufactured in the United States of America

10 9 8 7 6 5 4 3 2 1

ISBN 978-1-4767-2237-5
ISBN 978-1-4767-3061-5 (ebook)

For Darlene Ryan,
with love and gratitude.
Fortitudine vincimus.

CHAPTER ONE

"Morning, miss." Damp-cheeked and rosy from the steam rising from her cart, my favorite tealass, Sally, handed over a mug of her strongest morning brew. "Sold out me sticky buns early today, sorry. Crumpets are quite nice."

"Then I'll have two." I took a grateful sip of my tea and glanced at a gang of brickies patching the west wall of an assayer's building. "Business picking up now that they've carted out the rubble?"

"Oh, yes, miss. Tho' even after our boys sunk all them Talian ships what blasted us, me da wanted me to sell from the bakery, but I told him Rumsen'd be back to rights in no time." She sniffed. "Batty lot, sailing in at dawn, banners flapping bold as you please. What'd they think we'd do, run off to Settle?"

"Well, they certainly weren't expecting a fight." Indeed, the Talians had been promised quite the opposite: to find every soul in the city rendered helpless by magic. Fortunately the massive, nightmarish spell that would have enslaved our citizens had never been cast— but if I explained to Sally how I knew those details, she'd think *I* was the loon. "Morning paper out yet?"

"Just dropped off. Oy, Jimmy." She whistled to catch the attention of the little newsboy working the corner. "Bring us a daily for the missus."

Jimmy trotted over and offered me a string-tied bundle. "Couple of beaters were 'tacked last night, miss. Savaged, they were, by the beastie chap again—you know, the Wolfman. S'all front page."

"I imagine it is." I handed him some coins. "And did they lock up this beastie chap?"

"Couldn't catch him." He scratched the side of his face, connecting some of his freckles with smudges from his inky fingers. "Thing is, they said they had him last Tuesday, and some say he were even kilt."

I exchanged an amused look with Sally. "Maybe they caught the wrong beastie."

"Aye. Or there could be two." Looking hopeful, he touched the rim of his cap before he scurried back to his patch by the lamppost.

"Beastie men my aunt Frances," Sally said, shaking her head. "Some drunken brave in a fur, more like."

I watched an elegant young lady and her mother stroll by with a gleaming brass lamb on a tether. The animech bleated and wagged its tail, although it had been placed on a wheeled cart to prevent it from having to be rewound to walk every block. "Maybe it was a clockwork beast," I joked.

"I don't think they make them that big yet. Although I did have a gentleman stop yesterday who had a hawk. Covered the mech with real feathers." She tilted her head to one side. "Miss, you know that grand mage chap all the nobs fancy? The one what can kill with a blink, all legal like?"

"Lord Lucien Dredmore." I had killed him once, but then had been daft enough to bring him back to life; as a result I couldn't deny the acquaintance. "He can be a beast, but I doubt he's the Wolfman. All that fur, too vulgar for him."

"I don't mean the beast, I mean him." She lifted her chin toward my office building. "He's standing right over there, watching you."

So much for my pleasant morning. "Best sell me another crumpet then, Sally."

I took my time finishing my tea before I bid the cartlass good day and crossed the street. While I should have politely acknowledged the dark and brooding presence of Toriana's much-acclaimed and endlessly feted grand master of the dark arts, I didn't care to start my workday by bobbing before Lord Dredmore.

"Morning, Lucien." I managed a civil nod. "Are you lost, or slumming?"

"I am never the former, and only for you the latter." He gave my building one of his snide looks before he inspected me. "You've been avoiding me, Charmian."

Once I had, like the plague, until certain events had been set into motion by a phony curse, a nasty possession, and an invasion of the city. Mayhem and magic had solved most of the lot, but since then things between Lucien Dredmore and me had become rather more than less complicated.

"I've been busy." Partly true; now to choose the rest of my words with care. "How may I direct you to a better part of town?"

He took hold of my arm. "We should talk in your office."

I allowed Dredmore to escort me to the fourth floor but stopped him at the hall entry. "Wait here."

"Why?"

"Not all the crumpets are for you." I walked down to where an old woman sat huddled on my threshold. The skirts of her shabby gown had been patched so many times they resembled a mad checkerboard, and they were dirtier than usual. From the whistling rattle of her wheezing, I concluded that Gert had dozed off while waiting on me.

I reached down to give her shoulder a pat. "Come on, love. You'll get a neck crick, sleeping like that."

Two bleary eyes nestled in nests of wrinkled skin fluttered and then peered. "What? Where? Oh." She scowled. "It's you, demon's harlot. What vile work have you been at? I've been waiting hours, I have."

"I'm afraid Satan delayed me this morning." I helped her up and glanced at the glass window that she hadn't yet defaced. "Run out of death curses, or is this your half day?"

"Lost me grease pencil." She pushed out her lower lip. "Old tosser at the mission likely nicked it. They've all sticky fingers down there." She fumbled with her reticule before she extracted her wand and gave it a shake. "I cast this spell of doom on you, unwholesome soul, that you be swallowed up"—she trailed off into a damp cough, and had to clear her throat several times before she could continue—"I mean, devoured entirely by the blackest bottomless pit in the Netherside." She gave my arm a halfhearted swat.

After the few seconds of silence that out of respect I afforded her spells, I handed her the spare crumpet. "Straight from the cart, I promise. Now what are you doing at the mission?"

"Can't get work, and lost me room in the attack." She

tore open the wrapping and took a big bite. "Wretched Talians turned half the city into scram."

The damp cough meant she'd probably been sleeping outside, too. I thought for a moment. "Tinker Elias on Kearney Street always needs good rags. He'll want clean, but he pays in coin."

"Does he now?" Crumbs rained from Gert's chin as she gobbled up the rest of the crumpet. "I'll get to it, then." She hesitated before she added, "Might not be here tomorrow, but you'll not dodge my wrath forever, mind."

"Wouldn't dream of it." I watched her scurry off, feeling satisfied over my good deed until a long shadow crossed my own. "I asked for a minute."

The black slashes of his eyebrows elevated. "Do you always provide tea to vagrants who wish you ill?"

I gave him my sweetest smile. "You're here, aren't you?"

Once inside the office I opened the shades and checked the tube port. Along with the usual pile of post there were some fly-ads from the neighborhood merchants and a small box wrapped in brown paper. I put the post on my desk with the remaining crumpets, tossed the ads into the rubbish, and set the package in my coal bucket before covering it with the lid.

Dredmore watched from the doorway. "No sender's name on the parcel?"

"On that sort, there never is." I filled the kettle at the pipe basin.

"Why not open it?"

"I used to. The ones they pack with runes or stones or

spell packets are harmless enough, but occasionally"—I paused as a thump came from inside the bucket—"there's something with teeth."

Dredmore glanced at the window. "So the local mages still want you out."

"Aye, and you'd think they'd occasionally try a bribe. Don't bother," I added as he moved toward it. "I give the live ones to Docket when I go downstairs for coal."

"What does he do with them?"

"You know, I've never asked. I worry dining might be involved." I brought the kettle over to my tea stand and set it on the steamdog. "Now why don't you tell me what can't be heard outside my office?"

He joined me. "One of my clients is in need of your services."

"*My* services." I pondered that along with my selection of tea. "Did you eat your breakfast, Dredmore, or drink it from a flask?"

He took the teaheart from me and removed a silver packet from his coat. "Under ordinary circumstances I would attend to it personally." He thumbed open the infuser and shook in some gray-green leaves. "The lady in question, however, wishes to employ a discreet woman."

There it was, his real motive. "So you want me because I'm a female." I watched him place the infuser in my kettle and close the lid. "I can't believe I just said that."

He loomed a little closer. "Your gender is a significant part of your allure."

I could feel his body heat now. "Here I thought you fancied me for my mind." I switched on the BrewsMaid and moved to my desk, only to be halted by his hand on my wrist. "Please, Lucien. It's far too early in the day for a wrestling bout."

"Stop struggling." He touched my hair, from which he extracted a small brown leaf. "Your mop is a veritable magnet for detritus. You should wear a hat when you're out of doors."

"Ladies wear hats," I reminded him. "I'm a working gel."

He smoothed back the tress he'd deleafed before he murmured, "You don't have to be, Charmian."

If we continued down this conversational avenue I'd likely hit him, so I stepped away. "Moving back to business," I said briskly, "I have a full schedule today. Who or what does your client wish dispelled?"

"Your spell-breaker powers are not wanted this time." He walked over to my window and looked down at the street. "The lady recently lost her husband under abrupt and distressing circumstances. While the coroner ruled his death the result of natural causes, the widow believes it was quite the opposite, and wants proof to that effect. Naturally such an investigation must be conducted with the utmost discretion."

Oh, naturally. Dredmore moved in the highest and most exclusive circles in Rumsen society, so the lady was likely fabulous wealthy, titled, or both. In the past I'd done some work for his sort of patron, but I always ended up regretting it.

"If she's your client, why won't she let you manage it?" Before he replied something occurred to me. "Did *you* kill him?"

"No." He gave me an indifferent glance; death was

7

LYNN VIEHL

his business. "And if I had, I might have easily bespelled her to forget the matter."

He made it sound as if he'd wanted to. "This really isn't the type of work I do. If the lady suspects her husband was murdered, then she should go to the police."

"She has, and they are unwilling to pursue the matter." He came toward me, and now seemed slightly agitated. "I cannot tell you any more than I have; she is adamant about confiding the details of her suspicions only to another woman. All I ask is that you hear what she has to say. If after the interview you still wish to refuse, then I will not press you." He took my hand in his. "Please."

Lucien Dredmore did not employ that particular word with any frequency; I could count on one hand the number of times I'd heard him utter it.

"Very well." I checked my brooch watch. "Have the lady here at noon and I'll talk to her."

"The matter requires more privacy than your office can afford," Dredmore said. "I'll send my driver for you at four."

I shook my head. "I haven't time for tea. Besides, anyone who sees me on the Hill will know I'm working for her."

"It won't be on the Hill." He lifted my hand, and before I could snatch it back brushed a kiss across my knuckles. "Until later."

He swept out of my office, leaving me alone with my misgivings and whatever was thumping inside the coal bucket.

I glanced down at the rocking parcel. "I should have slipped you into his coat pocket."

Since I didn't want to drink whatever potion Dredmore

8

had brewed with his strange-colored leaves I emptied the kettle into the bucket. As soon as the greenish tea soaked into the box it gave a violent jump and bubbled furiously before going still. From the metallic stink that rose from rapidly blackening tea, whatever was inside the box might have more gears than teeth.

I picked up the bucket. "We'd better pay a visit to the Dungeon and find out just what sort of surprise you are."

I went downstairs, nodding to some of the other tenants who passed me as they arrived to begin their workday. Among them was my former ardent suitor and present good friend, Horace Gremley IV. Mr. Gremley, whom I had long ago privately nicknamed Fourth, hardly blinked at the sight of me lugging a smelly bucket of evil-looking tea across the lobby. It was a sad fact that becoming one of my acquaintances meant growing accustomed to such bizarre encounters.

Fourth doffed his hat and grinned. "Good day to you, Miss Kittredge." He gave the bucket a dubious glance. "Ah, problem with your tea this morning?"

"Yes. I let someone else make it up." I halted at the basement access door to the understair. "How is your dear lady friend, Miss Skolnik?"

"Wondrous and delightful. A lily truly beyond the gild." His eyes grew dreamy. "She is teaching me to speak her native tongue, you know. I daresay it is almost as lovely as she is."

"I wish you all the joy in the world, Mr. Gremley." Of course I did; I'd arranged the introduction in order to stave off his endless, awkward attempts to court me.

I nodded toward the entrance to the Dungeon. "Would you be so kind?"

He opened and held the door for me. "Go slowly and carefully, Miss Kittredge. You would not wish to spill that concoction on the steps."

No, but I might save some to pour over Dredmore's head. "I will, thank you, Mr. Gremley."

As I took Fourth's advice and made my way down into the gloom, the sounds of clanking metals and hissing steam enveloped me. The Dungeon, home and business of the Honorable Reginald Docket, also housed the building's boiler and furnace. The hot, murky air smelled of old grease and well-used tools, with a top-note of new mech.

"Docket?" I called out, lugging the bucket over toward the maze of his workbenches. "It's Kit. Got a minute, mate?"

"Hang on." A trolley slid out from under the undercarriage of a decrepit carri, revealing the old man with a wrench in one hand and a hammer in the other. He tossed the tools aside and sat up, sniffing the air as he did. "Phew. What is that stench?"

"I've had another anonymous parcel." I covered my nose and mouth with my hand. "I've soaked it in tea but it's not helping."

"Park it on the bench there." Docket brought over a large glass case and lowered it over the bucket, cutting off the stink. "That's better. Not a gift from a friend, is it?"

I grimaced. "The tea, perhaps. The parcel, doubtful."

"Let's have a look." He perched a battered pair of spectacles on the end of his nose and peered through a glass panel. "When I was a boy a skunk got in the barn. Our best mouser killed it, but not before it sprayed the cat, the plow horse, and half the bloody hayloft."

I peered at the tea, which had grown very black. "That must have been . . . aromatic."

"Not so bad as this." He reached under the bench, pulled out a pair of noz masks, and passed one to me. "Best put this on."

I pulled the mask over my head and adjusted the protective lenses until I could see clearly, then tightened the chin strap until the noz sealed off my nose. "Do we need tanks?"

"Got a couple minutes of air in the canisters." Once he'd donned his mask he lifted the glass cover and used long tongs to remove the soaked parcel. "Put this down and cover it," Docket said, pushing the bucket toward me.

I found a square of tin and a large rag to drape over the bucket, which I stowed to one side. By the time I returned to the bench, Docket was peeling away the sodden, stained paper from some coiled wires. "It was rigged?"

He nodded. "To explode. The tea saved you from decorating the walls of your office with your insides." Gingerly he opened the box's sagging top flap and bent closer. "Well, what have we here?" He used the tongs to extract a dripping, twitching device no bigger than my fist. "Looks to be a rat after all."

The tiny animech had been painstakingly crafted to resemble the real rodent, from the hair-thin wires sprouting from its riveted snout to the narrow length of leather crimped over tiny rollers.

I knew animech was all the rage in Rumsen now, but

this was a bit too realistic—I could almost feel the bite of the razor blades fashioned into its two long teeth. "Why would you want to make a bomb look like a rat?"

"You're a female, love." Docket made my gender sound like an incurable disease. "I'll guess the villain thought you'd open the package, scream, drop it, and leap onto a chair while it went scurrying about."

I'd be more likely to trap it under my coal bucket and send for the vermage. "It would have done that without winding?"

"Was wound before it was parceled. Had to, to trigger the boomer. These wires"—he pointed to the outside of the box—"are likely attached to a coil inside wound about the roller shaft. Soon as you opened it they'd trigger the coil to unwind and turn the rollers. Would make it scuttle about like the real thing for a minute or two. And then . . ." His cheeks puffed out as he made an exploding sound.

Docket was a marvel with mech, and what he said made complete sense. It also made me suspicious. "You can guess all that simply by looking at it?"

"I might have seen something like this during the war. Bad times, no one ever questions seeing a rat." He put down the animech on its back, pressed a rivet by its ear, and a hinged belly plate popped open. "This is where they put the charge." He frowned. "Hand me those pluckers in the tray, Kit. Yes, the smallest ones."

I passed him the tweezers and watched him extract a hunk of something pink, torn and definitely not mech. Even with the mask on the smell suddenly became unbearable. "Bloody hell. That's what stinks. What did it eat, a dead rat?"

"Looks to be a gland of some sort." Apparently immune to the stench, Docket examined it from all sides. "Not rat, not this big. Not skunk, either. Could be stag."

"Whatever it is, get rid of it," I begged.

He took an empty jar from the rack above the bench, dropped the chunk of flesh inside, and sealed it. "Aye, that was the source of the stench. You can take off the mask now."

I didn't want to breathe again until I was at least a mile away, but I'd run out of air and had to remove the mask. When I did I could still smell a trace of the noxious odor, but a moment later it seemed to disappear completely. "They needn't have used a bomb. That reek would have done me in."

"Might have made you faint, you being a female and all, but it were tucked inside a capsule. Wouldn't have smelled anything until after you've been blown to smithereens." Docket scratched the three days of beard stubbling his jaw. "You'd have smelled right pungent, though. Or whatever was left of you."

"Perhaps they wished to spoil the funeral as well as the current arrangement of my parts." I handed him the mask. "I should take it over to Rumsen Main and make a report."

"Best I keep it here. Chief Inspector Doyle won't thank you for smelling up New Scotland Yard." He studied the animech again. "This didn't come cheap, neither. Workmanship's too bloody fine for a toy. To get this detail, whoever put it together had to hand-work the brass while it was heated nearly to the melting point."

I knew next to nothing about metal workers. "Who would have that level of skill?"

"Someone who works with metals regular, like me,"

he admitted. "A watchmaker or a jeweler might, too; they can do this sort of wee mech. But they likely wouldn't know how to sort out the charge or the fuse."

"A mage?" I watched Docket shake his head. "Anyone else?"

"I'd put my coin on a blast master." He saw my expression and grimaced. "That's what they called the torpedo makers during the Insurrection. Those lads could make most anything into a bomb—stones, flowers, even shoes."

"I've had no dealings with the militia." I prodded the rat with a finger. "I'm not a hostile or a rebel. I pay my taxes and my rent on time."

"This is the sort of thing they do to get rid of turncoats." Docket was regarding the rat so he didn't see my expression change. "Give us a day to take this apart, love, see what else there is to it. Might find something useful for the Yard."

I wasn't going anywhere near Rumsen Main now. "I owe you one, mate."

Docket winked. "Let me keep the rat's works after, and we'll call it even."

I spent the remainder of the day visiting two new clients and solving their dilemmas. The ghost supposedly haunting a cobbler's shop turned out to be a cat sneaking in at night to escape the cold; I found the felonious feline snoozing in a bin of laces. My proof of his crimes, bits of leather from the shoes he'd scratched and chewed, still lay caught in his claws. The fishmonger who'd hired me to dispel the curse on his dockside stand wasn't too pleased to learn that the ridiculously high prices being demanded by his avaricious new wife, not evil magic, were chasing away his best customers. She denied everything and blamed me for trying to swindle her husband and ruin her marriage with my false accusations.

Relocating the cat and mediating a truce between the unhappy couple took more time than I expected, and I had to rush to return to the office in time to meet Dredmore's driver, who sat waiting beside his master's finest coach and four, all perfectly matched in the most depressing shade of gray.

"I don't suppose I could reschedule this for tomorrow." I stepped aside as Connell, silent and impassive as always, opened the door to the coach. "No, of course not."

I climbed in and sat down, leaning back against the fine leather cushions as Connell climbed up and started off. Once the horses' hooves were making sufficient noise I pulled down the window shades and closed my eyes before I spoke the only incantation I ever used.

"Harry, we need to talk."

CHAPTER TWO

My breath whitened the air as the temperature of the interior abruptly plummeted. The shadows before me moved in strange patterns, lightening and solidifying as a man's form took shape: a thinning mane of silver hair, a smart suit that had been fashionable some twenty years past, and two bright, dark eyes peering out from a narrow, clever old man's face.

The face lied, for he was not a man, but a spirit, and an immortal Aramanthan at that.

The first time the elderly specter had materialized he'd told me that his name was Harry White, but that alias (like Harry Houdini and Ehrich Weiss) was just another of the many he'd used throughout time to conceal his true name: Merlin. Among other things, he could possess the bodies of mortals, which was how he'd sired my mother. While I had no intentions of calling Harry "Grandda," to keep safe footing I'd made him my business partner. When taking on an associate, I reckoned, you could do much worse than the most powerful magician of all time.

At present, Harry looked about with visible disapproval. "You had to summon me in his coach? What has the bastard done now, kidnapped you again?"

Harry hated Dredmore, but then, Dredmore hated

him. What I hated was not knowing the cause of all the hostility and drama between them. "Not that it's any of your business, but I voluntarily accepted Lord Dredmore's kind invitation to meet with one of his clients. She wishes to hire me."

"Sounds so legitimate, too, doesn't it? I'll remind you of this kind invitation when he locks you up in his great tomb of a mansion to serve as his personal harem girl." Harry looked quite satisfied. "Again."

"I didn't call on you to discuss Lucien." I sat back and rubbed my eyes. "Someone tried to kill me this morning by sending an animech with a bomb inside to my office."

"Must not have been a very good one." Harry reached across and poked my arm. "You're still among the living."

"Pure daft luck, I assure you. My friend Docket said the device might have been made by a soldier. Which is odd, considering I've done nothing to annoy the militia. Unlike some occupants of this vehicle." I folded my hands in my lap and gave him an expectant look.

Harry hunched his shoulders. "I told you, Charm, I never actually spied for the Crown. I used the body of one of their spies to travel to Toriana to look after your mother and you. That's all."

I leaned forward. "The point is, that bomb was sent to the office. Our office, Harry. Your name is on the door now, too."

"That was your idea, not mine." He sniffed. "You shouldn't have used my true name anyway. Now all my enemies know we're partners." He frowned. "Did you find that cat at the cobbler's I told you about last night?"

"Yes. I found the cat." Getting my grandfather to

focus on the problem at hand was like trying to herd a dozen rabbits in an open field scattered with carrots. "What have you been doing that you haven't told me?"

"Oh, this and that." He avoided my gaze by examining the state of his cuffs. "I spend most of my time in the Netherside, as well you know. It would be much more convenient if you were to find a body for me to occupy."

"Let's be clear on something, old man," I said. "I am your granddaughter, your business partner, and, I suspect, the only friend you have left on the planet. What I will never be is your personal body snatcher."

"Calm yourself, gel." He sighed. "I'm not some demon spirit come straight from Hades to destroy the world. I was only thinking of the convenience."

While Harry could take on solid form for short periods, as he did now with me, the only way he could get about in the world was to possess a living person and turn him into his personal carri. Fearing Harry would do that and much worse to me, my parents had imprisoned him in a nightstone pendant I'd worn most of my life. Since no magic worked anywhere near my person, Harry had been unable to work a spell to free himself, and had remained trapped for decades like a genie in a bottle.

My parents had been wrong about his intentions, but I couldn't blame them. If Harry stayed in the body for longer than a day and a night, the possession became permanent and lasted until the body died . . . or someone killed it.

And there was one possible explanation for my vastly unpleasant delivery.

"Mother of God." I braced my forehead against my hand. "Someone thinks you've possessed me."

"I'll look into it," Harry said. As the horses slowed, his body began turning transparent. "You've arrived at the evil sod's lair. Have a care, gel. If you're not home by midnight I'll be quite annoyed—and I still remember how to turn an ass into a toad." He disappeared.

I glanced out the window and saw the soaring heights of Morehaven, the enormous cliff-side mansion Dredmore called home. "Fabulous."

Connell escorted me to the main entry, where Dredmore's butler stood waiting with a lantern. "Good evening, miss. The master is waiting for you in the draw-ing room."

I followed the butler through the foyer and down a long hall scented with beeswax candles and adorned with some of Dredmore's extensive art collection. It was so silent and gloomy I had to say something. "How have you been, Winslow? Plotting with your master to over-throw any governments lately?"

"Not this week, miss." The servant didn't miss a step, although his expression grew puzzled. "Forgive me, miss, but how could you know my name? Have we met before tonight?"

Actually we had, not that he or anyone else in the house would remember. Our meeting, which had taken place during Dredmore's abduction and seduction of me, had been erased when I'd been thrown back in time. "You know, I can't recall," I lied.

He stopped before a massive oak panel, knocking once before sliding it to one side. "Miss Kittredge, milord."

I walked in to the beast's lair, which immediately lived up to Dredmore's reputation for the fantastic. Magical-looking relics occupied stands and cases scattered about the room's many polished tables. Glittering light from a seven-tiered crystal chandelier illuminated the brass-studded dark leather furnishings and vases of hothouse roses. Everything was spotless, expensive, and mysterious—exactly the sort of atmosphere in which Dredmore thrived.

The master himself stood near a roaring fire in a gray-stone hearth, his arm braced against the mantel. It surprised me to see he had put on a white tie in my honor, almost as much as if I'd found him in his shirtsleeves swilling ale.

"Thank you, Winslow." Dredmore inspected me. "Bring our guest tea and sandwiches, if you would."

"Yes, milord." The butler withdrew and shut me in.

I occupied myself by placing my reticule on a table and then taking a turn of the room. "Did your client beg off at the last minute, or was it all a ruse to get me here?"

"The lady will be arriving shortly." He moved to an armchair and gestured for me to take a matching seat across from his. "Did you enjoy the tea this morning?"

"You know, I did, thank you. It turned out to be a genuine lifesaver." I disdained the facing seat and wandered over to an orrery fashioned of nested astrolab turntables with the suspended planets made of polished spell stone spheres. "Someone sent an animech rat containing a bomb to the office. It didn't go off because I poured your tea over the parcel instead of opening it. Don't glower like that, I'm fine."

A muscle twitched along his jaw. "Do you still have the mech?"

"Docket's having a look," I said. "Lucien, have you told anyone about my grandfather?"

"Who would believe me?"

I watched as the mech's rotagears turned and the tiny planets floated round the goldstone sun. "I know precisely how persuasive you can be. You could stand in the market square, announce the sky was the earth, and everyone within earshot would stand on their heads." I'd personally experienced what he called his mind power to charm the spirit-born, and combined with his reputation as a deathmage, it wasn't much of an exaggeration.

He appeared on the other side of the orrery. "You believe the parcel bomb was meant for Harry."

"Since I've done nothing to— Bloody hell." I glared at him. "You're *still* having me watched?"

"You are one of the most powerful mortal spell breakers ever born, Charmian. Of course I'm having you watched. Come here." He took my arm and guided me over to the armchair, making me sit. "The surveillance is only for your protection," he added in a gentler tone. "The Reapers have learned that a spirit-born mortal defeated their warlord Zarath, and in so doing prevented the conquest of Toriana. Thanks to your adjustments to the timeline, however, that is all they know. I cannot allow them to discover who you are, or that it was your doing."

I wanted to tell him I could look after myself, but he was right. "If the Reapers didn't send the bomb for me, then it must have been meant for Harry."

"I'll make some inquiries. I should know something by tomorrow." Dredmore looked up as Winslow carried in a large silver tray laden with a steaming porcelain pot, matching cups, and enough dainty sandwiches to feed a small fussy army. "Now eat before you wilt from hunger."

I eyed the pot. "I really can't drink anything green. Even on Saint Patrick's Day."

"This blend is called Golden Afternoon, miss," Winslow said as he poured and handed me a cup. "Indian amber leaf, touch of honey. Very smooth."

I took a cautious sip as he served his master. "So it is, Winslow. Quite delightful. Be warned, I might try to nick a tin or two before I leave."

"If you can get past Cook, miss, it's in the dry-goods pantry. Third shelf on the left." He inclined his head as he departed.

Dredmore added a slice of lemon to his tea. "I never knew Winslow to have a sense of humor."

"We all of us have hidden depths, Lucien." I selected a round of brioche filled with shaved ham and cranberry relish.

"I heard you talking to Winslow in the corridor," he said. "How *did* you know his name?"

More dangerous territory, for like Winslow, Dredmore had no memory of the night I'd spent at Morehaven before I'd mangled time. "As I told your man, I can't recollect. Perhaps you mentioned it in passing, or I met him once in town. Or it could be that I'm having *you* watched."

"I never speak of my servants to anyone. Your memory is flawless, and any meaningful surveillance of

22

me is quite beyond your financial means." He regarded me over the rim of his teacup. "And Winslow never leaves the estate."

"You should let the staff out now and then, Lucien," I said mildly. "I'm sure most of them will come back."

"You came to Morehaven before today." He set down his cup and gave me his full attention. "I know when. The question is, why?"

He could be annoyingly direct. "I cannot tell you what never happened."

"But you remember it." He stood and came over to me, cupping my chin in his hand and making me look up at him. "You may subvert the past as often as you like, my sweet, but you cannot escape your fate."

"My fate my foot. Leave off, Lucien. All this to-do is giving me indigestion." I pushed his hand away and took a bite of my sandwich.

He brushed a crumb from my lips. "Ah, but it's my fate, too, Charmian. The portents have made that unwaveringly clear."

Before I could tell him what I thought of his taking magical peeks into the future Winslow returned. "Your guest has arrived, milord."

Dredmore dropped his hand. "Show the lady to the Orchid Room, and inform her that Miss Kittredge will attend to her momentarily."

I wolfed down the rest of the sandwich, drained my cup, and stood. "I'll see her now."

"Before you meet my client," Dredmore said, "I have some additional information about the widow to impart."

I folded my arms. "Well? What is it? Do you think she killed him?"

"Naturally you would assume that, Kittredge." A tall, heavily veiled woman in dark blue strode into the room, her swirling red pin-striped skirts rocking along with the hitch in her step. "You've always been exceptionally commonplace."

I knew that voice, better than my own, and it explained why my host had been so reluctant to use her name. I faced Dredmore and uttered the only word I could reasonably produce without screaming. "No."

"You see?" Lady Eugenia Bestly removed her hat and veils and tossed them at Winslow. I glanced at her, and saw that to improve her color she had put on a great deal of face paint. The rice powder she'd used to disguise its shine had also brought out every tiny wrinkle round her eyes and mouth. "Did I not tell you, Lucien? She will never give me a fair hearing. She is not capable of compassion."

Compassion? No. Murder? Absolutely. "In regard to you, madam, you are quite correct. Good day." I stalked past her.

Dredmore reached the panel before I did and closed it in my face. "You assured me that you would listen to her."

I was trembling, panting, and I could hardly see straight. "That is a promise I am utterly overjoyed to break." I jerked aside the panel and stepped out into the hall.

Dredmore followed, closing the panel and catching my arm. "I am aware that you and Lady Bestly have had some unfortunate dealings in the past—"

"Unfortunate dealings. Such a lovely pair of words." I jerked my arm in an attempt to free it. "They make what that bloody harpy did to me sound almost pleasant. Like saying a beating is a lot of love taps."

"You may as well leave her go, Lucien," Lady Bestly called through the panel. "She will have none of me and my troubles."

That did it. I went back in to face the witch. "Are you in trouble, my lady? How terrible for you." I advanced on her, taking great satisfaction in watching her retreat. "Has someone repeatedly and viciously maligned your character? Have they registered dozens of complaints about you to the magistrate, or the police? Did they dare accuse you of crimes that you've never committed? Or did they send their servants to attack you in public, and then try to have you arrested for defending yourself against them?"

Lady Bestly backed into a settee and dropped. "Dredmore, for God's sake."

The gentleman stepped between us. "Charmian, stop this. You're frightening her."

"I doubt it," I told him. "Seeing as Lady Bestly and her friends did all of that—and quite a bit more—to me."

Dredmore gave my old nemesis an uncertain look. "Eugenia?"

"I never sent anyone to attack the gel." She fussed with the jet buttons on her gloves. "As for the rest, well, my position as president of the society required me to act ardently in order to preserve civil decency and safeguard the ladies of Rumsen against the influence of a decidedly unnatural young woman."

"Woman?" I hooted. "I was seventeen years old. I'd just come to the city with nothing more than the clothes on my back. Your campaign to smear my name cost me my job, and ruined any hope I had of obtaining new employment. By the time you were through with me, milady, I was reduced to sleeping on park benches and digging through rubbish cans for scraps so I wouldn't starve."

Lady Bestly raised her chin. "That was certainly not my doing. You should have left Rumsen and gone back to your people."

"My people. *My people*, milady, were all dead," I said softly. "I was a penniless orphan without a friend in the world. You had everything, and I nothing, and still you inflicted all that pointless cruelty on me. I imagine you were quite proud of how thoroughly you squashed me."

She paled a little. "There is no pride left to me in my present situation, Kittredge. Very soon *I* shall be the object of ridicule and scorn. I'm sure you will take great delight in that." One of her gloved hands fluttered to her throat. "Lord Dredmore, would you kindly call for . . . my . . ." She closed her eyes and slumped against the side of the settee.

"Eugenia." He stepped toward her.

I reached her first and checked her wrist to find her pulse strong and steady. In my line of work I had often watched other females succumb to hysterics or horror, and Lady Bestly showed no genuine signs of being overwhelmed by her emotions. Which meant she had another motive for faking the collapse, and I could only think of one.

"It seems she's fainted," I told Dredmore, shaking my head at the same time. "Can you bring some swooning salts, milord?"

He regarded me. "It will take a few minutes to find them." When I nodded, he gave the lady a final glance before leaving us and closing the panel.

I waited another moment before I said, "You can stop pretending now. He's gone."

Lady Bestly sat up at once and tugged straight the lay of her skirt. "My mother always claimed that men could not tolerate screaming infants, quarreling children, and swooning women. It seems she was correct."

I nodded. "Now tell me what you didn't want to say in front of him."

"I can no longer prevent publication of the exact circumstances surrounding my husband's demise." Lady Bestly took a folded paper from her reticule and handed it to me. "The editor of the *Rumsen Daily* had a copy of the story delivered to me this morning, along with a note advising me to dispense with my mourning and depart the city at once."

I unfolded the newspaper to read the headline of the front-page story, which was beyond stunning. I then skimmed the first paragraph before I looked up at her. "I don't understand."

She made a negligent gesture. "It is all there, in black and white. You can read, can't you?"

I read the rest of the article. "Is it true?"

"My husband was many things, Kittredge, but he was not what is printed in that paper. Yet tomorrow my family, my friends, indeed the whole world will believe him to be a monster." She touched her wedding ring and her voice went low. "How am I to mourn him?"

That was tragic, but nothing compared to what the lady was about to endure. As soon as the story broke, the good citizens of Rumsen would react with outrage; some would demand justice. Since the gentleman in question was deceased, they'd go after the person closest to him.

"The editor was right." I refolded the paper and handed it back to her. "You must leave town, tonight."

"I cannot go. I must have the truth." She straightened her shoulders. "My husband was a good man, compelled by unnatural means to commit these terrible crimes. Whatever magic was used also killed him."

Since he'd been married to her I was inclined to believe it; she was president of the Rumsen Ladies Decency Society. "Do you have any proof of that?"

"At present, no." Her lips thinned. "Lord Dredmore led me to believe that you have some expertise in these matters. He persuaded me to confide in you and engage you to investigate the matter. I must have the evidence necessary to prove my husband's innocence and restore his good name, which you would acquire."

"And by doing so, save your reputation from ruin," I guessed.

She folded her arms under her bosom. "Be assured, Kittredge, that I shall not be the only soul made to suffer."

What she meant was that everyone employed by, connected to, or acquainted with the Bestlys would be tainted by association. She hadn't wanted Dredmore to hear about this probably because she believed he would immediately sever his own connection with her. "Aye, but as his wife you'll suffer the worst. No decent person will ever again acknowledge your existence." I permitted myself a tiny smirk. "Such an ironic turn of events, wouldn't you say, milady?"

"I knew you would revel in your petty triumph over me. How tiresome to be proven so exactly correct. This interview is finished." Lady Bestly's hand trembled as she shoved the paper back into her reticule. "Good day to you."

I waited until she'd almost reached the panel. "I charge ten shillings a week plus reasonable expenses. I'll need that article to read again before I call on you tomorrow. I require unrestricted access to all of his lordship's rooms and possessions, which I will be searching from top to bottom, as well as a list of his friends and associates, each of whom I will personally interview. I will also have to question your household staff as soon as possible." When she said nothing, I added, "Does any of that present a problem for you?"

Lady Bestly turned round, and for a moment something shimmered in her steely eyes. "I reduced you to a beggar, and now you would help me? I cannot put faith in that."

"You're very fond of making assumptions about me based on nothing but your own narrow-mindedness." I smiled. "I did sleep in the park, and had my meals from rubbish bins. I lived so for a month and a fortnight. But as cold and hungry and hopeless as my wretched situation was, I never begged. Never once."

"Neither shall I." She handed me the newspaper.

"Ten shillings per week, Kittredge, plus reasonable expenses." She held out a gloved hand.

As we shook on it, Dredmore appeared in the doorway. "Eugenia. You are recovered?"

"I am, thank you, Lucien." The lady removed a card from her reticule and offered it to me. "You may call on me in the morning, Kittredge. If you wish to avoid the mob, I suggest earlier rather than later."

"There will be no mob tomorrow," I told her. "Lord Dredmore will see to it."

Lady Bestly's chin dropped. "Lucien can do nothing—"

"On the contrary." I smiled at him. "He has formidable powers of persuasion, and he owes me a rather enormous favor. Don't you, milord?"

Dredmore's mouth curled. "So it would seem." To Lady Bestly, he said, "Whatever you need from me to solve this dilemma, Eugenia, it is yours."

A flicker of hope passed over her features before they turned to stone once more. "I rather think that would take a miracle, not your magic. Good evening, Lucien. Kittredge."

Once Lady Bestly had gone, Dredmore turned to me. "Why is she expecting a mob, and how am I to prevent it?"

"The editor of the *Rumsen Daily* intends to run a story tomorrow morning about Lord Bestly." I looked down at the article. "You must convince him not to, at least for a week. I expect you will also have to attend to the reporter who wrote the story, and perhaps some of the police—"

"Before you arrange to have me bespell the entire

city," Dredmore said, "why don't you first tell me about this story?"

"You can read it for yourself." I handed him the article. "It seems his lordship died shortly after going on a rampage so savage that they've renamed him 'Lord Beastly.'"

Dredmore unfolded the paper and read the headline. "This is insane."

"So was the lady's husband," I said, "the night he became the Wolfman."

CHAPTER THREE

Discovering his client's once highly regarded and imminently respectable husband had died after murdering two strangers and mauling a dozen others unsettled Dredmore, but only for a few moments. Once he recovered from the shock of the unpleasant revelation he promptly tried to assume control of the case—and me, naturally.

"I can see to it that the editor delays printing the story on Lord Bestly until next week." He returned the article to me. "I will accompany you to Bestly House in the morning. You may interview the servants while I inspect the premises."

"You certainly will not," I snapped. "Lady Bestly confided her suspicions in *me*, not you. She also engaged *my* services, not yours. The investigation into Lord Bestly's death is my job, and I work alone."

Dredmore didn't like that. "Using my power to influence the editor already involves me. If the dark arts were used to compel Lord Bestly to this madness—"

"—they will have no effect on me," I finished for him. "I am immune to all magic."

A strange light glittered in his eyes. "All but mine."

I gave him a complacent smile. "Oh, yes. Except for yours, which you promised never again to use on me."

"How strange." His hands encircled my wrists. "I cannot remember ever making such a promise."

From here I'd have to be very diplomatic. "You don't want to have me as your mindless love slave, Lucien," I scoffed. "I'd hang all over you, become entirely useless outside the bedchamber, and talk of nothing but my undying and eternal love for you. You'd be bored witless within a day."

He caught my face between his palms. "I've wanted you, Charmian, from the first moment I saw you. Nothing has altered that; I've thought of little else these five years." His thumb brushed across my lips. "But you, you have changed. The old hostility is gone. You don't threaten, you listen. You even discuss. You don't look at me with hatred anymore. You see me. And now you've asked me to help you."

I could not explain the reasons for that. That while Dredmore knew nothing of me, I knew everything of him. Every dark and lonely secret, every lost wish, every hopeless longing. Of course I saw him now; the man had bared his very heart to me—and that I could never tell him, for only I had traveled back in time.

For Dredmore, it had never happened.

"I have changed, in my opinion of you," I told the third button on his evening shirt. "It has greatly improved."

"Why should it?"

"I did kill you to free you from Zarath," I reminded him. "I know in the past I threatened you with death a dozen times, but I never meant to do it. I didn't know that I could end another life. And when you were dead, when

I believed there was no hope of ever . . ." My throat tightened, and I swallowed hard before I continued. "Time has so generously provided us with a second chance, Lucien. Let's not make the same mistakes again, shall we?"

He bent his head to mine. "You and I are not a mistake, Charmian."

I never felt particularly feminine or small until Dredmore kissed me. In the past, such kisses had been part of his annoyingly regular attempts to seduce me, and knowing that they were for that expressed purpose had given me enough resolve to resist. He would always kiss well; I was sure his mouth had been fashioned for exactly this sort of activity. He definitely still knew what he was about, coaxing my lips apart and tasting me with his wickedly talented tongue. But as he filled his hands with my hair, I realized he was not being at all deliberate about it.

This, too, had changed.

I could feel the pounding of his heart beneath my palms, and trembled along with the unsteadiness of his fingers. He made a sound I'd never heard, or perhaps it came from me. I could not fathom it. He was all over me, arms folding, lips caressing, and the feel and the smell and the taste of him drugged my senses and slowly unraveled the tight and tangled thing hammering beneath my own breast.

"Stay with me." His murmured incantation whispered across my cheek as he chased it, trailing more gentle caresses across my burning skin. "Only for tonight."

If only it would be, I might have agreed, and in that moment I despised the pudding he had made of my own will.

Under my skirts my knees shook as I drew back. "You have an editor to bespell, Lucien." My voice wobbled, too, and I cleared my throat. "I must go."

He held on to me, and for a moment I feared he would sweep me up into his arms and carry me off to some dark room where I would be spending this and many other nights. I did not anticipate resisting any of that. Beneath his garments his muscles tightened, and then he set me fully away from him to ring for Winslow.

His butler must have had an ear to the door, for he arrived an instant later with my cloak.

"Connell is waiting to drive you back to the city, miss." He glanced at his master. "Shall I escort the young lady out, milord?"

Dredmore looked ready to throttle both of us. "We will continue our discussion tomorrow, Charmian."

Now he was threatening, thank God. A hostile Dredmore I could easily manage. "Deal with the editor and find out who sent that parcel to me," I countered, "and then we can have a chat."

Winslow dutifully ushered me out of the mansion. "Will you be returning to your office, or your home, miss?"

"Neither yet." Once outside I walked to the front of the coach. "Connell, do you know the Eagle's Nest?" He gave me a jaded look. "I see that you do. That is my destination. Winslow, your pantry is safe once more."

"Until your next visit, miss." He helped me into the coach. "Er, you are aware that you are having Connell take you to a house of ill-repute."

"You mean a brothel," I corrected. "Oh, yes, Winslow. My best friend owns it."

I rarely visited the Eagle's Nest after dark. My best friend, Carina Eagle, did conduct the bulk of her business at night, and I didn't care to be mistaken as one of her employees. Given that she operated the most popular brothel in Rumsen, her clients could be forgiven for assuming any female on the premises was there to trade the pleasures of the flesh for their coin. To avoid disillusioning them I pulled my hood up over my head and presented myself at the side entrance.

A slot in the door opened a few seconds after my knock. "No deliveries after six—oh, sorry, Miss Kit." The slot closed, the door opened, and the blond behemoth known as Wrecker waved me in. "Late for you to be calling on herself."

"Can't wait till morning for this, Wreck." I grimaced at him. "Would you take me up to her?"

He offered me his arm as nicely as any posh, and guided me to the back stairs. "We've a full house tonight, I'll warn you."

"I can see that." I stopped on the second-floor landing to permit a half-naked brunette and her rotund companion to pass in front of me. "Is Rina personally engaged?"

"Not likely. Last I seen she were working on the ledgers." He rolled his eyes. "Not in her best mood, either."

We dodged a few more unlikely couples in various states of undress before arriving at Rina's office. Wrecker knocked and opened the door.

"Beg your pardon, milady, but your"—he ducked quickly as an inkwell sailed over his head and smashed against the back wall—"friend's come to call."

"I said no interruptions, you nummox." Rina appeared, surveyed me, and made a disgusted sound. "Do you know how to balance six columns of figures to the pence?"

"No," I admitted, "but I can rub your neck and make pretty, soothing noises."

"I hate accounting. I hate pence. And now, I hate you." She turned on her heel and stalked back to her desk. "Tea for two, Wreck. Best you make it very strong and scalding hot, or you'll be breathing it."

"Yes, milady." The big man gave me a sympathetic look before he trudged back to the stairs.

I cautiously entered Rina's chamber and gently closed the door behind me. "Problem with the books?"

"You might say that. And when they summon you to court and ask who was most likely to have choked my bookkeeper to death with bare hands, you'll have to lie." Rina slammed shut a large green book and flung herself into her desk chair. "So what do you want now? Money, gowns, sanctuary from someone who wishes to strangle you . . . ?"

"I need only some information." I perched on the arm of her sofa. "Anything you know about Lord Terrance Bestly."

"Bestly, Bestly." She concentrated, thinking for nearly a minute before she spoke again. "Father was an architect on the Hill; mother Viscount Radley's youngest gel. Bestly inherited a pile, married up and more, founded a gent's club. Probably to escape the missus, as it's said he practically lives there." She sat up. "Wait, not anymore. He dropped dead last week. I meant to attend the burial, but for some reason they're dragging their heels on it. Probably waiting for family to travel."

Rina adored pomp and ceremony, and regularly disguised herself to attend important weddings and funerals. "Was his lordship one of your regulars?" I asked.

That startled a laugh out of her. "God, no. Lady You Best Not, his wife, runs that decency society. She and her priggish friends have come after me and my gels more times than I can count. She probably sewed Bestly into his trousers every morning and had him piss out his ear." Her eyes narrowed. "Did she kill him? Is that why you're on the case?"

I shook my head. "Lady Eugenia hired me to investigate her husband's death."

"Get your money up front," Rina advised. "Prudes like that one have short memories and tight fists."

"Oh, she'll pay." I rubbed my tired eyes. "Her husband was the Wolfman."

"What?" Rina shrieked and laughed, instantly delighted. "Blind my Cupid— Bestly, a murdering loon?"

I nodded. "His lordship went from posh nob to rampaging killer, all in one night. The story's coming out in the *Daily*. Hopefully next week, but possibly tomorrow morning."

"Capital." She chuckled. "I'll send Wreck to buy fifty copies and use it to wallpaper my loo." Her grin evaporated. "You're not going to ruin that, now, are you?"

I turned my hand from side to side. "The lady believes her husband was bespelled—that someone made him into the Wolfman."

"Come on, Kit." Rina kicked the tuffet in front of her feet. "He ripped apart two chaps, right in the street. There were dozens of witnesses. No black magic in the world can make a man do that." She gave me a suspicious look. "Why would you hire out to her anyway? You don't believe in any of that nonsense."

I couldn't tell her that I did because that would mean explaining the hows and the whys, none of which she remembered. "I took the case as a favor to Lucien Dredmore."

"Oh, that makes perfect sense. Of course." She lobbed a throw pillow at me. "You brainless bint. Doing favors for a deathmage who wants nothing more than to toss up your skirts? Have you gone off?"

"It gets worse," I said. "I met Lady Bestly once before, just after I came here from Middy. I was working at a tea shop as a counter lass, and I caught one of the lady's friends spiking a deb's cup with gut toss."

"Nasty." Rina pursed her lips. "Daughter's rival for some posh lad, I wager?"

I nodded. "I put a stop to it and told her to leave. Got a nice tip from the deb, but Lady Bestly showed up the next day. Called me a witch, got me sacked, and saw to it I couldn't work anywhere else."

"Bleeding Christ, Kit." Rina went still. "You were barely out of the schoolroom when you got here."

Wrecker knocked and came in with the still-steaming tea and two golden-brown turnovers. "Warmed up some meat pies for you and Miss Kit. Thought it best, her looking peaked and all."

Rina would have snapped at him, but my stomach chose that moment to growl. "You're like a stray. My staff is always feeding you."

"That's why you're my best friend," I told her, and smiled at Wrecker. "Thanks, mate."

"Pleasure." He ducked his head and shuffled out.

"Wrecker's never fancied the ladies, you know," Rina said. "Wouldn't guess it to look at him, but he's quite cozy with some kneecapper of the same persuasion."

I took a bite of my pasty and shrugged. "None of my business. If he's happy, isn't that all that matters?"

"To you and me," she allowed. "Your fine lady Bestly, however, would have him strung up by his smalls in market square and flogged for it. Now tell me truly: why have you hired yourself out to that right bitch?"

"She's about to go through hell, thanks to her husband." I tried my tea and winced as it parboiled my tongue. "Working for her, I get a front-row seat to it all. Should be vastly entertaining."

"Nicely put." Rina studied me. "But I know you better than that, you silly cow. Out with it."

"After your bastard fiancé lost your maiden night in a card game, you made good on the wager. Even when you knew it would ruin you forever, and your parents would toss you out on the street, you handed over your virtue to the winner." I cocked my head. "So you know *exactly* why I'm working for Lady Bestly."

"Revenge by honor. Daft twit." Her expression softened. "She won't thank you for it."

"Then it's good that I'm not doing it for her." I sipped my tea. "Now tell me everything else you've heard about Terrance Bestly."

I took a carri-cab from the Eagle's Nest to my home in one of the oldest sections in town. At first I'd rented a flat in the simple goldstone, saving every pence I could until circumstances and my bank account allowed me to purchase the building. I'd then helped the remaining tenants find new lodgings, adding an incentive for them to move out quickly by offering to pay their first month's rent if they relocated at once. Since the last had gone I'd been slowly renovating each floor; in a few more years I'd have one of the most spacious homes in the district.

The goldstone had been built first to serve as a granary, and a faint scent of wheat and barley still permeated its walls. I'd ignored all the current fashions in decor—not that I could afford them anyway—and furnished the first floor with the minimal comforts, most of which I'd taken in trade for my services. Secondhand shops and the thrift market had provided the rest, and what I couldn't manage to buy I did without.

Being reminded by Lady Bestly of my wretched days of dwelling in the parks gave me rather a better appreciation of how far I'd come since I'd arrived in Rumsen. Every rug, curtain, and stick of furniture under my roof had come to me through diligence, hard work, and self-sacrifice. My home might be humble by the lady's standards, but I hadn't gotten it by charity or marriage. No, I'd earned every damned inch of it myself.

Revenge by honor, Rina had called it. I liked that quite

a bit, I thought as I tossed my reticule on a side table and dropped onto my chaise longue. I might even have it chiseled above my front entry as a personal motto.

The chime of my doorbell got me back on my feet to look through the street-facing window, which gave me an excellent view of anyone on the stoop. The man standing outside my door wore a plain long coat that almost hid the lines of the pistol harness beneath it. Gaslight caught some of the gilded strands of his fair hair, which badly wanted trimming, and glowed along the hard line of his set jaw.

Chief Inspector Thomas Doyle didn't appear happy, either.

As children, Tommy Doyle and I had been playmates for a time. Twenty years later we'd met again, this time as copper and suspect. Although he'd harassed me, detained me, questioned me, and arrested me (twice), I'd considered him a friend—none of which he remembered now.

From his view this would be only our second meeting, so I composed myself accordingly before I answered the bell.

"Hello, Chief Inspector Doyle." I didn't have to fake the smile; I liked Tommy. "What brings the Yard to my door at so late an hour?"

He removed his bowler. "I'm sorry to disturb you, Miss Kittredge. Might I come in and have a word?"

"I live alone and I don't keep servants," I said. "This could irreparably tarnish your reputation on the Hill."

His mouth twisted. "I'm a policeman, Miss Kittredge. My official duties take precedence over society, among which I am respected nearly as much as the average footman."

"Butler, I should think." I opened the door.

Doyle refused my offer of tea and a comfortable seat, instead taking a position by the window I'd just checked. "Good view of the street here," he mentioned as I sat down. "Still, you should have a slot or a peek hole installed in your entry. You living alone here and all."

The man noticed everything. He also smelled very nice; a bit like the sea on a clear day. "I will take that under advisement." I sat down and watched him extract a notebook from his coat pocket. "But you didn't come here to inspect my vantage points."

"We received a complaint from a tenant in your office building." He flipped through some pages. "This morning you were observed carrying a bucket down into the basement level. Is that correct?"

Not the damned bucket. "Yes."

"For what purpose?"

"I had to dispose of some undrinkable tea." And now I'd have to get rid of him. "Is that all?"

"No." He rooted in his pocket for a pencil. "What sort of tea was this, then?"

"I can't say. It was a gift from a client." I pretended to think. "I can tell you that it was a very disturbing shade of green."

"Green tea."

I nodded. "Is there a law against tea of unusual hues?"

"Not to my knowledge," he said with a perfectly straight face. "Why didn't you drink it?"

I smiled. "Would you drink green tea?"

"Not if it smelled like"—he turned to another page and began to read from it—"'twenty rotting, maggot-infested carcasses,' according to the complainant's description."

"Not twenty, surely." I yawned. "One, two at the most—and as I said, I did dispose of it."

"You did not." Doyle closed and pocketed his notebook. "You left the bucket in the basement."

"Yes, with instructions for Mr. Docket to dispose of the contents," I tacked on.

"He did not," Doyle said. "According to the statement I obtained from Mr. Docket, he forgot about the bucket until he bumped it with his foot, knocked it over, and the contents spilled all over his floor."

"But his floor has a drain," I offered. "All basements do."

"It does," he agreed. "At the time of the spill, however, it was obstructed by some discarded rags, tools, and other items, so your green tea formed a pool."

I sighed. "There was hardly enough to make a puddle, Chief Inspector."

"A pool," he repeated, "which spread out directly beneath the building's ventilation system."

I rested my brow against my hand. "Did Docket shut the vents?"

"I believe he tried," Doyle said, "before he fainted and had to be carried out."

"Docket will be fine. He's practically indestructible." This day's disasters were never going to end, it seemed, so I stood up. "Right, then. I'll pop over now and tidy the spill myself."

"You cannot," he said. "The building had to be evacuated and sealed, which it will remain until we can safely determine the exact composition and nature of this tea of yours, and how best to remove it and the stench it is producing."

I sat back down. "Is it really that bad?"

"I have been on battlefields, Miss Kittredge, littered with hundreds of bodies of the fallen, that by comparison to your bucket of brew smelled like a lawn sprinkled with fresh-cut roses." He came to stand over me. "Now: who made the tea, and what in God's name was put in it?"

"There was a parcel I accidentally dropped in the tea," I said meekly. "It contained an animech rat."

He blinked. "What?"

"There was also a bomb in the rat, and some sort of glandular flesh, possibly stag, that seemed to be the source of the smell." I regarded him. "At least, that was Mr. Docket's theory."

Doyle turned his back on me and stood like that for a lengthy period of silence. "Why did you immerse a bomb in the tea?"

"Well I didn't know it was a bomb at the time," I pointed out. "I only wanted to be rid of the parcel, and the tea. I put both in the bucket and, well, here we are."

He faced me. "Why didn't you report the bomb?"

"I intended to, tomorrow." I gazed up at him. "I didn't know any of this building evacuation business had happened, Tommy. I've been out working since this morning; I've only just got back."

"Are you telling me the truth?" When I nodded, he retrieved my cloak and handed it to me. "Come on."

I hesitated. "Am I under arrest?"

"No," he said. "You're going to show me this rat bomb."

Two beaters stood outside the entry to my office building, and both came to attention as Doyle and I approached. I also saw someone standing at the corner; a short figure in a funny-looking blue cape.

"Any activity?" Doyle asked.

"We've had a few of the tenants come by to ask what's to be done," one of the cops replied. "Not a happy lot, any of them."

"You don't want to go in there, sir," the other beater said quickly as Doyle climbed the steps. "I tried to nick in round the back to use the facilities, but the air's so putrid I lost me dinner." He grimaced at me. "Begging your pardon, miss."

"No worries, mate." I wrinkled my nose back at him. "Sorry about your stomach." When I glanced at the corner again the oddly-caped man was gone.

"Stand back." Doyle took out a blade and used it to cut through the sealing tape stretched across the doors. As he opened them I covered my mouth and nose with a kerchief, but the stench I expected never came.

Doyle breathed in several times before rubbing the back of his neck. "You're sure no one's slipped inside?" he asked his men.

"Landlord locked it up tight, sir, and gave us the keys," the first beater said.

To me Doyle said, "Do you or any of the tenants have keys?"

"Only to our own offices," I told him. "The landlord sends his man to open and close the building each day."

He took the beater's lantern. "Let's have a look in the basement, then."

I led the inspector downstairs to the Dungeon, which like the rest of the building held no trace of the noxious smell. I walked over to the workbench where Docket and I had examined the rat, but except for a few tools it stood empty.

"Docket was working on the animech here." I turned round to examine the floor, and pointed to a bare spot. "That's where I left the bucket." Like the rat and the stink it also had vanished. "This burglar would make an excellent janitor."

"I saw the spill here." Doyle knelt down, moving some of Docket's things aside to run his hand over the boards. "Bone dry." He glanced up at me. "There's not even a stain on the wood."

I crouched down and put my hand next to his. As soon as I touched the wood a dark stain spread out from my fingers.

Doyle hissed something vile and snatched my hand back. "Magic."

"Won't hurt me, Tommy." Curious marks scratched into the boards also appeared, but they were unlike any wards I'd ever encountered. "It must be some kind of concealment spell." I tried to take my hand from his but he held on. "You know I'm immune to magic."

"And how should I know that?" he demanded.

He couldn't, thanks to my time traveling. The cost of what I'd done to save Rumsen from invasion and bring Dredmore back from death was well and truly grating on my nerves now. "Uncle Arthur told you that my mother was a spell breaker, a gift I inherited from her."

"You're lying to me again." A muscle twitched under his right eye. "You never sound more truthful than when you are."

"How do I sound when I tell the truth? Like a liar?" I stood up and touched the workbench, but the rat didn't materialize. "So they mopped up and took the mech. Why go to all this trouble?"

"Removing the evidence of their crime." Doyle stood and scanned the workshop. "What I'd like to know is, why bother to erase the stench?"

"To prevent you from arresting me, or me from finding them," I said without thinking. "Or my would-be assassin truly is a janitor and quite devoted to his calling to clean."

He cupped my elbow and guided me toward the stairs. "Not an occupation I'd imagine an assassin like Lord Lucien Dredmore pursuing."

"That was beautifully done, Tommy," I said with very real admiration. "Should I stutter my astonishment first, then give you all the details about his completely innocent visit to my office this morning?"

"He's a deathmage, Kit," he reminded me, seemingly unaware that he'd used my given name. "He wasn't even born innocent."

That didn't seem fair to me. "Dredmore can't be blamed for the unfortunate circumstances of his birth, any more than you can scrub Uncle Arthur's blood out of your veins. Does anyone at the Yard know you're the grandson of a duke?"

"Grandda relinquished all claim to the title before he left the Motherland." His upper lip curled. "As for the lads, they know me to be what I am, the son of a farmer and their chief."

I liked that he wasn't a snob, although he would have done much better for himself by using his family's connections. If he hadn't become a cop, he might have been the perfect man for me. Not that I wanted a husband; they always expected wives to clean and cook and carry children. On the list of things I disliked immensely, those three ranked in the top ten.

Back outside the building Doyle informed his beaters that the premises were safe to reoccupy, and to notify the landlord of the same. He then drove me to the goldstone, and even walked me to the door.

"Thank you for the ride, Chief Inspector." I felt too tired to work up a properly cheeky grin. "I promise to report any suspicious parcels delivered to my office in the future. After I immerse them in my tea, of course. I don't think it matters what color it is."

He didn't laugh. "I'm assigning a beater to stand watch at your office."

I suppressed a groan. "For how long?"

"As long as I bloody wish." He saw my face and sighed. "Look, Kit, when I was assigned here my parents came along. The bought a farm just outside the city. I know Ma would love to have you there for a long visit. Let me arrange it." When I didn't reply he put a hand on my shoulder. "This sort doesn't like to fail, Kit. They will be coming for you again."

"Then I had better find out who they are before they do," I said lightly. "Good night, Chief Inspector."

CHAPTER FOUR

I took a carri-cab to the Hill the next morning and gave the driver a good tip along with instructions to return for me at noon.

"You sure you want to stay here so long, miss?" he asked, casting a wary eye at the windows of Bestly House, all of which had been draped from the inside with dark blue mourning blinds. "They've not even put out the doves yet."

"Noon, if you please," I said firmly, hefting my case before I took the walk round the house to the servants' door.

It took several minutes before my knock was answered by a very young maid with disheveled hair and a soot-dusted apron. She looked me up and down. "The house ain't receiving, miss. Master's died. Don't you see the windows?"

From her appearance and tone she was probably the scullery gel, which meant the butler had already abandoned his post. "I'm Miss Kittredge, and your mistress is expecting me. Let me in, and go and tell her I'm here."

Doubt screwed up her face. "Not supposed to go upstairs. 'Sides, I've got to see to the cooking."

"Come on." I pushed past her and led her through the storeroom and into the kitchens. Unwashed crockery, leftover food, and other rubbish covered nearly every flat surface. On the stove something was busily burning. "Cook leave with the butler, then?"

"Aye, slipped out last night after her ladyship told us about the master becoming a beast before he died." The gel fiddled with the sides of her apron. "All the maids are gone, too. Still got a footman, but I think he's only here 'cause he's due wages."

Scandal turned servants into rats; they never stayed to sink with the ship. I went over and removed a smoking pan of charred sausages from the stove. "What's your name, gel?"

"Annie." She flapped her hands about trying to dispel the smoke. "Annie Hartley."

I put the lid back on the open burner. "Why didn't you go with the others, Annie?"

"Ain't been in service but two months. Got no references but what her ladyship might give me, but I didn't want to ask. Seemed a bit mean-hearted." She coughed into her sleeve and then gestured at the mess. "'Sides, someone's got to look after herself, right?"

"Very commendable of you," I said. "I'll go upstairs and wake her ladyship. You put on the kettle, see what's in the cold pantry for tea, and set it up in whatever she uses as her morning room. And for God's sake, don't cook."

On my way to wake Lady Bestly I noticed other glaring signs of the staff's negligence: vases of dead flowers, blackened lamp glasses, and doors standing ajar or open. None of the family portraits in the halls had been veiled yet, and as I passed the butler's room I spotted unopened post and several packages sitting in several heaps on his writing table. I found her ladyship's bedchamber by following the trail of footprints left on the unswept rugs.

The neglect of the house should have made me feel

a bit smug; servants sneaking out in the middle of the night was only the opening ceremony of the ordeal yet to come. Lady Bestly had always been popular among the ton, for whom there could never be enough rules or kowtowing; to protect their own reputations they'd see to it that her fall from grace was immediate and ugly.

In a week or less Lady Bestly would occupy hell on earth, or as close to it as her friends and neighbors could make it.

I rapped on the door. "Milady, it's Kittredge." After hearing a muffled "Enter," I walked in.

Some sort of fruity cologne saturated the air but failed to disguise the sour scent of puke. A full blue-and-red-striped mourning gown stood at the foot of an unmade bed; something trapped inside it writhed before sighing.

"It seems my maid has chosen to pursue another position," the gown said, "and I have never dressed myself. Would you be so kind, Kittredge, as to provide some assistance?"

I set down my case and went to her, straightening the wadded bodice and sleeves. "Annie Hartley, your scullery gel, was playing at cook when I arrived. You might have her bathe and bring her upstairs before she sets fire to the place." I glanced at the necessary pot sitting beside the bed and the dark, damp spots on the rug where she'd missed it. "Are you unwell, milady?"

The face that popped through the high collar of the bodice looked pale and tired under the thick paint and powder. "I am grieving, Kittredge. It does not put roses in one's cheeks. I can manage the sleeves, thank you." She presented her back to me so I could button, and

I frowned at a large bruise covering her shoulder. "So Cook has vacated her post? And without notice, like the others. How do they expect to find suitable employment without a reference, I wonder."

"They'll use whatever you accepted when you hired them." I started at the top button and worked my way down. "Everyone will know they were working for you, but once word gets out they'll all pretend it never happened."

"I should have suspected as much when Jarvis left last week." She tugged at the scarlet lace of her cuffs. "Thirty-two years of service to my husband, and not so much as a farewell to me. Perhaps he'll have second thoughts."

I could have lied to her, but it was time the woman faced facts. "None of them will be back, milady. To return to this house after the story about Lord Bestly is printed would be the same as publicly condoning what your husband did. They'd load bricks in their pockets and jump into the bay first."

Her shoulders slumped a little. "I cannot acquire any new servants until after the end of my first mourning. Even then, no one will wish to serve a maniac's widow."

"Lord Dredmore might arrange something, or there are the day-service agencies in town. Their hires aren't as respectable as live-ins, but they'll look after you." As was the custom I left one button unfastened and surveyed the length of her untidy night braid. If she'd never gotten dressed by herself she'd probably never touched a brush, either. "Come and sit by the vanity, and I'll do your hair."

She faced me. "You, attend to my person? I think not."

"I can fetch Annie to do it, if you'd rather," I offered. "Or the footman waiting on his wage packet."

"There's no one else?" When I shook my head she closed her eyes and swayed a little. "I cannot bear this. It is intolerable. It is *indecent*."

"Don't dwell on it, milady. You'll only be sick again." I took her by the arm and led her over to the vanity, where I eased her into the chair. "I can manage something simple," I said as I untied the end of her braid. "I won't pin it too tight; that will only make the throbbing worse."

She watched me in the mirror. "How did you know I have a headache?"

"I always do after I, ah, have bouts of indigestion." I picked up a brush and began working on the ends. "We do have to talk about your husband, and how he was before he died. All right?" When she nodded, I asked, "Did you notice anything out of the ordinary with him before the incident?"

She sat back and closed her eyes. "If you mean did he behave differently toward me, no. He spent much of the day in his study, of course, but we always shared luncheon and dinner together. Our conversations were normal. He did not mistreat me or the servants."

She was presenting a rather rosy image of her husband, but few wished to speak ill of the dead, who often became such angels in memory. I ran the brush through the white curtain of her hair before I reached for the pin minder. "Where was he spending his nights? At the club, or with a friend?"

Her shoulders went rigid. "That is not your business."

"None of this is," I agreed. "But if your husband had a particular friend, I will have to know."

She pressed her fingers to her mouth before she

dropped her hand. "My husband did not seek out such women. He regarded the vows of marriage as sacred, and when he felt need of conjugal intimacy, he came to me." She caught my gaze in the mirror. "You may regard this as fantastic, Kittredge, but Terrance was an excellent man and a devoted husband."

She said that in her president-of-the-Rumsen-Ladies'-Decency-Society tone, which told me two things: either the late Lord Bestly had been genuinely devoted to his wife, or he had shown his deference to her by being extremely discreet. Given that she had as much personal warmth as a mountaintop in December, I'd put my stakes on the latter.

"Very well, no particular friends." I tucked a hairpin in place. "Can you recall what he did on the day before he died?"

"I can't say for the morning. I hadn't slept well so I rose rather late that day." She cleared her throat. "I had luncheon with Terrance at one, and we discussed the weather and gardens. I was concerned about another frost harming the sweet pea vines. He directed Jarvis to speak to the groundsman and have him blanket the new blooms—it was all very normal, Kittredge. Nothing to indicate he entertained violent plans, or felt guilty or remorseful."

"Why would he? He hadn't done anything yet." I tucked some stray strands under the coil of her chignon. "After your luncheon, did he return to his study?"

"Yes. No. I believe he went direct to his dressing room to change. I spoke to him in the hall a little before three." She frowned. "He left shortly after that, and he didn't return."

I picked up a comb and came round to smooth out the front of her hair. "What did you say to him in the hall, exactly?"

"If you must know, I told him he looked deplorable." Her jaw tightened. "My last words to my husband were to suggest he sack the valet. Such a warm memory to cherish, don't you think?"

"You weren't to know you'd never see him again. There." I lowered the comb and stepped back. "I've done as much damage as I can."

Lady Bestly examined her reflection. "This is good work. Somewhat simple but quite tolerable." Her eyes narrowed. "You're very familiar with a maid's duties for someone who has never been in service."

"I've played the part a time or two, most often for my mother. Mum loved having her hair brushed." I let the comb fall onto the vanity table with a clatter. "I directed Annie to put together morning tea for you. She can't cook so you shouldn't expect anything hot. While you're downstairs I'll have a look at his lordship's rooms, with your permission."

"Of course," she said. "His bedchamber and dressing room are at the end of the hall. The study is at the back of the house, across from the dining room."

"Thank you, milady." I retrieved my case.

"Kittredge, any evidence you might locate must be brought to me directly, that I may examine it for myself," Lady Bestly said. "Nothing you find is to leave the house, is that understood?"

She doled out insults much more deftly than she did compliments—and she was also frightened, maybe even terrified, of what I might find. "Absolutely, milady."

I started my search in Lord Bestly's bedchamber, which appeared to have been tidied but smelled musty, as if no one had entered since the night of his death. I drew back the curtains only to confront the dark blue funeral blind that had been tacked to the frame. Removing it would only further scandalize her ladyship's neighbors, so I left it in place and instead lit the lamps.

The chamber could have belonged to any successful gentleman. Several carefully polished trophies marched along the marble mantel above the cold hearth; I read one engraved plaque that proclaimed a hunting victory some thirty years past. The others were of the same age and boasted of his lordship's prowess at shooting, archery, and tracking.

"Quite the sportsman in your youth." Lady Bestly had likely put an end to all that after their wedding; an unfortunate clash with some native hunters twenty years ago had made outdoor sport uncongenial, and therefore unfashionable, among the tonners.

After taking the magnifying glass and some other tools from my case I looked through Lord Bestly's armoire, secretary, and boot cases, finding nothing but costly garments and ruthlessly polished leather. He'd dressed mainly in the dark, conservative style of his rank with some startling contradictions; he'd liked complicated cravats that must have bedeviled his valet, and had amassed an astonishing variety of bejeweled lapel pins. I also found a watch case containing a dozen pocket watches, all solid gold and set with diamonds, emeralds, rubies, and other precious stones.

If he'd left the house on the day of his death looking deplorable, as her ladyship had indicated, it hadn't been because of his wardrobe.

The stark cut and sober color of his clothing didn't fit with the flashiness of his neckties and personal adornments; pairing them would have made him resemble a magpie. Perhaps that was what his wife had found so objectionable. The garments were intended for wearing at home, definitely, but the pins and the watches . . .

When I went downstairs I'd have to ask her to explain what exactly about his garments had prompted her withering observation.

The silk coverlet on the bed appeared unwrinkled and spotless, and when I drew it back I found his linens in the same condition. Beneath the bed the necessary was bone dry and occupied by a small, deceased house spider, a dusty web, and a tiny broken egg sac, indicating the pot hadn't been used or cleaned for quite some time.

I bent over the bed and sniffed the linens, detecting a strong version of the musty odor. The bed hadn't been stripped or slept in for weeks, perhaps months. I lifted the mattress on either side to probe it with my ticking pick, but found no cache beneath the edges, and nothing stuffed or hidden in the ticking.

"The only thing really living in here was that poor spinner," I muttered.

I went from the bedchamber to the dressing room, which I found in much the same state. The adjoining lavatory held a large bath, sink, and washstand that hadn't known water in months. An expensive assortment of pomades, colognes, and soaps filled the toiletry cabinet, but most were dried up or showed the cracks of nonuse. His hairbrush held plenty of dust but not a single hair; his straight razor sported an edge of uneven rust, and lay resting beside a cake of shaving soap so desiccated it had shrunk from the edges of its porcelain dish.

I made a second sweep of both rooms, this time searching for any cashsafes or hidey-hole in which Lord Bestly might have stashed his secrets and warded with concealment magic. After running my echo across every wall and finding nothing, I stomped downstairs to the study.

The cold of the interior gave me pause on the threshold, and I took a moment to take it in. Here was a room that had been regularly occupied, unlike what I'd seen upstairs; signs of Lord Bestly's presence were everywhere. A copy of the *Rumsen Daily* lay partially unfolded on a table by the hearth-side armchair; a half-empty carafe of some dark amber liquor stood sparkling by several crystal tumblers. Neat stacks of correspondence sat on one side of the desk opposite a hefty book with a monogrammed brass marker poking out of its pages. A pair of riding boots, shining with a mirror finish, stood near a cloak stand hung with three different gentleman's coats.

Years of the master smoking cigars, handling paper, and sipping strong drink had permeated the study with the pungent but not unpleasant scent of all three. According to his wife, Lord Bestly had spent much of his time in his study. My impression was that his lordship had practically lived in here, although Rina had said lately he'd been entrenched at his club. Perhaps he'd divided his time between both. . . .

Because this was where I would likely find any real

evidence of what had happened to the gentleman, I moved into the room with slow, deliberate steps, turning my head from side to side to inspect everything. I studied the arrangement of the furnishings, read the titles of the books in the glass-fronted shelfairs, and eyed the measures of liquor left in each bottle standing on the libation trolley.

With the latter I saw something very wrong: three of the decanters had less than an inch of liquor in them. Tonners prided themselves on being able to offer their cronies a drink whenever they came to call; whenever a bottle ran low Lord Bestly would have ordered the butler to refill it.

The apple and pear brandies remained full, as did all of the smaller schnapps. Only one bottle had been completely emptied, and I picked it up and lifted the stopper to smell it. The strong odor of blue ruin still clung to the inside of the decanter. The selection of spirits made it plain that Bestly often drank at home, but why bother when he could freely indulge at his club? Unless he went there for other reasons. . . .

The door behind me opened. "Fancy a drink, miss?"

I turned round to see a younger man grinning at me. His livery identified him as the lingering footman and, judging by the badly wrinkled state of his sleeves, trousers, and jacket, he'd evidently slept in it. His bloodshot eyes were a light blue made disagreeably insipid by the darkness of his olive skin and the greasy gleam of his heavily pomaded black hair. The distinctive bridge of his nose suggested that at least one of his parents had been Talian.

"I don't drink spirits. They make my eyes red." I replaced the gin bottle on the trolley. "And what is your name?"

"Roger Akins, at your service, miss." He abstained from a bow and tramped toward me. "The pretty gels all call me Jolly. 'Cause I am, you see."

The smell rolling toward me told me what fate Lord Bestly's blue ruin had met.

"Is this jolliness a perpetual state," I asked, "or something you enjoy only after you help yourself to the master's liquor?"

"Posh talk for a shopgel," he said with a sneer. "What you come here to sell her? Gloves? Hats? Sashes? Give it up, she can't wear nothing new." He squinted at me. "Or are you one them what chases out unwholesome spirits? What they call them, exormages?"

"I am here to tidy up," I agreed.

"Should have said." Giving me more of a wary look he veered away and went to the trolley, where he filled a tumbler with whiskey. "Sure you don't want a sip? It's top notch, best quality. Still burns going down, but won't leave you with a raw gullet."

"I never indulge, thank you." I saw Lady Bestly appear in the doorway behind him. "It's also rather early to be drinking."

"Bah." He swatted at the air between us. "Herself's like you, don't take no spirits. Rest of household's run off in the night." He leaned forward and added in a mock-whisper, "So if someone has a bit of a nightcap when the day's work's done, or even before it starts, who's to know, ay?"

"As you say, mate." I kept my gaze on him. "What did you sample besides the drink?"

"Couple of them cigars." He made a hideous face at the humidor. "Don't smoke easy like cigs. Couldn't hardly keep them lit."

He hadn't been in the upstairs chambers or he'd have stuffed his pockets with his lordship's pins and watches. "Nicked anything good for yourself?"

"Stealing from a widow's a sin." He drained his glass and belched. "I did see some of her good silver's gone. Bet it walked off with that Jarvis, the coin-grubber." He nodded as if he'd just convinced himself of that fact before giving me a leer. "Want to give the brandy a taste, then? It's wretched sweet, but you might fancy it."

I glanced past him. "I believe that's all, milady, but I recommend you have his cases checked before he leaves."

"What? Who?" Akins spun round, staggering as he saw Lady Bestly and grabbing a chair to right himself. "Your ladyship, I—I—I found this shopgel in here, drinking up the master's gin—"

"Forgot to say," I murmured to him. "Not a shopgel."

Lady Bestly strode into the room. "You are dismissed for drunkenness and thievery, Mr. Akins. Collect your belongings and leave the house at once."

"Blind me, I wouldn't steal from you, milady—"

"She heard everything you told me," I advised him. "Dunce."

"I'm owed wages, I am," Akins whined. "It's the only reason I stayed long as I have." He gave Lady Bestly an ugly look. "And I ain't leaving till I get what's due me."

I coshed him smartly with the empty gin container and watched him pitch forward into a heap. "Is Mr. Akins due anything more, milady?"

"I should think that will suffice, Kittredge." Lady Bestly gave the unconscious footman a final glance before ringing the bell. When Annie trotted in she ignored the scullery's wide-eyed gasp and said, "Hartley, please summon a patrolman to remove Akins and his belongings. Oh, and before he is taken away, do see that none of the family silver has fallen into his baggage."

"Right away, milady." Annie scurried off.

Lady Bestly regarded me. "If you would join me in the drawing room, Hartley has kindly prepared tea."

"Thank you, milady." I put the decanter back on the trolley. "I am a little thirsty."

Once in the drawing room I accepted a dainty cup of the blackest tea I'd ever seen, and held it as I surveyed what appeared to be a feast for twenty crammed haphazardly on the serving table. I counted five loaves of bread, seven bowls of fruits and nuts, a quivering gold and pink tower of diced ham in aspic, and more crumpets, scones, and cakes than a busy bakery could sell on a morning before a holiday.

"You will need a cook, milady," I said as I stared at one platter containing a cold roast of beef as big as my head that Annie had surrounded with a dozen unpeeled red apples. "Tonight at the very—is this *everything* in your cold panty?"

Lady Bestly's expression was serene as she offered me the cream pot. "I do believe it is."

∽

Once Akins's baggage had been searched and his person removed by the nobber, I returned to the study to continue my search. I rechecked the decanters of spirits, this time with dippers, but found no trace of poison or drugs. I also went through every paper, letter, and other document in Lord Bestly's desk, all of which pertained to either his social schedule or his household routine. His lordship had not kept a journal or diary, and reading his brief, dry personal correspondence made me yawn so often I nearly nodded off.

Bored, I performed a final, methodic search of the furnishings, cabinets, and walls, but once more I found nothing hidden or bespelled. Everything was as it should have been, and it frustrated me. This was not the lair of a lunatic killer; nothing suggested Lord Bestly had been committing atrocities in secret or making a slow descent into madness. Everything indicated he'd lived a proper gentleman's life occupied by the usual pursuits of his class, one that was so ordinary it seemed colorless.

"What life?" I muttered as I paced the room. "The man had no life here. He didn't sleep in his bed or shave or bathe or—" I stopped in my tracks.

Lord Bestly hadn't lived in the house. He'd put on a ruse of it, but he'd been sleeping and bathing elsewhere. But where?

Rina's voice echoed in my head. *Founded a gent's club . . . practically lives there . . .*

"Miss?" Annie peeked in at me. "Your carri's waiting outside."

"Thank you, Annie." Distracted now, I turned to her. "Where is Lady Bestly?"

"Milady went into town to see her physick. She's been feeling poorly in the mornings." Annie twisted her hands in her apron. "Sorry about the tea, miss. I didn't know what to put out from the panty, so I put out everything. That was wrong, I knew it, but . . ." She hesitated before she said, "Will she give me the sack for it, you think?"

"She'd be daft if she did. You're the only one who hasn't walked out on her. But if she does"—I dug a calling card out of my reticule and offered it to her—"you come and see me in town. I'll find another position for you."

"Would you, really?" Her face brightened as she took the card. "That's ever so nice of you, miss." She hesitated before she added, "I know what they been saying the master done, but he weren't like that at all. He always had a kind word for everyone, even me."

"Is that right?" In any other household a scullery would never have had any dealings with family. "When did his lordship speak with you last, Annie?"

She smiled. "Every day, miss. He liked to come through the kitchens when he was leaving for town. Once, when Cook was at market, he stayed and had a talk with me."

I nodded. "And what did he say to you that day?"

"He asked after me parents, and said he was sorry when I told him they'd passed on. Then he wanted to know what I been doing on me half days. He told me about this nice place for a picnic." She sighed. "Honestly, miss, he made me so nervous I forgot to watch the fire. Burned a whole pot of stew. Thought Cook would pull me ear off when she got back."

Bestly had been up to something, but with the scullery? "Did you ever go and have a picnic, Annie?"

"Oh, no, miss." Annie shook her head. "I stay in me room on me half day. Only chance I get to sleep past dawn."

"This nice place he told you about," I persisted, "did it have a name?"

She nodded. "Rosings Park. The master liked to visit it, too." Her face clouded. "It's where they found him when he died."

CHAPTER FIVE

When I returned to the city I went to the office and paid a visit to the Dungeon to see if Docket had recovered, but the old mechanic was nowhere to be found. I spent the next hour going door to door to make my apologies to the other tenants. Most of them were familiar with my business, and gracious enough to accept my explanation, which was a politic retelling of some of the truth: a poorly addressed parcel of powerful farming fertilizer had been sent through the tubes for weeks before being accidentally delivered to me. My clumsiness had caused the parcel to fall into a bucket of old tea, which had saturated it, activated the fertilizer, and resulted in the unpleasant smell.

I would have given myself the credit for eradicating the stink, too, but I couldn't think of a lie to explain how and instead credited an unnamed mage of my acquaintance whom I'd brought in for the cleanup.

Everyone seemed to believe my tale except for Fourth, who was having none of it.

"There are no farms or farmers in the city," Gremley informed me, "and even if there were, the merchants who sell to them do so in such quantities as would never fit in a tube."

I hadn't thought of that. "Perhaps it was a sample of some sort."

"I should say not. The properties of fertilizer are universally known." He regarded me. "To my mind I think this some sort of attack on you and your business, Miss Kittredge, and if it was, that cannot be tolerated."

"Your concern does you credit, Mr. Gremley." And wishing he was a little stupider wouldn't make it so. "I have met with Chief Inspector Doyle of Rumsen Main, however, and I know the police will be looking into the matter."

"I do not mean to badger you, Miss Kittredge," he said, "but it is ever a gentleman's strictest duty to protect the fair sex."

I smiled. "I feel safer already, Mr. Gremley. Now I will stop taking up your valuable time and return to my own labors."

"Oh, please, not just yet." His cheeks pinked as he added, "Forgive me, I dislike imposing on you, but would it be terribly inconvenient to ask for your opinion on a matter of feminine taste?"

"I am the least feminine woman I know," I admitted, "but I certainly have more opinions than New Parliament. Please, ask."

"It is only this." Fourth opened his desk drawer, from which he removed a small white velvet-flocked box. He held it as if he expected it to explode. "I intend to ask Mr. Skolnick for permission to marry Maritza." His hand trembled as he held out the box. "This is what I shall be offering my beloved. Unless you think it hideous."

I took it and removed the lid to reveal the contents.

"I know it is not especially grand," Fourth said quickly, "but I rather liked it."

I held up the thin filigree engagement ring. The dainty thing sported five small citrines and a garnet fashioned into the shape of a bloom.

"Why do you choose a daisy?" I asked, looking up at him.

He went red. "Maritza is always picking them when we take a turn in the park. She has never said, but I think it her favorite Torian flower." His Adam's apple bobbed. "I would give her diamonds and rubies, but such are beyond my means. Is it too humble, do you think?"

"On the contrary, sir. I think it the most lovely and thoughtful engagement ring I have ever beheld." Carefully I returned it to its case and handed it back to him. "I also predict that Miss Skolnick will be offering much in the way of gratitude to the luckiest of her stars. Just after she says yes."

He beamed. "Oh, you are very good, and surely the best of friends, Miss Kittredge." He seized my hand and tried to shake it off my arm.

As soon as I could politely extract myself I said, "I must get on with my business at hand. I meant to ask, did you see Mr. Docket this morning?"

Sorrow replaced his joy. "Mr. Billson from Talbot's Shipping on two told me that he'd seen the poor old gent last night at hospital, when he went there to visit his brother. From what he described I fear Mr. Docket is very ill."

"Hospital." My throat tightened and I hurried out, turning round and dashing back in to ask, "Did Mr. Talbot say which hospital he visited, Mr. Gremley?"

"I believe it was Saint Albert's on the North."

I gave him my thanks and ran out to the street, where there were no carri-cabs in sight. Going on foot was out of the question; Saint Albert's on the North lay on the other side of the city, at least twenty miles away.

An only too-familiar gray coach stopped at the curb in front of me, and the door with Dredmore's spike-and-fist crest swung open. At the same time a carri trundled to a stop just behind it, and Doyle peered round the back of the coach at me.

Here then were my prospects of immediate transportation; I had only to decide if I wanted to go with the assassin or the copper.

I spotted a trolley coming to a stop on the other side of the street and darted between the two. "Another time, Inspector," I called back to Doyle. I glanced over at Dredmore's coach, shrugged, and ran to board the trolley.

I paid the fare for two transfer exchanges and a return before I went to the back and sat in a rear-facer so I could watch the back. I didn't think Tommy would follow me crosstown, but Dredmore might. Once the coast was clear I heard the sound of huffing on my left and glanced at the pudgy clerk occupying the other half of the seat. "Afternoon."

He sniffed and turned his face away, watching the buildings we passed with a permanent glower of disapproval.

The older man seated across from us lowered the top half of the newspaper he was reading. "You should have a maid with you, young woman."

What he meant was I shouldn't have been on the trolley at all; real ladies never stooped to make use of such public transport.

"I just learned that a friend of mine is in hospital, sir," I told him. "I couldn't wait for a maid, even if I did have one." '

"The violence of one's affections must be tempered with the proper attention to one's reputation." He snapped his newspaper back up.

What he said made me go still, but not because I took it to heart. The violence of one's affections . . .

Lord Bestly hadn't been sleeping or bathing at his home for months, but he'd maintained the appearance that he was. I sensed that his facade hadn't been merely for his wife's benefit, either. Everything at the house had felt staged, as if Bestly hadn't wanted to leave a single clue about the life he had been living elsewhere.

I didn't know his reason for such absolute conceal-ment; they could be anything from a gambling problem to a second, bigamous marriage. It wasn't a penchant for the company of harlots; Rina would have known about that. Whatever his lordship had been up to, however, had been something so unworthy as to make him beyond reticent; he'd probably gone to great lengths to erase all evidence of it.

"Because if he hadn't, his reputation would have been destroyed," I muttered to myself. "But what could be so ruinous?"

The clerk gave a second, stronger sniff and shifted another inch away from me.

It took another hour and two changes of trolleys to reach Saint Albert's on the North, which like so many across the territories had once been called something else but was renamed in honor of Her Majesty's father, Prince Albert. We had so many, in fact, that some people had taken to calling all hospitals Berties for short.

This one was very old, the very first built in the province after the occupation. It had always been run by the Conscientious Claires, an odd order of nuns who had long ago broken from the papists to take up marriage, nursing, and an unwavering devotion to the Church of England. They were easy to spot in the city, for they always wore bright blue frocks with red-and-white-striped pinafores.

I was met in the front entry by a young, brisk-looking nurse holding a notebook and pen. "Welcome to Saint Albert, miss," she said, looking me over with expectant eyes. "Patient or visitor?"

"I've come to see Reginald Docket." If he was very ill they would only permit family access, so I added, "I'm his niece, Kit."

She consulted her notes. "Docket, Docket, ah yes. Sir Reginald is in the Recovery Hall."

Sir Reginald? "Where is that, please?"

She used her pencil to point to the right. "Just down that hall, on the left at the end. Your uncle's room is on the right, 714. Visiting hours end at six, but you'll hear the bell."

I thanked her and followed her directions to a narrow hall of patients' rooms, and nodded to some other nurses pushing linen and medicine carts. Although most of the rooms stood open, I found the door to room 714 closed, and knocked twice before I stepped inside.

Two beds stood divided by a hanging blue-and-white-striped curtain, and the first was empty. I approached silently, drawing back the curtain with a trembling hand as I braced myself for the worst.

Docket lay huddled with his back to me, his body shrouded beneath a heavy wool blanket. I'd never realized how old he was until now, seeing him like this, so frail and helpless. I didn't want to wake him, but if he was dying . . .

Slowly Docket turned over, groaning a little as one eyelid lifted. "My dear gel," he said, his voice a thready whisper. "Have you come alone?"

"Yes, as soon I heard." I moved quickly to the bed and took hold of his head. "I'm so sorry, mate. I never should have brought that wretched animech down to you."

He tried to look round me. "Did you close the door?" When I nodded, both of his eyes opened and he sat straight up. "Good on you. Bloody nurses have eyes like hawks."

I let go of his hand. "You're not dying."

"Course I'm not." He wriggled, reaching back to adjust his pillows before he reclined again, tucking his hands behind his head. "Felt good as new, soon as I woke up. Haven't slept so comfortable in years. Pity that mech stunk so bad, or I'd jar it and sell it as a slumber potion."

I peered down at him. "If you're not dying, why are you here?"

"Can't go back, building's been shut up." He regarded me. "I don't have a nice house like you, Kit. I live in the Dungeon."

Now I understood. "You're faking it so you can sleep here."

He beamed. "Not just sleep, my gel. They feed me three meals a day, change me sheets every morning— do you know, they even bathe me, with sponges. Right here in the bed, like an infant." He sighed with contentment. "If this is what heaven is like, I'll have to leave off sinning."

I sank down on the chair beside the bed. "I flew across town because I thought you were done for, Doc." I glared at him. "Or should I be calling you Sir Reginald?"

"Them bloody do-gooders." He tried to look indignant. "Pulled me papers out of me wallet. I told them it don't mean nothing here."

"It means you're either gentry or knighted," I countered. "So which is it?"

"Knighted," he mumbled. "Fat lot of good it's done me. Herself taps me shoulder with a sword one minute, and the next I'm tossed on a boat to Toriana."

"You were knighted and deported on the same day." Some of my temper eased. "Only you, Doc."

"Explosion only wrecked a little bit of Buckingham, and I did save Herself, didn't I?" He waved a hand. "Sod them all, ungrateful bastards. Now what about you? Did you find out who sent the rat?"

"Not yet. While the building was shut up someone nicked everything we had, even the smell." I related what had occurred when I'd visited the Dungeon with Doyle. "The only thing left was a stain on the floorboards where the tea spilled, and they tried to cover that up with a concealment spell."

"The stench came from that bit of flesh inside the rat. Stag. I'm sure of it." His expression darkened. "After you left that day I checked a few of me books. Can't be certain, but I think it was native magic."

Doc's suggestion set every wheel in my head to spin with a fury. I should have guessed a tribal mage was involved; the smelly gland from the stag or whatever animal they'd killed was an unmistakable giveaway. Natives used blood ritual and animal sacrifice to work their magic, which I found disgusting. For that and other reasons I'd always steered clear of the local shamans, and now I felt perplexed. "Why would a native want me dead?"

"Probably don't. Could have been part of the ploy," Docket suggested. "Everyone knows Torian mages won't dirty their hands with animal magic. So you use a native spell to work your mischief, and afterward everyone blames them."

"No one knows native magic but the shamans," I pointed out, "and they guard their spells and rituals like the Crown jewels."

He nodded. "Could be why they came back to clean up. They got that stag gland, but they didn't nick the mech. Just before I blacked out I put the rat in my pocket." He nodded toward the trunk sitting at the foot of the bed. "Should still be in me coat."

I went to the trunk to search his coat, and removed a small cloth sack containing the mech. "You're brilliant, mate."

"Ah, go on with you." He looked pleased. "You should take it. That speller might come here looking for it."

I nodded. "What about you?"

"Since the Dungeon's been tidied up I expect I'll be

taking a startling turn for the better." He winked at me. "Right after me evening bathe."

I left Docket to enjoy his last night with the sisters and took the market square tram instead of returning to the office. Until I ferreted out who was responsible for the mech rat, the safest place for it was in my wall cache at home.

Unlike the city trolleys, the tram was packed with females; mostly wives or daughters of merchants and work-men returning from an afternoon at market. Handbaskets filled with vegetables and fruits occupied every lap that didn't hold a baby too young to be left at home. I found a space between an old lady snapping the ends off a pile of pole beans and a tired-looking young mother trying to rock an equally exhausted toddler to sleep.

"Got kin at hospital, then?" the older lady asked me. When I nodded she gave me a pained smile. "That's too bad. No worries, love. Sisters looked after me Rob in his last months, God rest. They're good and gentle souls."

"Says you," the young mother put in. "I had little Charlie here at Berties, and ghastly it was, them hushing me and saying it were natural. Natural, to feel like you're being split in half. And what came out after!"

I cringed a little and glanced outside. A well-known duchess was walking out of a hat shop with two of her maids carrying stacks of boxes. Her Grace held a diamond-studded leash attached to a long, large feline animech made of gold. When it lifted its head I saw the eyes, fashioned from enormous orange topazes, blink.

A hoot from the old lady drew my attention back to my tram companions.

"At least you had nurses to look after you. I birthed all six of mine at home, with no one but me husband to help." The old lady gave me a jaded look. "I loved him, dearly I did, but Rob were like all men in a pinch. Useless."

As I nodded, I silently renewed my lifelong vow never to procreate if I could help it.

"Here." The old lady wound up the simple tin animech butterfly pendant hanging from a chain round her neck and let the boy hold it and watch the blunted wings flutter. As the child's eyes drooped closed the young mother whispered her thanks.

The sky gradually darkened as the tram crossed the city into the poorer sections, and then came to a sudden, violent stop. Pole beans rained over my skirts, and as I reached to right the old lady's basket I saw the driver stand up and reach for the trunch club hanging beside the door pull.

"What is it?" Plastering her now-screaming little Charlie to her breast, the young mother tried to peer round the other passengers who were scrambling to pick up what they'd spilled. "Another carri crash?"

A terrible howl ripped through the air, silencing everyone for three seconds. As several women erupted into shrieks, I got up and pushed my way down the aisle to the door.

"Are you daft, gel?" The driver caught my arm and tried to shove me back. "There's a mob out there—"

I caught a glimpse of people running or cowering away as others were tossed into the air like rag dolls. Before I could make out what was tossing them the

77

driver and I were both thrown against his perch as something slammed into the side of the tram.

Someone screamed, "It's the Wolfman" as glass shattered and chaos ensued.

I pushed myself up and saw the driver had been knocked unconscious. I turned to the passengers. "Stay in your seats and keep your heads down." I had to shout to be heard above the din they were making. "Put the children between you. Do not try to get off the tram." I grabbed the driver's trunch and peered through the door panel.

A massive fist covered in dark brown hair punched through the panel, pelting me with shattered glass. I dodged the groping hand and brought down the trunch on the wrist as hard as I could. Bone cracked, flesh split, and sparks flew up in my face. At the same time a horrible screech sounded, but the monstrous hand kept snatching at me.

I darted back out of reach and clutched whatever I could, bracing myself as the entire front of the tram began to shake. The hairy brown hand pulled back, grasping the edge of the door panel. Despite the sharp glass cutting into its flesh it jerked wildly at the frame, flinging gouts of blood as it tried to yank the panel from its frame.

If this thing could do that to a door, I couldn't allow it to board a tram filled with women and children.

I turned my head toward the passengers and raised my voice again, this time to be heard over the snarling outside.

"Pass all your baggage and belongings to the front," I told them. "When I go out, stack them up on the stair and block the door with them." As the terrified women stared at me, I added, "Come on, he's nearly got in now. We can't let him at the kids, can we?"

Half the women immediately surged out of their seats to stand in the aisle, and quickly formed a brigade to pass their parcels to the front. Somehow the old lady with the beans had worked her way up to me, and gripped my shoulder hard.

"When you get out, dearie, you run for your life," she told me, and pressed her paring knife into my hand. "But if he catches you, you give him a good jab with this. Side of the neck or into the eye will do the job."

I nodded, tucking the blade into my sleeve before I gripped the roof pole to my right and the glasshield divider to my left. Using them to support my weight, I brought up both legs, kicking out the door panel and onto the thing tearing at it, knocking it back.

I landed just to the right of it as I jumped out of the tram, and in the few heartbeats it took me to gather up my skirts it threw off the broken panel and got up on all fours.

I backed away, glancing at the tram to see the women stacking and cramming their baskets and parcels to block the broken door before I regarded the thing on the ground.

It looked something like a man, and the shredded, bloodstained clothes he wore had once been very fine. Long, shaggy brown hair covered every inch of its face, neck, and hands, and more sprouted through the rents in his sleeves and trousers. White eyes with tiny black pupils stared back at me, and his flattened, blackened nose hitched as froth-white lips peeled back from jagged teeth.

It snarled again as it took a step toward me, lowering

its head and using its human hands like paws. I heard a grinding noise as one of its shoulders dropped and it partly collapsed again, until it thrust itself up on its legs and swayed, dripping blood from its torn hands onto the pavement.

"Easy now," I murmured and inched backward, wondering if I'd live long enough to tell Lady Bestly that her husband had not, in fact, been the Wolfman. "You're hurt. I can get help for you." As I said that, I slipped the knife from my sleeve into my hand.

The Wolfman staggered forward, stepping out of the shadows and into a shaft of moonlight, where it went still. A horrible crackling sound grated against my ears as its nose began to thrust forward, growing out of its face and reshaping itself into a snout. At the same time the tips of the creature's brown ears shot up in two points, and its pelt of brown hair grew heavier and thicker.

The silence round me told me everyone had fled the street, which made the crackling and crunching noises coming from the Wolfman seem even louder. The cause seemed to be its limbs, which were twitching as muscles bulged out, splitting the few intact seams of its jacket and causing it to fall away from its expanding torso in shreds.

Whatever was causing the transformation held the beast mesmerized, and from the way it stared up at the sky it had to be the moon. I backed away unnoticed, reaching the end of the block before the Wolfman dropped its head and fixed its mad gaze on me.

Slowly its jaw lowered, and what began as a low snarl grew into an unearthly roar.

I hitched up my skirts, whirling and running as fast

as I could into the alley, looking frantically for some open door or high perch I could climb. Howling echoed off the brick walls, and heavy running steps scraped against the cobblestones. I felt the bellow of hot breath against my shoulders just before I was snatched off my feet and thrown into a pile of crates.

The impact knocked the knife from my hand and the breath from my lungs. Pain shot through me as I tried to push myself upright, but the rough hairy hands were already latching onto my bodice.

The Wolfman seized me by the throat and then went still, the hair covering its face receding into his flesh, along with extruding snout and sharp claws. Now a man again, he looked down at me and then bared his teeth like an animal. I felt him dragging up my skirts, and screamed as his head came down to sink his blunt teeth into my shoulder.

Before he bit me something hit him and threw him off me, coming at him a second time and tumbling over and over with him down the alley.

I pushed myself out of the pile of broken crates to see a second Wolfman attacking the one who had been changed back into a man. Rigid with terror, I crawled upward, pressing myself against the wall. The one who had attacked me transformed again into a beast and fought wildly. As they savaged each other, their jaws ripping and claws rending, sparks flew from between them and bounced off the bricks and stones, impossibly bright.

The second Wolfman uttered a gurgling shriek as the first latched onto its throat with inhuman fangs and crunched down. I turned my head away as a wide swath of blood sprayed from the wound, and saw the knife I'd dropped. I dragged myself over to it, reaching down to swipe it up and cradle it against my breast as I stood.

Something heavy fell, and when I looked I saw both Wolfmen had fallen to the ground, still locked together. Their bodies writhed, then twitched, and then went motionless. Blood misted the air and seeped out round them in a dark, gleaming pool.

I didn't move. I didn't think I could move again. I gulped the air and watched them, my knuckles white as I gripped the knife. I didn't understand why my eyes felt so hot and dry until I realized I'd stopped blinking, and closed them.

I slid down the wall, landing on my bruised bottom in a billow of torn skirts. When more footsteps came into the alley, I looked over at the two beaters who had come.

"Have a care." I had to swallow twice before I could get the rest of the words out. "I'm not sure they're dead."

"Hang back a bit, Donny." The one who said that came to me, his callused hands gentle as he helped me up. "Give us the blade, love. That's it." He carefully pried it from my fist and handed it to his partner. "I saw how you lured him away from the tram. Wee gel like you, taking on that monster. You're an angel."

The alley darkened as the clouds obscured the moon, and I heard wet, sucking sounds coming from the bodies of the Wolfmen. As the beater turned I moved past him, lurching over to the pair, whose faces and bodies now appeared completely human. The first slid away from the second, revealing a familiar face above a throat that had been torn away—and what lay inside.

I recognized it, and heard the sound it made, and still I didn't believe it.

As the beaters flanked me I shook my head. "Do you see it?" I tried to stand again, but my legs had gone to jelly, and the beaters had to grab me as I fell. "Do you hear it?"

The wretched sound kept time with the pounding in my head, growing softer and more distant as the night closed in. From a distance I felt myself lifted off my feet, and then I fell into the shadows and knew no more.

CHAPTER SIX

"She should be dead," a stern voice said somewhere close to me. It sounded very much like Chief Inspector Doyle. "She took on two of the bastards alone, with nothing more than her wits and a peeler."

"With that she could conquer a small nation," a second, dry voice observed, and that I knew at once to belong to Lucien Dredmore. "Has she been examined by the physick?"

"Aye. She's all over bruises and scratches, but nothing worse. He won't give her anything for pain until she wakes and he can assess her sense." He made a rude sound. "Not that she has any."

I didn't feel any pain, but then I wasn't precisely awake. I felt like the old lady's animech butterfly, floating somewhere between Doyle's and Dredmore's voices, away from my body, or perhaps above it. I was reasonably sure I wasn't dead, but making certain seemed too much trouble. By comparison being a butterfly, even a tin one, was much more pleasant.

"I should like to have a moment alone with her, Inspector," Dredmore said.

"Leave her alone and unconscious with a deathmage who appears out of nowhere but half an hour after she's attacked and near torn to pieces by two monsters?"

Doyle's tone went frosty. "I'm thinking never, milord."

"Charmian is under my protection." Now Dredmore sounded ready to exercise his official powers. "The shock of the attack has bruised more than her body. Her spirit is untethered and trapped between here and the Netherside. I can bring her back, but I must be alone with her."

No magic worked on me, so that had to be a lie. But why would Dredmore want to be alone with me?

"You're an assassin, not a healer," Doyle said, but he sounded less certain now.

"The longer her spirit drifts, the more difficult it will be to wake her." Something thumped. "Damn it, man. If I don't bring her back soon she may never wake again. Is that what you want?"

Doyle's voice became a disgruntled murmur, and whatever Dredmore replied dwindled to a hum. I lost interest in them and glided through the dark toward a cool, blue light. It looked like a veil made of the thinnest silk, each strand illuminated from within, and as I grew closer it stretched out, impossibly long and heavenly wide, and when I reached for it I could feel the brilliance of what lay beyond it tugging at me with a million little silvery hooks.

A shadow welled up round me, blocking the light and enveloping me. It was as thrilling as the veil, but warmer and closer, and definitely darker.

Charmian, you must return. It is not your time to cross over. Your body is still alive.

The words hurt my heart, and I tried to shrug away the shadow. *I don't want to. Those things. They were horrid.*

*I know they hurt you, but you are stronger than this.
Your work here is not finished.*

Work. That was all I ever did there. Work and struggle and suffer and despair, and why? I was alone in the world. There would be no little Charlies for me. Those women on the tram, they'd sacrificed me. That was all I was good for—being thrown to the wolves.

No, Charmian. He was angry and kind, all at once.
You are wrong. You have me. I am yours. You come back to me.

I opened my eyes, and the light was no longer cool and blue but golden and flickering. It gilded the midnight eyes looking down into mine, glinting off the fine, straight black lashes and softening the slash of his brows. In the lamplight Lucien Dredmore looked like a much younger version of himself, a handsome boy. For a moment I was so enchanted I lifted my hand to touch his face.

Deep, throbbing pain raced up my arm into my shoulder and skidded down my back. I felt as if I'd been dashed across a brick wall, and groaned as I tried to sit up and made it worse.

"Be still now." His hand came over my face, his fingers spreading out as his warmth sank into my skin. "Your spirit was battered out of your body. It will take a few moments to enmesh yourself."

"Just shut up and kill me," I begged. I'd have bitten his hand but I thought my teeth might fall out, my jaw was aching so. "The women and the kids on the tram?"

"Hysterical, but safe." He stroked my forehead, and everywhere he touched the pain diminished. "You are not to think about it."

"I don't want to." The horror of what I had seen bloomed back in my mind, however, and I had to tell him. "They were like animals, Lucien. Wolves with the bodies of men. But it wasn't natural. Someone made them. They made animech beasts out of those men."

He hushed me and pulled me close, and only then did I realize he lay beside me on the bed, our limbs entwined and nearly every part of us touching somewhere. Even his hair had tangled with mine, falling against my cheek like black and brown silk.

I drew back, looking at him. "You're in bed with me. That can't be right." I turned my head to see a room very much like the one in which I visited Docket. "Hospital?"

He nodded. "When they couldn't rouse you the beaters brought you here." He moved his hand over my shoulder and along my arm. "I nearly lost you twice in one night. You should be locked up for your own good."

I should have pushed him off the bed for that, but the effort required was beyond me. "Why was I floating off like that?"

"You're spirit-born, Charmian. In times of great duress part of you will always seek out your other kind and their realm." He lifted his head. "Your friend the inspector will be rejoining us in a minute. Is there anything I should know before he does?"

"I didn't kill the Wolfmen. They killed each other." I shuddered as I added, "One of them was named Akins. Until this morning, he was Lady Bestly's footman."

Dredmore departed with a promise—one that sounded like a threat—to return, ignoring Doyle entirely as he stalked from my hospital room. The chief inspector came to sit at my bedside, looking more troubled than annoyed.

"You have interesting friends, Miss Kittredge." His fair hair glinted as he turned to regard me directly. "How are you feeling?"

"Knocked about, but I'll live." Carefully I moved onto my side so I could face him. "Your men in the alley, they were very kind to look after me."

"They say you deserve a medal or two." Instead of taking out his notebook or spouting something official, he reached for my hand. "Do you feel well enough to tell me what happened, Kit?"

I didn't, but I did. Describing what I had seen sounded ridiculous, even to my own ears, but I gave him nearly every detail, leaving out only two facts: what I'd seen just before I'd fainted, and the fact that the second Wolfman had been the footman sacked earlier that day by my new client.

To his credit, Doyle didn't laugh at me, although when I spoke of the physical transformations I'd witnessed his expression grew doubtful.

"I know it sounds like something out of a bad dream," I said once I'd finished. "I can't tell you how they did it, or God knows why, but their bodies changed shape. I could hear their bones cracking. And they were so fast, and so terribly strong."

"My men said as much, at least the ones who survived." His jaw tightened. "Those bastards killed six of them in the streets before they got to you. It's a miracle you survived."

That hadn't been my doing. "Why did they fight each other, Tommy? Why didn't they both attack me?"

"Those men were insane, Kit. You'll never fathom it." He gave my hand a squeeze and stood. "I have to go now and see the families of the men who died. Try and get some rest."

What I wanted was to get up, get dressed, and get out of here—and never to sleep again. Fortunately my body would have none of that, and after a few minutes of fighting to stay awake I nodded off and slept without dreams, nightmares, Doyles, or Dredmores.

Sometime later a sister woke me for the physick's exam, which was a quick but somewhat painful business.

"No signs of addlement or rupture," the iron-haired, hatchet-faced surgeon told the nurse, who jotted the same down on the chart she carried. "I am Mr. Brecourt, Miss Kittredge. I expect you in some amount of pain, given the buffeting you've taken. You may have some opiate if you wish."

What polite names doctors had for ruddy joy. "It's tolerable, sir, so I'd rather not." He must be a surgeon; they were called Mr. instead of Lord like other doctors because they were obliged to use their hands to work on patients, and no lord performed manual labor. "Is there some question of surgery?"

"Not at present. When you came in I was obliged to extract some splinters of wood from your back and buttocks," he said bluntly. "They were not lodged very deep, however, and the wounds should heal in a few days."

That explained why my back was sorest of all. "When can I be discharged?"

He considered that. "You lay senseless for most of the night, and there is always the possibility of relapse. You also cannot reach the wounds on your other side, and such are prone to turn septic. I would keep you at least three days more. Why do you frown?"

I told him the truth. "I appreciate your concern for me, sir, but I can't afford that long a stay."

His expression cleared. "That is not a worry, my dear," he advised me. "Your account has already been paid in full."

Doyle couldn't have managed it. Dredmore could. "By whom, sir?"

Brecourt glanced at the nurse, who consulted the chart before she said, "There is no name, sir, only a notation that it was a grateful mother."

He nodded. "I understand this morning many mothers are grateful to you, Miss Kittredge. Now, Nurse will change your bandages and see to some breakfast for you. I will look in on you during my afternoon rounds."

Brecourt left me with the sister, who helped me to lay on my front while she dampened my dressings with warm water before carefully removing them.

"You're a very good healer, miss," she said. "Most of these gashes are beginning to mend." She gasped, and I felt her touch a tender spot. "Goodness, this one's already closed over."

I'd always healed very quickly, but I couldn't tell her having an immortal Aramanthan grandfather was the reason for it. "I'm sure it was just a scratch."

"As you say, miss." She finished her work quickly, however, and after replacing my bandages she practically ran from the room, nearly bumping into someone who was coming in.

I eased over onto my side to see it was Docket, who gave me a sheepish grin as he produced a bouquet of wild lavender. "Heard you'd taken a leaf from my book." His voice dropped to a softer register. "How are you doing, love?"

"I've had better nights." I pillowed my head on my arm and watched him arrange the fragrant bunch in my water carafe. "They tell you what put me here?"

"You playing catch-me with two Wolfmen, beaters said." He dropped into the chair beside my bed. "You look awful, but they're much worse. Made me vow never to get on your bad side."

"You saw the Wolfmen?" I sat up. "When?"

"Just before I come up to see you. They brought the bodies here, and I know the cutter down in the morgue. He let me have a look." His expression grew serious. "I know you didn't do all that to them. Were someone too wicked for words."

"You saw the mech, too." I sat up quickly, biting my lip as my body punished me for it. "I thought I'd gone daft. Did you recognize what it was put there for?"

He moved his shoulders. "Didn't take that close of a look."

I eyed the wheeled chair sitting in the corner. "Can you help get in that, and push me down there, to the morgue?"

He sighed. "Now why would you want to look at dead monsters, best forgotten? Good riddance to the rubbish."

"I need to talk to your cutter friend. Please, Doc," I tacked on when he shook his head. "It's for a case I have going. I need to learn as much as I can about these Wolfmen, and by the time I'm released the bodies will be gone and buried."

He pursed his lips. "The sisters'll have me head and hide."

"They're too busy serving breakfast to the other patients. I'm a patient, not a prisoner. If any of them ask I'll say I needed some air." I swung my legs over the side of the bed. "Please, Doc. Help me. Can't do it without you."

"So you're always nattering. Very well, stay there." He retrieved the wheeled chair and positioned it beside me, and then helped move me from the bed to its caned seat. He then realized my bare legs were poking out from under the knee-length gown and snatched up the blanket from the bed, swaddling me with it. "If they haul me off to lockup for this, you're bailing me out."

"In a heartbeat," I said, gritting my teeth against the pains stabbing my back and bottom. "Oh, you should say you're my da, if they ask."

"If I were your da, I'd give us both a proper thrashing." He pushed me out of the room.

My guess that the sisters would be too busy to notice us proved correct; only one glanced our way as Docket wheeled me down the hall.

"She should be in bed," the nurse said as she shifted her tray to one hip so she could open a door.

"Getting my gel some fresh air," Docket said, pushing my chair a little faster.

He wheeled me to a cage-front box and lifted the

cage. "This is the lift they use for downstairs," he said. "I'll lower you and your chair down in it and then take the stairs myself. Unless you want me to carry you?"

That would draw too much attention. "No, put me on the lift—and don't drop me."

He patted my hand. "Not a chance, love."

The box, meant to transport items to the basement level, creaked a little as Docket wheeled me inside. I looked at him through the cage he lowered and crossed my fingers and my toes.

"Set that pulley brake when it stops," he said, nodding to a lever to one side of me. "Else someone might bring it up while we're off ogling the dead."

I nodded, and winced as he released the pulley ropes and began lowering me down. The lift worked like a gigantic dumbwaiter, and as I descended into the shaft the light from the hall disappeared. I'd never been afraid of the dark, but suddenly I realized what the lift was really used for—moving dead bodies down to the morgue.

The box round me shuddered and landed with a heavy thump, jolting me to one side. I set the brake, and wheeled myself over to the cage panel to raise it.

"Oy." Someone beat me to the cage, and jerked it to reveal a blocky man dressed in his shirtsleeves and spattered coveralls. A brass helmet covered his hair, but he lifted its hinged front glassine shield to reveal a very young face with very old eyes. "What you doing on my lift, miss? Someone pull a prank on you?"

"No. Hello." I wheeled myself out, extended a hand, and beamed up at him. "How do you do? I'm Charmian Kittredge."

"I don't care if you're the bloody queen of Talia," he said frankly. "You can't be coming down here like this. Not until you're dead." He peered at my face. "That'll be awhile, I expect."

"Your optimism is comforting." I felt a surge of relief as Docket appeared behind him. "I think I've met your friend, Doc."

"Dez, there you are." Docket clapped a hand to his shoulder. "Kit, this is Desmond Holloway, known to one and all as Dez. Dez, my good friend Kit. We've a bit of a favor to ask, old chap."

Dez looked from Docket to me and back again. "Is she the one they ravaged? What you bring her down here for? They're still laid out on the bloody tables. I haven't even stitched them up yet."

Docket grimaced. "She needs to have a proper look at them, Dez."

That request horrified the cutter. "No, she don't. Sodding Christ, Doc, *I* don't want to look at them, not after seeing . . ." Dez shook his head and turned to me. "See here, miss, you can't be down here. I'll take you back upstairs meself. We'll find the physick and he'll give you something, help you sleep. By morning you'll forget all about it—"

"Both men have wounds all over them; deep claw marks and bite marks, broken bones in their faces, fractured ribs, and dislocated joints," I stated calmly. "One has most of his throat torn out, and the other has a shattered wrist."

His jaw dropped. "How'd you know all that?"

"I shattered the wrist," I told him, "and I watched the

rest happen. You let me look at the bodies, and I'll tell you everything I saw them do before they died."

"But you've already seen them," Dez countered.

"The outside of them, yes." I met his gaze. "I need to see the mech that was put *inside* them."

Dez took charge of my chair while Docket walked ahead of us to hold open the swinging doors. "You ever been in a morgue, miss?"

"A few times." The smell of preservative, sharp and sickly sweet, was growing stronger. "Why did you take a job as a hospital cutter? Are you hoping to become a surgeon?"

"Cut into live people? I don't fancy that." He turned a corner. "My da was a butcher, like his da, and his da before him. I only took this job 'cause it pays more, and I don't have to be neat or sell what I cut to no one."

I tried to appreciate the advantages, ghastly as they were. "But they're people, not cows or pigs or chickens. Doesn't that, ah . . ."

"Bother me? Sure, it did for a long while. Still does, when they send down a little one. But someone's got to look after them, and I don't make a hash of it." He stopped in front of a set of closely fitted doors. "This is the cutting room." He handed me a cloth mask that smelled of peppermint. "Tie this over your nose and mouth; it'll help. If you feel sick, tell me. I've plenty of basins."

Docket opened the doors and Dez wheeled me inside the brightly lit room. Five metal tables, two of them occupied by draped bodies, took up the center area. Each table had a perforated surface elevated over a long, broad drip basin. There were trays of knives and tools scattered about, as well as some open books displaying anatomical etchings.

I heard something dripping and looked beneath the shrouded bodies; the basins under them were half filled with dark, congealing blood.

Dez went to the nearest body and looked back at me for a long moment before he said to Doc, "Bring her closer."

Docket wheeled me to the side of the table as Dez pulled down the draping cloth to expose the upper torso of the first Wolfman, which had been cut open from shoulder to shoulder and down to the waist; the skin and muscles were neatly folded back from an apparatus gleaming over the organs and the inner cavity.

The stink of the decaying body turned my stomach, so I pressed the cloth mask over my nose and mouth as I inspected the mech. A fist-sized sphere of riveted brass had been embedded in the breastbone, and layers of it moved in time with a loud ticking. From the sphere it sprang a dozen different geared, jointed shafts. The shafts narrowed as they spread out and disappeared into the arms and lower abdomen. A web of cords, some of them frayed, had been strung along the shafts, and vibrated slightly in time with the sphere.

I frowned. "Why is it ticking like that?"

Docket leaned over to take a better look at the sphere, and then turned his head to listen. "I don't hear nothing, Kit."

"The other one has the same mech in his chest, but it was smashed." Dez turned the Wolfman's head and peeled back a flap of skin. "There's a recess here that goes right to the spine. I found a piece of brass stuck inside."

He took a pair of tongs and fished a bloody chunk of metal from a dish fastened to the side of the table and held it up. "Looks like part of a key," I said.

"Aye, to wind up the works, I'll wager." Docket glanced at me. "You've gone plaster-white, Kit."

I ignored the acidic roiling in my belly and rolled closer. "Show me the rest of the body."

"He's naked," Dez protested. "It ain't decent."

"Cover up what you think is indecent and let me see the legs," I said.

Dez hadn't cut open the corpse's lower limbs, and when he drew up the bottom half of the drape I saw they were mostly intact.

"There's something under the skin." I pointed to a long ridge of bulges running from midthigh to ankle. "More broken bones?"

"Could be a shattered femur, but there's no swelling." Dez took a long metal pick attached to a handle and probed one of the bulges. "That's metal. Has to be more of the mech." He put down the probe and reached for a small blade. "Docket, move her out of the way."

I rolled backward a few feet and watched as Dez cut open the leg, exposing more gears, four interconnected shafts, and cording weaving through all of it.

"How could he live through having so much mech put inside him like this?" I asked.

"He couldn't. The metal alone would have turned his blood septic." Dez used the back of his hand to wipe the sweat from his upper lip. "It weren't put inside him. Look at the skin on the legs. There's not a single surgical scar."

Docket nodded. "And there was no swallowing it, unless it was in bits, and then once inside it all would still have to be fitted together. Although if you did use long probes through some of the other body cavities—"

I recoiled. "Doc."

"The shafts have welds at the joints. You can't weld a man together from the inside or out." Dez tossed down the knife and covered up the body. "I've shown you the bodies, Miss Kit. Now you tell me what you saw."

He listened as I repeated what I had told Doyle. Unlike the inspector, he stopped me to ask very specific questions about the Wolfmen's anatomy. I described everything as best I could, and then lapsed into silence.

The dripping into the basin slowed to a stop before Dez looked over at Docket. "You still on the outs with the city's guild master?"

"I can get a word to him." Docket eyed the shrouded bodies. "No names in the report, Dez. Once the details get out I expect Bonnie to be all over this."

They were talking over my head, and I didn't like it. "Would you mind explaining to me what you're saying, because I can't make it out."

"Take her back now, mate. Good night, Miss Kit." Dez turned on his heel and left.

As Docket wheeled me out of the room I craned my head up to look at his grim expression. "What was all that about the guild master and no names? Who is this blasted Bonnie?"

"I have to tell the master of the city's magic guild about the mech inside these Wolfmen," Docket said slowly.

"He'll know if one of his animech mages has wits and the power to have put it inside them. I asked Dez to keep our names out of his report because if he doesn't, you and I will be summoned by Bonnie—the Bureau of Native Affairs—to be questioned during the tribal inquest."

As he stopped at the lift I sat back. "I still don't understand. How could a mage put mech inside men that turns them into beasts, and why would the natives be involved?"

"The mech inside those poor blighters made them strong, and the only way it could have been put there was by the dark arts," he said. "But another kind of magic was used, too. The kind that turns men into beasts, Kit. The kind of magic only native shamans know how to use."

CHAPTER SEVEN

My surreptitious trip to the morgue earned me a sound scolding from the ward sister once she'd ordered Docket to leave the facility and return only when he'd regained his sanity. I meekly accepted every stern word as she checked my bandages and helped me into bed.

I would have apologized, too, but my temporary escape had left me exhausted, and I fell asleep just as the sister was trying to decide if she should put me in restraints or have me transferred to the local loony bin where she suspected the rest of my relations surely must be residing.

I had troubling dreams of wolves turning into men, and men turning into animech beasts.

I woke briefly when they brought luncheon, some of which a much kinder nurse helped me eat, and then slept through a visit from the physick and the remainder of the day.

I felt much better in body than in spirit when I finally woke and saw Rina dozing in the bedside chair. She was wearing a brand-new gown, of course (Rina had long ago resolved never to wear the same garment twice, and earned more than enough from her pleasure palace to keep that vow), but the prudish style of it was no more Rina than the size of her new and somewhat pendulous bosom. The staid lace cap and heavily silvered brown wig concealing her angelic golden hair and most of her face completed the costume, and utterly perplexed me.

"Stop staring at me," she muttered without opening her eyes. "It was the only way I could get in to see you."

"By dressing like my grandmother?" I lifted my head to peer at the top of her ensemble. "What on earth did you put inside your bodice?"

"I had to be a convincing old lady, didn't I?" She took off the hat, extracted some strategically placed hair grips, and slid off the wig. "Mary Mother, this itches. I hope I never go bald." She regarded me as she drew off her gloves. "You're the heroine of the hour, or so I hear. Fighting off hordes of monsters in the streets to protect helpless women and innocent babies, are we? What was it, a slow day at the office, or did you just get bored with breathing again?"

"There were only *two* monsters," I admitted, "and they did the fighting. I was busy crashing into crates and walls and having hysterics."

She nodded, her expression satisfied. "That sounds more like it. I won't ask you why you were such an idiot as to go after two Wolfmen by yourself because then you'll tell me and I'll want to finish the job."

"The part about saving the women and children was true," I offered meekly.

"Twit." She slapped her gloves against the edge of my bed. "Bloody stupid mule-headed reckless thoughtless blundering cow."

"Come on, Rina, I can't be a *mule*-headed cow—"

"Shut up." She rose and began pacing. "I don't need

101

a friend like you. I've *never* needed you. I'm the richest woman in the province, aren't I? Nearly a hundred gels working for me, and there are twice as many men—some of them bloody important—who would kill for me. Cheerfully. Do you know, I could sell the business tomorrow, buy myself an island, build a bloody grand mansion on it, and have a herd of handsome strapping young chaps feed me grapes and rub my feet for the next fifty years? But no, I'm dressing up like a granny and sneaking past the good sisters to see my friend Kit, the mule-headed cow." She faced me and put her hands on her hips. "Don't you grin at me like that. I stuffed two butternut squashes in me bodice for you."

I wisely swallowed a laugh. "And I can never adequately express my gratitude, Carina. Now come and sit down."

She glared at me for a long moment before she plopped onto the side of the bed next to me. "So they knocked you about, then? That was all?"

"Cut up my back and bottom." The relief on her face made me ask, "Why were you worried there was more?"

"Felicity and Janice, a couple of my gels, went out for a house call last night. They were coming back when they met up with one of your monsters. It got them both before they could blink. Dragged them into the bushes, knocked them on their backs, bit them and tore at their clothes some, but it didn't kill them." She met my gaze. "Or the woman they saw it catch after it was done with them."

A memory of the Wolfman tearing at my skirts came back to me. "You mean it raped them?"

"Aye."

The horror of what her gels must have suffered—what I'd almost endured—made bile rise in my throat. "Oh, Rina. I'm sorry."

"So you should be. I was thinking the same had been done to you." She rested her hand on my brow for a moment. "Felicity's only been in the game two years, and she's still too terrified to make a peep, but Janice, she's been on the stroll since before you or me made our first wail. She told me everything." Her expression darkened. "Janice couldn't see much, it being dark and her skirts in her face, but she said while he were at her she heard gears turning, and some kind of ticking. As if he were carrying a clock."

Or had one inside his chest. "Did she notice anything else?"

"Janice had enough sense left to try to talk her way out of it. It never spoke or stopped once, not even when she grabbed a branch to cosh it in the head. Once it was done with her she tried to drag it back from Felicity, but she couldn't budge it. She said it weighed as much as three men."

That also sounded right. "Did you bring the gels here?"

"To this house of prudes? Not on your life. I have a physick who comes round the Nest when he's needed; he's looking after them now." She tucked my blanket round me. "So how long are the sisters keeping you from your next act of breathtaking idiocy?"

"The city should be safe for a few more days." I heard footsteps out in the corridor and reached for her wig and hat, handing them to her. "Did Wrecker drive you here?"

"He did, and he's waiting outside for me." She put on the rest of her disguise and grimaced. "Oh, and I ferreted out the name of that club your old ponce Bestly founded. It's called the White Lupine, and you're not to go anywhere near it."

I frowned. "Why not?"

"Aside from the fact that it's a gentlemen's club and they wouldn't let you stand on the stoop," she said, "it's cross the street from the park where that Wolfman got my gels."

"A park." I searched through my memory. "Not Rosings Park."

"That's it." She eyed me. "How did you know?"

Although I trusted Rina, I didn't confide to her that Lord Bestly had died after his transformation into a Wolfman. As fiercely protective as she was of her gels, and women in general, she'd want to know more than I could tell her. The fact that both Dez and Docket believed native magic was involved also troubled me.

Over time Torians and the tribes had learned to tolerate each other, and had come to many useful compromises in order to coexist, yet each side remained very suspicious of the other. If any rumor got out that the Wolfmen were the result of native magic I felt sure the city would turn on the shamans.

No Torian cared for the native mages and their strange blood rituals, but among their tribes the shamans were deeply respected and held in high esteem as holy men. If they were blamed for the Wolfmen, their people would be outraged. It was that sort of ignorance and mutual hostility that had resulted in the horrid massacres of Rumsen settlers and the tribal villages seventy years ago, during the old native wars.

I still felt sick over what Rina had told me about the attacks, but when a new sister brought in my dinner I forced myself to eat. This was no time to languish weakly in a hospital bed; I had to heal and get out of here. After praising me for my efforts the sister went to change my bandages but decided against replacing them.

"Your wounds are all closed, Miss Kittredge. I can hardly make out some of them." She helped me into a clean gown. "I'm sure Mr. Brecourt will be very pleased when he comes in the morning."

She didn't sound uneasy, and when I glanced at her face I saw no fear or disapproval like the other nurse had demonstrated. "You don't think it's odd, my rapid healing?"

"Not at all. You're spirit-born." She bundled up my old gown, saw my expression, and suppressed a chuckle. "You didn't think you were the only one, surely?"

"No, but I've never heard anyone talk openly about it." Suddenly I realized why she knew. "You're the same."

"Me, me brothers and sisters, *and* me mum." She glanced at the door before she said, "It's a family matter, so we don't blurt it out to just anyone. You've likely found out already that most magic folk don't care for our kind. If they get wise to you, they can be very unpleasant."

I thought of Gert. "Why do they hate us so much?"

"Jealousy, I expect," the nurse said, her tone wry. "We're born magical, miss, and they're not. Folk in the mage trade, they have to be taught spells and how to work the stones and such, but they've no power of their own to use. Can't stand it that they're limited when we're not."

The thought of having magical power had done nothing but annoy me, but now I was intrigued. "How are we . . . so unlimited?"

"Why, because our magic is natural to us, like breathing is. Even when I was a baby, if someone who was in pain held me in their arms, the hurt went away. That's why I became a nurse." She gave me a sympathetic look. "I tried to help you last night when you were brought in, but as soon as I touched you I knew it wouldn't work. I could feel my magic coming back to me, like it bounced off you."

"It did."

Her eyes widened, but before she could say any more the ward sister came in. "Sister James, you're needed in Miss Percher's room now."

"Yes, Sister Bailey." The younger nurse gave me a quick smile before she trotted out.

The ward nurse came to the foot of my bed and inspected me. "Your color is better, Miss Kittredge. I expect the visit by your dear grandmother"—she gave the last word deliberate emphasis—"lifted your spirits."

"It did." I squirmed a little. "And I do feel much improved, Sister."

"So that nothing impairs this remarkable recovery, I am putting you on strict bed rest until you are released. That means, Miss Kittredge, that you are not to take a turn in the hallways, or ride the lift down to the morgue, or do anything besides remain in this bed." She tapped the foot railing. "Is that clear?"

I sank back on the pillows and pulled my blankets up to my chin. "Completely, Sister."

"Excellent. I bid you good night." She turned down the bedside lamp and marched out.

"She's very good at that." Light filtered through the shadows, forming itself into a brightly glowing version of my grandfather. "Comes from her past life as a general. Conquered most of Europe, as I recall."

"Harry." I threw a pillow at his head, which passed through him and thumped against the wall. "I've been summoning you since dawn. Where have you been?"

"Having tea with the queen. She sends her regards." He took on solid form and settled into the wheeled chair, which he rolled round the bed. "I say, I do like this contraption. In my day one only got about in procession litters carried by slaves. Very bumpy." He peered at me. "What?"

I'd have thrown another pillow but that would leave me with none to smother myself with. "Oh, nothing at all. Someone sent a bomb to my office, and then I was attacked in the street and nearly killed last night, but you needn't worry."

His expression turned indignant. "And who do you think led that second beastie into the alley? Father Christmas?"

"*You* brought the second Wolfman after me. Of course you did." I closed my eyes. "Harry, I am *mortal*. I can be *killed*. You do remember this?"

"I saw the first one going after you and lured the second there so they'd fight over you like the animals they are. Without a body, it was all I could do to save you." He sighed heavily. "Once they'd done each other in, I intended to materialize and comfort you—as much as I could in spirit form—but then the beaters came, and you fainted, and I thought I'd be more useful tracking those two dogs."

"Those two dogs were dead," I pointed out. "They didn't go anywhere."

"When bodies die, spirits cross over," he reminded me. "I went to the Netherside to find them and have a word, but they weren't there."

"What does that mean?" I demanded. "They didn't have spirits?"

"They did, but they did not cross over to the Netherside," he said. "Before they were meddled with, your Wolfmen were ordinary mortals. Your lot goes elsewhere, and no, I don't know where. I'm not mortal."

"If magic turned them into Wolfmen, being near me should have broken the spell at once. It didn't. They had to be possessed. There's no other way they could have survived having the mech installed in their bodies. Or is there?"

Harry's brow furrowed. "They might have been killed first, meddled with, and then their bodies reanimated for a short time. Revenants are slow, mindless things, but the mech might have given them speed and purpose."

I thought of the footman. "How long does it take to work that kind of magic?"

"I may have helped myself to a dying body or two, but I'll have you know that I've never killed a mortal." He sniffed. "It's not sporting."

I felt impatient. "Very well. How long would it take

an Aramanthan who doesn't have your scruples to work the revenant spell?"

"The body has to be cured or it turns rotten and starts to fall apart, and then there's gathering everything for the ritual and finding the place for the altar . . ." He trailed off as he counted out something on his fingers. "It could be done in three months. Two, if they hurried and didn't care what the body looked like."

"Then they're not revenants," I said. "I saw one of the Wolfmen earlier that morning, and he wasn't dead or meddled with yet."

"It was not a revenant spell."

The deep voice made me jump and Harry scowl. "Dredmore." I looked over and spotted him standing by the window. "How did you get in here?"

"I climbed." He shut the window and regarded Harry. "Hello, Ehrich. How good of you to keep watch over Charmian. Perhaps if you'd done so yesterday, she wouldn't be here."

Harry glowered. "As it happens I *was* looking after her last night, unlike some evil conniving bastards who don't give a jot about anyone but themselves and amassing power they can't control and tossing it about to destroy the world."

Dredmore inclined his head. "I must bow to your authority on such matters."

"Charm, I lied," Harry said flatly. "I am going to kill a mortal. Be a love and close your eyes for a minute."

"This perpetual squabbling between you two is becoming exceptionally tedious." That got their attention. "Harry, we have to know who is responsible for creating these Wolfmen, and the night isn't getting any longer. You should go and see what you can find out about the mage behind these beasts before dawn sends you back to the Netherside."

"I can't leave you alone with him," my grandfather protested. "Think of your reputation, my gel."

"I haven't got one. Now go on." Once he dematerialized I turned to Dredmore. "Do you think it wise to continue baiting my grandfather the way you do? He is Merlin, remember. Greatest mage in the history of the world?"

"He *was* Merlin," Dredmore corrected. "Now he's mostly a blustering old fool interested only in creating chaos and dropping you in the middle of it."

I threw up my hands. "For pity's sake, Lucien, he's my grandfather, and the only family I have left in the world."

He came to the bed and loomed over me. "He's Aramanthan, Charmian, and more dangerous than you can imagine."

"What a coincidence, he says the exact same thing about you." All this drama was making me tired again. "Oh, do sit down. I'm getting a crick in my neck."

"Are you." He lifted me into his arms, blankets and all, and carried me over to the chair to sit with me on his lap. "Better?"

It was, not that I'd admit it. "I'm supposed to stay in the damn bed."

"I can have you moved to Morehaven tomorrow," he murmured as he adjusted my blanket. "My personal physick can supervise your recovery, and you'll be protected there."

"From everyone but you." I rested my cheek against his shoulder. "Did you call on Lady Bestly today?"

"I did. Some sooty little wench came to the door and said Eugenia was too ill to receive." He threaded his fingers through mine. "The ton has already begun questioning her reasons for delaying Bestly's mourning. It is only a matter of time before the truth comes out."

Another reason I was glad to be a commoner; the nobs always turned death into the social event of the season. "What is the protocol for a lady widow to mourn a husband who turned into a mad hairy killer just before he dropped dead?"

"Eugenia will be pitied by some, certainly, but the Hill must preserve its purity and dignity." His tone hardened. "In the eyes of the ton she will cease to exist. The invitations will stop immediately, and no one will ever call on her again. In public she will be given the cut direct."

Rina had endured much worse than that, and she'd survived. "That's not so bad."

"If it were only that, perhaps she could retire from society and live a quiet life," Dredmore agreed. "Bestly's actions will irrevocably taint her, however, and the ton has many ways of evicting those they considered undesirable from their proximity. She will be unable to replace her servants, and tradesmen will be directed to refuse her household orders. She will begin to receive anonymous suggestions that she leave Rumsen, polite at first, and then they will grow more direct. There will be no suitors to ask for her hand, of course, so in three months' time her husband's estate will revert to the Crown."

I hadn't thought of the inheritance laws. Because the Bestlys were childless, there was no male heir, and under Torian law wives and daughters could not inherit. In the early days of settlement, disease and warring with the natives had killed many Torian men before they could father any children, and their families had pressed New Parliament into changing the old English entailment laws. If she remarried within three months of her husband's death, Lady Bestly's new husband could petition the court to take possession of the estate, and if there were no liens against it he would inherit everything.

But Dredmore had said there would be no suitors, and that meant no remarriage. "What happens to her if they take it all away?"

"She will be served official notice to vacate the house within seven days. As neither she nor Bestly have any living family to provide for her, she will have nowhere to go. After a week if she is found at the house, she will be removed by the police and jailed for trespassing on Crown property." He glanced down at me. "If that happens, even you might pity her."

"I wouldn't put money on that." But I already did. "Anyway, if the worst happens, you'll look after her."

"I have already offered to help her leave Rumsen and settle elsewhere," he told me. "She has flatly refused my assistance. If we cannot clear her husband's name, I fear she will elect to take the avenue of last resort."

Disgraced gents usually put a bullet in their brains, but the ladies were a bit more genteel about it. "She'll walk off a cliff." Even if Lady Bestly survived the drop, which most didn't, the weight of water-laden skirts would drag her under the icy waters of the bay. "If it comes to that, you can use your mind-magic on her. Persuade her to believe cliffs are indecent. Shouldn't take much."

"Such compassion for Eugenia." He seemed bemused. "She had none for you when inflicting your suffering."

"Others did." I smiled a little, remembering. "There was this old gent who liked to feed the pigeons in the park. He bought me tea and a sticky bun every time he came. Some days that was all I had to eat. My friend Bridget and I met when she caught me rummaging through the remnants in the bins behind the mill. The weather had turned cold and I had nothing but the clothes on my back. She could have called a beater, but instead she brought out a brand-new wool blanket. To this day I still keep it on my bed."

He caressed my cheek. "Perhaps I shall toss Eugenia off a cliff."

"That's not why I told you, Lucien." I tried to think of how to put it. "If I were to take pleasure in Lady Bestly's misfortunes, I should be ashamed of myself. It would be the same as spitting on the people who were kind to me when she was not."

"Then it is a noble thing you do here." He studied my face. "You claim everything you do as a disenchanter is simply business, but I suspect more often than not you are as ruled by a soft heart as that hard head. It also makes me wonder how I shall ever repay my debt to you."

I pretended to think. "Well, you are very rich."

The door to my room flung open with a bang and

something dark and snarling barreled inside. Dredmore grabbed me up and leapt across the bed, setting me on my feet and shoving me behind him. When I darted round him I saw it was one of the Wolfmen from the morgue, his body still gaping open and the mech inside whirring and grinding. He began to advance on us, his jagged teeth snapping, and as he drew closer the hair on his body receded, revealing more of his ruined flesh.

"Climb out the window," Dredmore said to me, never taking his eyes from the beast. "*Now*, Charmian."

The magic spell making him a beast might not work in my presence, but my power had no effect on the mech inside him. Nothing would stop him, unless—

I picked up the curtain closer and pushed it in Dredmore's hand. "The sphere in the center of his chest. You must destroy it."

The Wolfman hurled himself at us, and Dredmore brought up the curtain closer just in time. I cringed as I heard the sickening sound of tearing flesh and shattering mech as the Wolfman impaled himself on the rod. The body thrashed wildly for several moments and then sagged, jerking and twitching. The sound of the ticking came to a halt, and the Wolfman hung motionless.

"Miss Kittredge, I thought we had an understanding." Sister Bailey marched in, halted, and stared at the Wolfman. "You are . . . to stay . . . in bed."

"I was in bed, Sister." I tried not to look at the body. "Um, is the morgue still receiving?"

Chapter Eight

"You are not well enough to be released," Sister Bailey said several hours later as she replaced the last bandage and began buttoning the nurse's uniform she'd found for me to wear home. "Mr. Brecourt will be absolutely furious in the morning when he finds you gone."

"I'm sorry about that, and I wish I could stay." I looked over at Sister James, who was gingerly collecting the last of the bloody parts that had exploded from the Wolfman's chest. "But if I did, this could happen again, and other patients might be hurt."

"That some mage would use a dead man for such wickedness—and in a hospital. It's absolutely revolting." She eyed the stains the Wolfman's oily blood had left on the floor. "Until the police capture this villain, Miss Kittredge, I fear you will not be safe anywhere. Where will you go?"

I heard the sound of angry voices arguing in the hall. "I believe that matter is still being discussed, Sister." As she came round to straighten my collar I met her worried gaze. "Would you believe me if I told you this was not the worst thing to happen to me?"

"Yes, I would." She surveyed me before nodding. "There, now you look respectable. You should leave the bandages on until morning, and if there is any fever or festering you must see a physick at once."

She helped me into the wheeled chair and after covering me with a blanket pushed me out into the hall. As soon as I emerged Dredmore and Doyle stopped quarreling and turned to me.

"Gentlemen." I smiled. "Have you come to a decision?"

"I am moving you to Morehaven," Dredmore said, at the same time Doyle announced, "You'll be taken into protective custody."

As my protectors glared at each other I looked up at Sister Bailey. "Does the hospital have a carri for patients who need transportation?"

"I took the liberty of sending word to your grandmother, Miss Kittredge, and she is providing a carri for you." She pushed me past the men toward the reception lobby.

Dredmore caught up with us first. "I will not permit you to go home, Charmian. You will be alone and entirely vulnerable to another attack there. Furthermore, you don't have a grandmother."

"I am not going home, Lucien, and you don't know everything about me." I nodded to the beaters we passed—Doyle had stationed more than a dozen on the ward—and took a moment to check what coin I had left in my reticule. As Tommy came trotting up beside my chair I said, "Inspector, it would be wise to post some men here tonight to keep watch. I trust Dredmore has advised you of how they might best incapacitate these Wolfmen."

"Be sensible, Kit," Doyle said, stepping out to block our path. "You can't just walk out of here after being attacked twice by these beasts."

"Three times, if you count the second one in the alley. But you're wrong, I can walk. Slowly." I reached back to touch Sister's hand. "Thank you for everything, Sister Bailey."

"You are welcome, Miss Kittredge." She helped me to my feet and pressed my hands in hers. "Our best wishes for a speedy recovery, my dear."

I did my best not to limp as I walked out of the hospital and down the steps to where a carri waited at the curb. The sight of Wrecker at the wheel made me sigh with relief.

"I *do* know everything about you, Charmian." Now Dredmore got in front of me. "I have made it my business to know. So I can tell you now that you are not spending the night in a house of ill repute."

"You're right—I'm *not* spending the night at Morehaven." I glanced back at Doyle, who had actually taken out a pair of manacles. "You can't arrest me, either, Tommy. Good night, gentlemen."

Wrecker lumbered down to help me into the carri, and when Dredmore came after me he stepped in his way. "Have you magical knees, milord?"

"What?" Dredmore stared at him. "No."

"Then don't make me smash them. It hurts, quite a bit." He tipped his hat and climbed back up behind the wheel.

As Wrecker pulled away from the curb I waved at both men and then sat back. "That was brilliant, mate, but you really shouldn't threaten to kneecap a death-mage."

"I can put him on his ass faster than he can spell me

dead," he said, unperturbed. "Milady gave me a message for you. She said if you're not coming to the Nest then you're, ah . . ." He cleared his throat. "Some things I don't care to repeat to a lady like you."

"Worse than a mule-headed cow?"

He nodded. "If you don't come back with me she's also prepared to wash her hands of you, dance naked at your funeral, piss on your grave, and so forth. I don't think you need to worry, though. When she were yelling all that at me her right eye weren't batting. Only does when she means it. So where will you go?"

I suspected only one place in the city would provide me with completely safe haven, but I was reluctant to name it. Instead I gave him a nearby address, which he recognized, given the way he eyed me. "It's not what you think. It's more like . . . a passage."

"If you say so, Miss Kit."

We arrived a few minutes later, and once Wrecker helped me out of the carri he studied the darkened windows. "You sure about this, miss? It still looks like a butcher's shop to me, that and it's locked up tight."

"The proprietor has me come once a month at night to check his shipments for rotting spells." I went over to the display window and felt along the bottom side of the ledge until I found the niche and tugged out the key hidden inside. "I can manage it from here. Tell Rina not to worry, and I'll see her soon. Thanks, Wreck."

I let myself inside, locking the door behind me and waiting until Wrecker drove off. Then I walked to the back of the shop and into the butcher's cold storage.

Blocks of ice packed in sawdust formed the floor

and kept cold the carcasses suspended from the ceiling. I tried not to look at them—they reminded me too much of what I'd seen in the hospital's morgue—as I stepped carefully round them to make my way to the back corner.

The huge barrel appeared too heavy to move, but was actually made of very thin wood that had been filled with cheesecloth, so it took only a bit of a push to shift it aside so I could get at the little hatch behind it.

I used the key for the second time on the hatch's lock and bent down to step into the room beyond where a massive coil of tubes snaked about a narrow ladder. I had to tuck up my skirts before I climbed down two levels into the old sewers.

Few citizens remembered when the city had been wholly dependent on an underground warren of tunnels to divert the population's waste; Rumsen's tube network had long ago rendered obsolete the old sewer system. Most of it had been sealed off or converted to housing tube junctions and jam dumps, and over time it had acquired an atmosphere of decrepit menace. In the course of my business I'd been obliged to pay several visits belowground, and while I knew enough to avoid falling down an old cesspit or becoming lost in the labyrinthine branch tunnels, I'd never grown accustomed to knowing I was walking beneath the unseen weight of countless tons of building stone, paved street, and every soul in the city.

The smell always made my stomach clench at first, but as before when I'd worked underground I knew I'd get used to it. I tried not to notice the whitish, blunted things growing in the corners, or how my footsteps set off the sounds of scrabbling and scampering in the shadows. What held off the bulk of my unease was assurance that I knew my presence would be quickly detected by the master of this domain, and so I waited in the dark until a bobbing lantern light approached me.

"Miss Kit." The stooped old man held up his light to have a better look at me. "What are ye doing here? 'Tis the middle of the night."

"Hello, Mr. Hedgeworth." I wrapped the blanket a little tighter round me. "I've come to collect on your debt, if I may."

I'd once done some work for the old scrammer, and instead of collecting payment—Hedger had no use for money—I'd taken a promise of his help in the future in exchange.

"Strange time to be doing that, but fair enough." Hedger grinned. "What'll it be, then? I've everything but coin and respectability."

"I need a place to stay for a day or more," I said. "Someone is trying to kill me."

After hearing my somewhat tailored explanation, Hedger insisted I come to his personal sanctuary.

"Not at all what ye're used to, I expect, Kit," he said as he led me deeper into the tunnels. "Still, I can keep watch while ye sleep, and even when I'm gone ye'll be all right. An army couldn't get at me place."

Hedger's home lay behind a massive junction station filled with more tubes than I could count. As I ducked and edged my way through, he pointed out the different traps he'd set for unwelcome visitors.

"Ye'll not want to bump that connection; that lets loose scalding steam from a bathhouse boiler. And that panel there gives way under any weight and ye'll end up in me old privy. Keep to the center of the walkway, that's right. Oh, no." He caught my arm before I touched an innocent-looking banister. "That's fashioned of paper, not wood. Ye'll fall right over the side."

I glanced over the phony railing at what appeared to be a black bottomless pit. "Mr. Hedgeworth, exactly what sort of unexpected visitors were you expecting?"

"The sort who'll take everything a man cares for," he said grimly. "Never again, says I."

Guilt knotted my tongue, for what Hedger didn't know was that Harry had been responsible for his misfortunes. I had learned of it before I'd defeated Zarath, and managed to persuade my grandfather to apologize, but I couldn't do the same now. Nor could I tell him I was Harry's granddaughter, or he might give me a hard push over the fake banister instead of the much-needed sanctuary.

Finally we arrived at an odd door patched together out of bits of planking and old shingles. He picked out one knotted loop from a tangle of many and tugged it, lifting the interior bar latch.

I stepped inside and smelled wood smoke, tea, and—"Apples?"

"Couple of crates got jammed in the market tubes," Hedger said. "Kept what got bruised and been pressing them into cider."

As Hedger moved about lighting his lamps things began to glitter, and I saw the plastered wall nearest to me had been artfully inlaid with thousands of pieces of colored glass, gleaming metal, and broken pottery, all polished and fitted together like some giant's puzzle.

I turned round to admire his handiwork, which the lamps revealed covering every inch of all the walls. "It's beautiful. Like Aladdin's cave."

He blushed. "Always been a magpie for shiny things. All the years down in the mines, I expect. Sleeping chamber's back here."

I followed him to a smaller adjoining chamber made up with sparse but comfortable-looking furnishings that resembled the door he'd built out of scraps. "I don't want to turn you out of your own bed, Hedger."

He waved a hand. "Nod off in my chair by the steam venting most days. Besides, ye'll sleep nights when I'm out minding the tubes."

Hedger insisted on making up the bed with clean sheets, something I protested until he showed me the enormous pile in his closet that he'd collected from hotel tubes (regularly overloading by the maids, he claimed, resulted in frequent jams and tons of linen scram). He also provided some wool-wrapped hot bricks from his hearth to warm the cold sheets. After I spread out my hospital blanket as a coverlet and refused his offer of warm cider, I sent him off to work.

Hedger's bed was a bit lumpish, and to be comfortable I had to turn on my side. When I had first arrived in Rumsen as a gel I'd had trouble sleeping in strange places; in Middy I'd always had the comfort of my own bed in my parents' house. Lady Bestly's success in turning me into a beggar had cured me of that; ever since those days I could sleep anywhere, even standing up if I had something to lean against while I dozed.

I certainly had my back to the wall now, in a manner of speaking. I closed my eyes. Why send the Wolfman after me again? Because he failed to kill me the first time? They didn't murder Rina's gels or the other woman in the park . . .

I knew I was dreaming when I found myself standing in the aisle of the market tram again. This time every seat stood empty except for that of the driver, who had turned round and was watching me. I couldn't see his face for the shadows, but his eyes shone, all black. Outside the tram I heard howling and saw moonlight bathing the streets in liquid silver.

"You are not like the others." The driver reached out and closed the door to the tram, breaking off the handle before allowing it to drop to the floor. "You are cunning. I can smell your power."

"I do need a bathe." Carefully I took a step back and heard a snarl just behind me. When I glanced over my shoulder I saw it was another Wolfman crouching at the end of the aisle. Blood made dark streaks through the gray-white hair covering his body.

"My soldiers die too quickly," the driver said as he approached me. "The magic will not hold for long, and not at all when they come to you." Long white teeth flashed as he grinned. "You will tell me why this is, mortal, that I may complete the spell."

"You're mistaken." He was Aramanthan and, I suspected, using my dreaming slumber to get into my mind. "I have no magic or spell advice."

The driver inched closer. "Tell me how to keep my soldiers alive. Tell me now, and I will not make you a vessel."

He stretched out his hand as if to touch me, and the moonlight gleamed along his long, daggerlike claws. I could feel the hot breath of the Wolfman, too, burning against the back of my neck. The prospect of being torn apart by the beast didn't frighten me as much as those claws coming ever closer to my face.

A cloud of black mist enveloped me, dragging me through the roof of the tram as though it were made of nothing but air. I flew through the night sky, cradled in no more than that dark cloud, and I had never felt so relieved, so safe—or so annoyed.

I drifted down to a wide cliff above the bay, where the mist carrying me set me gently on my feet and swirled away. "They couldn't hurt me," I grumbled as I turned, looking for him. "This is a dream. None of it is real." I frowned. "Your magic shouldn't have worked, either."

"I am miles away from you in the waking world." Dredmore materialized before me in a ghostly version of himself. "You cannot break my spells—or theirs—unless you touch us. Where are you, Charmian?"

"Here, obviously." His features were almost transparent, but still I could make out his scowl. "The driver on the tram was Aramanthan, and he called the Wolfmen his 'soldiers.' There's something wrong with the spell he's using on them, and the idiot seems to think I can fix it."

He moved to look out at the sea. "Did he offer you a bargain?"

"I think so." I tried to remember what he had said. "Something about not making me his vessel. Maybe by that he meant not putting any mech inside me to turn me into one of his creatures. They really can't hurt me when I'm sleeping, can they?"

"He can deceive you into believing whatever he wishes, and influence your waking decisions." Dredmore scanned the horizon. "I have the sense of him now. He is not coming to Toriana as I assumed. He is already here. I think he has been, for some time."

"An Aramanthan, working as a common tram driver?" I chuckled. "I hardly think so, Lucien. You know how snobby they are about the bodies they snatch for themselves." I thought of Lady Bestly's footman. "He must be creating the Wolfmen for something other than possession. He called them his soldiers. Does that mean they're to be his army?"

"It is possible." He came to me. "I will ward your dreams tonight, but the distance between us makes it difficult. You must come to Morehaven as soon as the sun rises, when the Aramanthan's power dwindles."

"Hiding in your house will only make things worse," I pointed out. "If I'm there your spells won't work, and your mind-power works only on spirit-born mortals. If he truly has an army of these Wolfmen, and he sends them to attack Morehaven, we're finished."

He looked down at me. "Then I will come and stay with you."

"You're that determined to protect me." I reached out to touch him and felt a cool tingle against my skin. "Unless you want to take up permanent residence in my house, we have to find him, Lucien, and stop him. It's the only way I'll ever be safe again."

"The last time you fought an immortal," he murmured, "you had to kill me."

"You told me to do it," I reminded him, "and I did alter the course of history to bring you back. Surely that made up for my driving a spike through your heart. So how do we ferret out this immortal during the daylight?"

"I will tell you when I see you tomorrow, at your office." He bowed his head to press a whisper of a ghostly kiss against my brow. "Sleep now, my heart. I will keep watch over your dreams."

So he would, I knew, and I closed my eyes and gave myself to the dark.

The sound of tubes clanging mixed with the scent of cinnamon to rouse me from my sleep, and I opened my eyes to see Hedger standing with a steaming mug at the foot of his bed.

"Morning, love." He brought the tea to me and studied my face. "Ye rested well?"

"I did, thank you, Mr. Hedgeworth." I sat up and took a sip from the mug, which was not tea but spiced cider. "This is very good."

"I've put a bit of breakfast out by the hearth for ye." He smothered a yawn. "Will ye be staying downside for the day, then?"

"I must go and meet someone at my office." Once I was topside I could catch a trolley, although the thought made me feel a little sick. "I'll return before dark. Do you know a shortcut through the tunnels that would bring me up close to the Davies building?"

He scratched his grizzled cheek. "Why would ye wish

to be close when ye could go right in through Docket's Dungeon? 'Tis only four passages and a junction skip south of here."

"You know Mr. Docket?" I grinned as he nodded. "That's marvelous. But I never knew there was an entry to tunnels in my building."

"'Twas none, till the old tinker melted a hole through the foundation," Hedger said.

I winced. "Melted?"

"Ye don't want to know, gel. I still have nightmares," he said. "Found him wandering about exploring and had a chat. Been selling mech scram to him ever since then. He were down right before ye came, looking for braces and gears and such."

So Doc was back at work, and I had another soul to worry over.

After Hedger walked me out of his booby-trapped lair and gave me precise directions on how to reach the Davies building, he produced a small bundle of red velvet and shook it out. "Found this cloak blocking one of the tubes to the Hill. Too small for me." He draped it over my shoulders and drew the hood up over my hair. "Fits ye much better."

I stroked the sinfully soft material. "This is silk velvet, Hedger. You could sell it to a dressmaker for quite a packet."

"Some things were meant to be sold, and others given." He fastened the frogs under my chin. "Now go on with ye so I can get some shut-eye."

I took care to follow Hedger's directions precisely as I made my way through the tunnels, and when I passed through the junction he'd described I spotted the ladder and hoist he'd told me Docket had installed. They led up into a slab of blackstone with a large, irregular opening. I climbed up the rungs, grimacing as I passed through glassy edges of the hole and emerged in the back corner of the Dungeon.

"Doc?" I called out over a whirring, pumping sound, and followed it to one of his wall racks, where the old mech was standing and making adjustments to a star-shaped frame of gears and pistons in motion. The sound drowned out my voice, so I stepped into his view and waved a hand.

"Kit?" He reached up to tug a switch and the mech shut off. "You shouldn't be here. Beautiful cloak, love the scarlet on you. Makes your eyes shine. Now why did you leave hospital?"

"I'm much better, and I have to meet someone." I glanced at the stairs leading up to the lobby. "I was wondering if I could borrow one of your swords."

"Who are you meeting, a Wolfman?" he joked, and then his smile faded. "Oh, God. Are you expecting one of the beasts to come here?"

"No, unless you consider Lord Dredmore beastly, which would be entirely understandable." I gave him a pained smile. "Actually the sword is more for personal protection after dark."

"You won't need a sword. I've been working on something much better." He gestured at the rack. "It's this. Well, I don't have a proper name for it yet, but it's a harness, built for you."

I glanced at the mech. "You want to harness me to a wall exactly why?"

"It doesn't stay on the wall. You wear it, like a suit of armor." He pointed to the uppermost extensions. "These fit over your arms, and the two lower on your legs. We will have to make some adjustments for your skirts, of course. Then this piece goes over your front, and there's another for your back. I have to fit a collar to shield your neck, and we should definitely think on some sort of helmet—"

"Doc, I do appreciate you inventing this for me." If I stayed another moment he'd want to put it on me. "But this harness as it is now must weigh three or four times as much I do. If I wore it, I couldn't take a step without falling on my face."

"No, dear gel, you don't understand. I've designed it to support your weight and respond to your movements. Watch." He threw on the switch, and the mech whirred into motion. He then had to shout to be heard over it. "The winders draw on your muscle motions in the harness to power the motors. All along the inside are levers I've preset to locomotion, but as soon as you kick, punch, or run, the gears shift into battle-or-be-off mode." He looked at my face and switched it off. "Once I've worked out a few snags it will protect you and make you much, much stronger." He beamed. "You should also be able to run a mile in a minute. Possibly less."

If it did all that, I was queen of Toriana. "And did you bang your head when you were testing it?"

"It sounds impossible, I know," he assured me. "But I based my design on the mech I saw inside that poor chap at the morgue." He patted the frame. "I've adapted what they're putting inside the Wolfmen, Kit, to be worn on your outside."

At last I understood. "Doc, just how powerful is this harness?"

He beamed. "If my calculations are right—and I know they are—it should make you as strong as three of them."

CHAPTER NINE

I left Docket to continue tinkering on his improbable harness and took the back stairs up to my office. I was so preoccupied that I forgot about Gert, who came rushing down the corridor as soon as I emerged from the landing.

"There you are, you wicked creature." She tossed some herbs from a small sack at me. "I knew if I kept my vigil you'd slither back from whatever corruption you've been visiting on the innocent. What evil have you wrought now?"

I stopped and looked at the scattered herbs and then at her face. "I have been chased and attacked by a man-beast." As I spoke I advanced on her. "I was taken to hospital to be treated for my wounds, where I was attacked again. Then the beast's master came after me in my dreams, and I had to spend last night hiding in the sewers." I stopped and lowered my head until we were on eye level. "The completely fantastic part of it, Gert, is that *none* of that evil was my doing."

Her chin wobbled. "'Tis the price of serving the devil, young miss."

"Evil is chasing me all round Rumsen," I assured her. "Evil wants me dead. A right shabby way to treat such a devoted servant, don't you think?"

Her eyes widened, and she squeaked before whirling about and skittering off.

I didn't have to look behind me to see what had frightened her. "Morning, Satan."

Dredmore followed me into the office, where he told me to stand and wait while he inspected the tube portal and the rest of the premises. No Wolfmen, rat bombs, or other unwelcome deliveries were found, but the pile of post he tossed onto my desk made me groan.

"If this keeps up it'll sink the business." I went over to fill the kettle. "We are not having green tea. We are having black, and I like it strong. Be warned, it may grow hair on your teeth."

He watched me bustle about. "I presume you spent the night in a sewer, as you smell like one."

"No, I don't." I took a surreptitious sniff of my sleeve; yes, I did. "I'll change and wash up when I go home." I thumped the kettle down on the steamdog and switched it on. "Why did the Aramanthan come after me in my sleep? Why not send another Wolfman to hunt me down? Or maybe those two were all he had and there aren't any more."

"Inspector Doyle told me that fifty-nine men have gone missing since Bestly died," Dredmore said. "A few are servants, but most were titled—and all of them resided on the Hill. The missing men's families have agreed to keep it quiet and out of the papers for now, but the ton is closing ranks and demanding answers."

"How could he have taken so many so fast?" I sat down and stared at my unopened post. "He couldn't have made them all into Wolfmen yet. He knows from what happened to Bestly and the other two that it will kill them. A dead army is useless to him." I thought of all the facts I'd gathered, and the one that kept nagging at me was Bestly's ornate tie pins and pocket watches. "Were the missing men taken from their homes?"

"According to Doyle, they all left their homes on their own volition and never returned." Dredmore gave me a shrewd look. "What are you thinking?"

"If they weren't taken, then the Aramanthan had to lure these men to him," I said slowly. "Lord Bestly was last seen leaving him home for the White Lupine. The immortal could be recruiting from the gentlemen's clubs, and why are you looking at me like that?"

"Sir Refrue, a former client of mine who is among the missing," Dredmore said, "is a founding member of the White Lupine."

"If the other missing men belonged to Bestly's club, then that is the connection. The Aramanthan could be posing as one of the members, too." I stood up. "We must go and question the manager."

"Women are not permitted inside a gentlemen's club. I will call on the manager." Dredmore brought me a cup of tea. "You will go home, take a bath, and burn that gown. Connell will drive you."

"Stop being so bloody high-handed. As long as the sun is up I'll be safe, and I have work to do." I cradled the cup between my hands. "I'll go and talk to Doyle. He'll have a list of who's gone missing." The thump of his cup on my desk made me frown. "If you break that, you're buying me another."

"This isn't a game of hide-and-find, Charmian," he

said through gritted teeth. "The Aramanthan will be using mortals. Mortals who can easily cut your throat at any hour of the day. He already has fifty-nine of them under his spell."

"After last night I'm not sure he wants me dead. Else why would he bother offering a bargain?" I watched him pace back and forth. "Locking me up in Morehaven won't solve this case. Lucien, this isn't only about Lady Bestly's reputation and ruin. He can't be permitted to change all those men into mindless beasts."

He turned on me. "You will agree to have Connell drive you. Furthermore, you will wait for me at your home, and you will not creep back into the sewers."

"He didn't find me there last night, did he?" I took a sip of my tea. "I can look after myself, milord. I always have."

"As you are so fond of reminding me." He leaned over the desk. "Do you know what it will do to me if I lose you?"

I pretended to think. "Your mood would improve in time, certainly. You'd go on as before, dazzling the nobs and amassing unimaginable wealth, until you retire to some tropical island to spend your golden years drinking coconut milk and eating a great many fish. By the way, Rina will probably be your next-door neighbor."

"*Charmian.*"

I met his dark glare. "You might miss me a little at first, but I expect in the end you'd be grateful to have me gone. After all, I've brought you nothing but grief."

"You are sadly mistaken, madam." He retrieved his cloak and shrugged into it. "We will meet at four, agreed?" When I nodded he picked up his tea and threw it across the room, where it smashed through the window. Before I could do more than gape he tossed a shilling on my desk. "Here. Perhaps you'll live long enough to buy another."

I watched him stalk out before I picked up the coin. "What about the window?" I called after him.

I temporarily patched the broken pane in my window with a bit of paperboard before I sorted out the post. Among the usual inquiries and payments was a list of the names and addresses of the Wolfmen's victims I'd purchased from a clerk at Rumsen Main (Doyle had no idea how simple it was to bribe some of his staff), as well as no less than ten invitations to tea on the Hill. I tucked away the list of victims for future reference and studied the invites. Since I'd never been the toast of the ton, I hadn't met any of the ladies requesting my attendance, but I recognized their names. All ten were well established, filthy rich, and married to the most important men in the territory.

The cream of Rumsen society also had no reason to know of my existence save one: my visit to Lady Bestly's home.

It would have only taken them a day to find out who I was and seize the opportunity to confirm the gossip doubtless spreading like wildfire among their servants. They couldn't ask Lady Bestly about the matter directly; that was bad ton. I, on the other, had no social standing, so they could interrogate me unmercifully the moment I stepped in the drawing room.

This put me in something of a pickle. I couldn't toss the invitations into the fire or pretend I'd never received them, but I couldn't respond to them, either. No one said no to these women; any refusal on my part would be considered a personal insult. Still, no one but Docket, Gert, and Dredmore knew I'd come to the office this morning; that would buy a little time.

I put on Hedger's red cloak and pulled the hood over my head before I departed. I took care to keep my face averted whenever I passed one of the other tenants, and while a few of them sniffed and muttered rude things about bathing and laundry, no one spoke to me. The lady dispeller on the fourth floor could hardly afford to wear silk velvet.

Outside Connell sat waiting for me in a hired carri, and for once clambered down to help me inside.

"You're looking very pale, miss."

He'd never before spoken to me, so I could be excused my moment of shock. "I'm all right." Then, because I couldn't help myself, I said, "I didn't know you could talk, Mr. Connell."

"His lordship don't like chatter." He tipped his hat and climbed up behind the wheel.

Small wonder Dredmore expected me to follow his orders without a quibble. Even Connell, another of his trusted servants, was expected to go about his duties with silent, absolute obedience.

As he started the engine, I leaned forward to ask, "Don't you ever get tired of him ordering you about, Mr. Connell?"

"Lord Dredmore pays me to do what he says, miss."

He gave me a sideways glance. "I'm to take you to your house and keep you there. He said to tie you up if need be."

"No need to resort to ropes." When this was over, I decided, Dredmore and I were going to have a very long talk about who was actually in charge of my life. "Do drive on, Mr. Connell."

Connell drove the carri as fast and skillfully as Dredmore's coach and four, and in a few minutes we reached my goldstone. Once he helped me down he insisted on going into the house first—also on his master's orders—and checked the premises as thoroughly as Dredmore had my office. He politely refused my offer of tea, bolted the back entry, and took position at the front.

I retreated to my bathing room, where I stripped out of my sewer-fragrant gown and ran a hot tub, adding a liberal amount of rose-scented soap flakes to the water. I had to stand on my footstool and hold a hand mirror to remove the bandages taped to my back, but my awkward inspection confirmed that the last of my wounds had closed over and most were healed, leaving only a few pinkish-white scars. In another day or two those would also disappear; thanks to Harry's blood I never scarred permanently.

I climbed down from the stool and put away the hand mirror, frowning at my reflection as I remembered the Wolfman's body in the morgue. *No surgical scars*, Dez had said. Yet the only logical way the mech might have been installed in the man's body would have required it to be cut open.

The men had not been immortal or possessed, but

could they have been spirit-born, like me and Dredmore? Able to heal without scars?

I tested the water in my old clearstone tub before I stepped in and carefully sank down beneath the pink bubbles, groaning a little as the heat spread over me. Every muscle in my body felt stretched and sore, as if I were some animech that had been wound up too tight. I folded and tucked a washing cloth under my neck and closed my eyes.

"Jolly fine time for you to be taking a nap," Harry said somewhere behind me. "The city is in imminent peril. We've crazed monsters running about the streets attacking the helpless. Not to mention you could nod off and drown."

I opened one eye. "Harry, I didn't summon you. I am naked, in my bath, and you're my grandfather." I closed my eye. "Go away."

"Don't be disgusting," he snapped. "I went to hospital to check on you, and you were gone, so I came here and waited. Once the sun came up I was trapped. Where have you been? Your gown smells like the sewers."

I was going to drown myself in my tub. "Never mind where I was, what have you learned? Do you know who is creating the Wolfmen?"

"I know what he is, but not who." He made a frustrated sound. "The Aramanthan who populate the Netherside are not very keen on mortals or me. Since I led the mortals who defeated them, I suppose it can't be helped."

I reached for my soap cake. "We already know the master of the Wolfmen is Aramanthan. What else is there?"

"This one is said to be earthbound, and has been since the immortal wars ended," Harry said. "Possessing one mortal body after another would have granted him the means and time to acquire whatever he needed to build his power and develop his magic. After so many centuries he may be unstoppable."

"That was what they said about Zarath," I reminded him, "and I not only stopped him, I made sure he'll never possess another mortal body again."

"If you're thinking of using your da's pocket watch again, forget it," Harry said. "You were lucky to live through your first trip through time. When you did, you created unnatural forces that still resonate inside you. Another such journey will add more, much more than you can contain in your mortal form. You can't risk another go."

Although Harry had often lied to me in the past, this time I sensed he was being completely honest. "Very well, no time travel. How then are we to defeat him?"

"I don't know."

"You're Merlin. You've *forgotten* more magic than anyone knows." The way he was avoiding my gaze made me suspicious—what could this beast-maker immortal do that would give Harry pause? Then suddenly I understood. "I see. He's like you, isn't he?"

He made a blustering sound. "No one is like me. I am the only one of my kind to have bothered to protect humanity. I even saved your world a time or two."

"I meant, he is as powerful as you." I waited for him to reply, and when he didn't I sat up, sloshing bubbles and water over the tub's rim. "I have to wash my hair and rinse off. Go out in the sitting room and wait for me there."

"It's daylight, and I can't go anywhere," he grumbled as he floated through the wall and disappeared.

I scrubbed my hair and scalp until all I could smell were roses, and then emptied the tub before filling my rinse bucket with cold water and pouring it over my head and body. I hated cold rinses, and shivered as I dried off and wrapped up my hair, but it woke me up and sharpened my thinking. Harry was right, this was no time to nap.

I pulled on my dressing gown and walked out to the sitting room. "You have to know some way of—" I stopped at the sight of Lady Bestly warming her hands over my stove. "Milady." I looked about but saw no visible sign of Harry, and then remembered only I or another spirit-born could see him. "I'm sorry to present myself in such a state. I wasn't expecting anyone to call."

"I would have sent a servant to warn you, but I have only Hartley now and she cannot drive." Lady Bestly took in the room. "This is a very pleasant home. You must bake bread quite often."

"I don't bake at all. The building was used as a granary before I bought it, and the scent of the wheat they stored here has never entirely disappeared." I gestured to the nicest chair I owned. "Do sit down. I'll just go and change—"

"Please don't trouble yourself on my account. I have intruded on your privacy, and . . ." She pressed her gloved fingers to her lips and swallowed. "Forgive me, but might I impose on you to use your lavatory?"

I saw the beads of perspiration pop out on her brow

and gestured quickly. "It's right through here, milady."

I showed her to the loo, and then stood outside and listened for a moment to the coughing and retching sounds she made before I returned to the sitting room. A few minutes later she rejoined me, apologizing again as she sat down and clasped her hands so tightly I thought the stitching in her gloves would pop.

"Annie told me that you have been seeing a physick in town," I said carefully. "You do look very ill. Might I summon a carri to take you to his office?"

"He can do nothing for me, Kittredge." She blotted her mouth with a lace-edged kerchief. "What I suffer is a natural condition, and in time, it will pass. One way or another." She saw my expression and crumpled the lacy linen in her fist. "As you have already guessed."

I nodded. "When do you expect your confinement?"

"Sometime in the fall, if I live that long." She regarded me steadily. "At my age there is no guarantee of that, of course. I barely survived the conception."

That was why she had waited a week before sending for me, why she had worn such heavy face paint, and walked like such an old woman. "Your husband attacked you."

"That *thing* was not my husband," she snapped. "But yes, yes it did. It came into my bedchamber, pinned me down, and had its way with me. It pummeled me and clawed me, and then it ran off into the night like the beast it was, attacking and murdering every poor soul in its path."

Now I felt sick. "I'm so sorry, milady. Truly."

"Terrance and I tried to have a family all the years of our marriage, but we could not. As much as I loathe the creature he became, he gave me a child." She ducked her head. "If it is in fact a child. I hardly know what to think, given what its father became."

"Magic made your husband into that beast, milady," I told her. "I believe Lord Bestly was deceived by a powerful mage, who for his own evil purposes forced the unnatural transformation on his lordship."

I expected my theory to shock and horrify Lady Bestly, and imagined she would have to use my loo again straightaway. Yet after a moment of visible confusion she only shook her head. "That could not be done to Terrance. He distrusted and despised magic and anyone who practiced it. He would not tolerate a mage in his presence. Indeed, the few times that Lord Dredmore called on me, my husband became so agitated he left the house."

And with that she threw my theory into the gutter—unless Lord Bestly had worried that a mage might expose him. "You are certain his prejudice was genuine?"

"Absolutely. In his youth Terrance was swindled by a mage who convinced him that unclean spirits haunted several of my husband's properties," she said. "The mage persuaded Terrance to sell him the properties for a pittance, as he claimed he could only use his power to force out the ghosts if the properties belonged to him. Once they were gone, he promised on his honor to sell them back to Terrance at the same price."

His greed must have overcome his common sense. "None of this was put in writing, I suppose."

"As I said, my husband was young and unfortunately, very trusting. The mage immediately sold all the properties for an enormous profit, took the money, and vanished. My husband was almost ruined, and worse, made a laughingstock." She touched the wedding ring she still wore. "I think he would have done harm to himself if we had not met."

Or if your dowry had not been so large, I thought with a tinge of cynicism. "The mage who did this to your husband may not have presented himself as a practitioner of magic. He probably would have gained his trust by posing as a gentleman or some other sort of intimate acquaintance. Before he died, did Lord Bestly mention to you any new particular friends?"

"He did not discuss such matters with me."

"I see." No, I didn't. New acquaintances were discussed endlessly on the Hill; it was how they assured no unworthy soul penetrated the iron ranks of their society—and their vetting process began at home.

"You have an unsavory interest in my private affairs," Lady Bestly snapped suddenly, as if I'd somehow insulted her. Before I could apologize her shoulders sagged. "No, I do not mean to say that. You have been remarkably tolerant, while I . . . I have acted disgracefully."

"Milady, what happened in the past is done."

"I do not refer to the past, Kittredge." She gave me a direct look. "I have lied to you more than once about my communications with my husband. He did not discuss his new friends with me because he barely spoke two words to me. Just before he died I discovered he was no longer spending his nights at home, and had not been for months. I checked his bank account books, and found he had regularly withdrawn large sums of money this past year as well."

I nearly groaned out loud; why had she concealed all this from me? "Did you confront him about it?"

"I already knew what it was," she said. "He was living at his club and spending inordinate amounts of money, probably on a younger woman. Even if he hadn't died, Terrance would have left me anyway."

"Or he was being swindled by another mage," I suggested. "One who was far more clever than the first. Under such influence, your husband might not have even known what he was doing."

A glimmer of determination appeared in her eyes. "You must find out the truth of it, Kittredge. For my sake as well as my child's. We have no hope of a future without it."

I promised Lady Bestly I would call on her as soon as I had something new to report, and asked Connell to summon a carri-cab to take her back to the Hill. As I watched Dredmore's man escort her out to the curb, the glare of the sun made me squint at the horizon. In a handful of hours twilight would fall, and the Aramanthan would again be able to roam about freely and use his powers. Sooner than that Dredmore would arrive, and I was still traipsing about in my dressing gown.

I'd never felt more useless as I turned to go to my dressing room. Being female was bad enough, but now I was a female in danger. Dredmore would lock me up and toss away the key, unless . . .

"I have a message for his lordship," I said, testing the words. "An urgent message for his lordship."

I walked past Harry as he was rematerializing,

stopped, and turned. "Do you have any useful magic during the daylight?"

"I can sit and listen to you natter on with that evil-minded harpy like she's as dear to you as your own mother." He folded his semitransparent arms. "If you weren't my own blood I'd believe you'd been spelled."

"You knew I was working for Lady Bestly before today." I went into my dressing room to find the appropriate costume.

"Aye, I knew the name, not the face that went with it," he called after me. "I watched everything she did to you eight years ago. I know exactly who she is."

"Who she *was*," I corrected as I took out a somewhat shabby suit and cap from the back of my armoire. "Now she's a pregnant widow fighting for her child and her life. That's who I'm working for." As Harry muttered something vile I added, "Besides eavesdropping on extremely private conversations that are none of your business, what more can you do?"

"I can leave."

"Wait, don't do that." I dressed as fast as I could and came out. "Harry, I need to get into— Ah, sorry." I backed a few steps away from Connell. "I like to talk to myself when I'm alone. Silly habit, really."

"It's me," Connell said in Harry's voice as he inspected himself. "You'd never know it to look at him, but he's fast as a snake and strong as an ox. In this body I could run round the city a few times before sunset."

It took all my self-control not to slug him. "Harry, get out of that man. Right this minute. *Harry.*"

"Stop being so bloody dramatic. You know I won't

keep him." He moved his head from side to side. "As if I'd spend the next fifty years serving the devil himself." He regarded me. "You wanted to get past him. It's this or cosh him over the head, and with this lad's training, you'd never get close enough to take the first swing."

I could have argued the point, but Harry usually kept his promises to me, and Connell would have no memory of being overtaken by my grandfather's spirit. "You will not let anything happen to Mr. Connell. If he winds up with so much as a bruise on his knuckles, our partnership is dissolved for good."

"No scratching the carri, got it." He gave me a cheeky grin that looked ridiculous on Connell's face. "So where to, miss?"

I jammed the messenger's cap over my damp curls. "The White Lupine."

CHAPTER TEN

Of course Harry didn't drive anything but horses, so I had to take the wheel of the hired carri. Fortunately in my messenger's garb I didn't attract the notice I certainly would have dressed as a female. Under city regulations, an unmarried woman could not apply for a driving permit, and a married woman could have one only if her husband signed his consent. Few were issued, as it was a common misconception among the men of the city that females were incapable of adequately operating mechanized transport.

Due to various emergency circumstances I'd risked driving a carri a few times—generally borrowing Bridget's carri when I did so I could produce her permit if stopped—but any beater who spied a young lass like me perambulating round town would give chase until they could jump on the back and order me to the curb—and the very last thing I needed now was to be arrested.

Naturally Harry made himself helpful by sitting beside me on the driver's bench and criticizing every turn I made. "You're cutting the corners too close. Look out for that chap there with the barrow. Slow down before you lose control of this bloody contraption."

"I know you'll survive being thrown under the wheels, Grandfather," I said through my teeth. "But I'll enjoy squishing you anyway."

Harry made a rude sound. "And I thought you liked this Connell lad."

Once I reached Rosings Park I slowed enough so I could examined the buildings on the other side of Mission Street. Most appeared to be vacant with boards on the windows and padlocks on the doors, but I spotted the glow of lights from inside one blackstone in the center of the block, and pulled to the curb opposite the front entry. I looked up and down the street but saw no sign of Dredmore's coach.

"Well?" Harry said after several minutes. "Are we going in or sitting here?"

"*I'm* going in. *You're* staying with the carri." I climbed down and straightened my jacket. "If I'm not back out by sunset, find Dredmore and tell him where I am."

"I'll do no such thing," he blustered, climbing down after me. "I'm going with."

"No one uses two couriers to send a message." I rubbed my forehead. "Harry, you know what I do for a living. For God's sake, shut up and let me do it."

He glowered. "If you're not out of there in thirty minutes, I'm coming in after you. It's as simple as that."

"Fine." I stalked across the street.

After I rang the bell I pulled my cap down an inch to better shade my face and thrust my hands into my pockets. Only a few seconds passed before the door opened and the scent of a pungent herb made me sneeze. Before I could apologize, a cadaverous-looking butler in black glared down his bony nose at me.

"No soliciting," he intoned as he began to close the door again.

"I been sent to deliver a message." Quickly I stepped up and put a foot on the threshold. "Urgent business."

The butler hesitated. "Well? What is it?"

"Confidential, sir." I tried to sound polite and scornful at the same time. "I'm to give it directly or not at all."

"To whom?" A loud burst of laughter from inside distracted the butler, who muttered under his breath before he tugged me inside and slammed the door. "Wait here," he said before he hurried off into a corridor.

I took in the front foyer, which was guarded by two massive brass standing urns filled to overflowing with white flowers. A expected portrait of the queen hung above one of the urns; the law required an image of Herself prominently displayed in any meeting place. No dust covered the frame, but there were odd bunches of some white-green dried leaves I didn't recognize affixed to the four corners. A step closer confirmed the funny smell was coming from them, and more of the leaves tucked in among the urns.

I reached into the urn, plucking out some of the leaves and tucking them into my jacket pocket. I'd show them to Harry later; he'd know if they had any magical properties.

Since this was a gentlemen's club, I expected to see painting or portints of the founders and more important members, but not a single portrait adorned the hall. Instead the heads of several wild animals sprung from the carved plaques; they were probably hunting trophies. I wandered over to a table on which a stuffed bobcat snarled silently at nothing and couldn't resist touch the striped, spotted fur. It was not as soft as it looked, and the cold, solid feel of the body beneath it reminded me I was handling a dead thing.

Lord Bestly had once been a keen hunter, judging by the number of trophies he'd collected as a lad. Perhaps he'd created the club to relive his childhood glories with like-minded chums. The longer I stood in the place, however, the more it bothered me—and not because I was a woman in disguise.

Something about the place grated on my every nerve.

The mounted trophies all seemed to be glaring at me as I noticed more animal symbols round me. Crude lions and tigers had been worked into the Turkish carpets covering the floors, and the twisted handles of the brass urns looked very much like snakes. Every door sported a handle shaped like a bear or a fox; the chandelier overhead sported no less than a dozen hawks worked in bronze, their wings seeming almost to move with the shadow play from the bulbs of lighted keroseel.

No lambs or rabbits for the manly members of the White Lupine, I thought, feeling a bit contemptuous—men were so enamored of things that killed. I stiffened as the thought made plain what bothered me so about the place.

Every animal rendered in the decor was a predator—a creature that attacked and devoured others to survive. Was that his lordship's secret? Had he agreed to the Wolfman transformation to indulge his love of hunting—to become the ultimate killer?

Laughter erupted again from the corridor, and then was abruptly cut off, as if a door had opened and closed. Shortly thereafter a young gentleman in a rumpled suit appeared in front of me, weaving slightly as he tried unsuccessfully not to spill the drink in his hand.

"Hallo," he said, breathing the fumes of very good whiskey in my face. "Who are you?"

"Courier, sir." I remembered to touch the rim of my hat. "Waiting to deliver an urgent message."

"Well, then, what are you standing about here for? Come on." He grabbed my arm and hauled me into the corridor opposite the one the butler had taken. When we reached the end of it, he yanked open the door and pushed me inside as he sang out, "Messenger, lads."

Smoke fogged the room, but not enough to hide its occupants or what they were doing to the half-naked women presently entertaining them. Champagne sparkled and red mouths laughed as the gentlemen drank from slippers and gobbled canapés perched on the slopes of bare breasts. In one corner a pair was coupling; in another a brass-haired harlot bobbed her head over her companion's open trousers.

The young man who'd dragged me in nudged me with an elbow. "Like a bit of that, wouldn't you, boy?"

I hardly knew to blink, much less speak. I began moving backward toward what I hoped was the door. I missed it and bumped into something hanging on a wall that stabbed through my jacket and into my back with tearing pain. I stumbled forward, biting my tongue to keep from crying out, and glanced back. I'd walked into some sort of fetish fashioned from a mass of talons embedded in a circular weaving of red and black fibers round a great skull with a fanged muzzle. Scarlet gleamed on several of the sharp claw tips, and I felt sick as I realized it was my own blood.

"Really, John," a silky voice said from the door I'd missed. "The child probably doesn't comprehend what he's seeing."

Never had I been so relieved to turn my back on a roomful of nobs. "I've a . . . a message."

The gent who'd spoken wore a bronze smoking jacket over his immaculate evening dress. Large topaz studs twinkled in his lobes, and more bejeweled pins studded his lapels. He had a well-groomed helmet of caramel-colored curls framing his angelic features, and altogether presented a respectable if somewhat casual appearance. Looking into his light brown eyes made my spine go to ice, for they had the same focused malevolence that I'd encountered in my tram dream.

"I am Louis Lykaon, the club manager," he said. "You may give your message to me."

"Yes, sir." He was the Aramanthan, I was sure of it. "I mean, no sir, I can't." I felt something trickle down my back and swallowed. "I was paid to deliver it directly to Lord Dredmore."

"Dredmore." His smooth, toffee-colored brows drew together. "His lordship is not a member of the club. Who sent this message?"

"A lady from the Hill, sir. I don't know her name." I began inching toward the door. "Since his lordship's not here, I'll just be on me way."

I almost made it before a strong hand seized my collar, lifted me off my feet, and swung me round.

Lykaon looked me up and down before setting me down. "What is your name, boy?"

I went blank on all but one. "Harry, sir."

The sound of two men shouting outside in the corridor drew his attention, and when he released me and went out to investigate I followed. There I saw the butler blustering at a beater, who was giving it right back to him while tapping his trunch against his palm. As soon as I emerged the beater shoved past the servant and seized my shoulder.

"I told you he was in here," the beater said to the butler, and glared down at me. "Chief inspector wants to talk to you, lad, and he'll not wait all day."

"I ain't done nothing," I protested, mostly for show, as I was marched down the corridor. I could feel Lykaon and his butler staring after us, and held my breath until we were outside. "Thank you, Officer."

"Shut it," he said pleasantly, hauling me down the steps to a waiting carri. Before I was shoved in I darted a look across the street, but Harry was gone.

I stumbled against the seat, groping to steady myself, and planted my hand on a hard chest. "Sorry." I shifted to the opposite bench and collapsed as my back throbbed. Once I'd caught my breath I looked at the inspector. "Afternoon, Tommy. You wanted a word?"

"Several." He leaned forward. "Why are you dressed like that?"

"I had to deliver a message to that gentlemen's club." I made a show of removing my hat and fluffing my matted hair. "They don't let you in if you're wearing skirts."

"What message, and for whom?" he persisted.

"It was for Lord Dredmore. Something about his laundry—I think someone may have used too much starch on his shirts." I glanced out the window before I gave him a cheery smile. "Could you drop me at the goldstone? I would like to change out of these trousers. Very scratchy, tweed." I could feel the wet stickiness of blood soaking through my shirt now. "I don't know how you men endure it in the summer."

He made a disgusted sound. "I should simply arrest you."

"For what? Dressing in men's garms isn't a crime." I thought for a moment. "Is it?"

"There is a law against impersonating a courier to gain access to private property." He smiled back at me. "It's called trespassing."

"Only if the club owner presses charges," I countered. "Which he won't because he's deceased and his estate has yet to be transferred. Come on, Tommy. It was only a bit of a lark."

"This time you larked your way into the middle of an official investigation," he said tightly. "So you'll tell me the real reason you went in that club, who you spoke with, and what you saw, or I'll toss you in the lockup until you do."

He would, too; I could see all the righteous resolve glittering in his eyes. "I went to find an acquaintance of Lord Bestly's whose name I have yet to learn. I spoke to the butler, a drunken man, and the manager, but nothing we said was of any consequence. As for the general debauchery, licentiousness, and heresy I saw in practice, I believe that the White Lupine is not a gentlemen's club but one of the lower levels of hell itself."

"Hellfire," he muttered, his features tightening with dislike. "They're called hellfire clubs."

"There's more than one in Rumsen?" When he didn't answer me I decided to press the issue. "I did recognize some faces well enough to put names to them. Perhaps I should call on their wives and share with them the details of what I witnessed."

"Issuing a threat to an officer of the court will earn you ninety days at a labor farm," he said. "Where you will *not* be growing flowers."

"To think you wanted to place me in protective custody only yesterday." From the corner of my eye I saw we were approaching Rumsen Main. "Why don't we agree to an even exchange of information on the way to my home, Inspector? You answer a question honestly, and in return I'll answer one of yours, and so forth until we reach the goldstone."

"You'll answer truthfully?" When I nodded, he said, "I ask first."

If he didn't hurry I was fairly certain I'd bleed through my jacket and all over the seat. "We can begin as soon as you give your driver my address."

Doyle instructed his man to take us to my home and then started in on me. "Why are you poking into Bestly's affairs?"

"His widow hired me to investigate the circumstances surrounding his death." I folded my hands. "What are you investigating at the White Lupine?"

His jaw tightened. "Some of the men who disappeared from the Hill were members of the club."

"Some?" I echoed. "Not all of them?"

"It's not your turn," he told me. "Where did you go last night?"

I made a face. "I stayed with a former client of mine who lives in the sewers."

"You slept in the sewers." He dragged a hand through his hair. "You *should* be locked up."

"No one came after me, did they? And just so you know, that wasn't my next question." I felt my jacket clinging and shifted forward from the seat back. "Are any of the servants at the club natives?"

"No, none of them are." He peered at me. "Why are you interested in native servants? The truth, Charmian, or I turn the carri back to the station."

"If I tell you this, it has to remain strictly confidential. Agreed?" When he inclined his head, I said, "I think the mage who is making the Wolfmen is using native magic."

He went very still. "You believe a shaman is responsible?"

"It's possible but unlikely, as the magic is being used incorrectly. And that's two questions." I felt the carri slowing and looked out to see my block. "You'll have to owe me the answers. Thank you for seeing me home, Inspector." I opened the door as soon as the carri stopped.

"Not so fast." Doyle pulled it shut again. "This is my case, Kit. You're to stay away from the White Lupine and anything to do with these Wolfmen. You may also tell your widow that the Yard will handle the investigation from here."

"Not hardly." When I saw how serious he was I sputtered. "Tommy, this is my job—my living. You can't order me off the case now. I'm too close to uncovering the truth."

"If you interfere in my investigation again, I will arrest you." He opened the door for me. "Good day, Miss Kittredge."

I stomped into the goldstone and slammed the door. I was just beginning to shed my jacket when Dredmore emerged from my sitting room, accompanied by Connell.

"Lucien. How prompt you are." I glanced at his driver, who looked almost as angry at me and his master. "Mr. Connell, I hope my brief sojourn didn't greatly inconvenience you."

"He knows I'm in possession, Charm," my grandfather said, giving Dredmore a filthy look. "Caught me outside the club, but I didn't tell him anything."

"He didn't have to," Dredmore said, eyeing my suit. "You went inside that cesspit. I can smell it on you. When you agreed to wait here for me."

I didn't care for his tone. "I said I would meet you here at four. Inspector Doyle delayed me only a few minutes."

Dredmore pointed to the stairs. "Go and change out of those clothes, immediately. When you do, burn them."

I had no intention of destroying a perfectly good disguise, although telling him that would only further provoke him. "The Yard is also investigating the club. Doyle told me that some of the missing men are members. Excuse me." I left him to chew on that and went to stoke up my coal boiler so I wouldn't have an ice-cold bathe.

Coaxing the old blackpot to produce enough steam

to heat my water gave me a few minutes to consider how to placate Dredmore. Admitting I was entirely in the wrong might right things, if I could convince him I meant it. Yet as I came back in, I saw no sign of Dredmore, and Connell sat snoring in my favorite arm-chair by the fire.

"Really, Harry," I muttered as I passed him. "If you want to nap, don't use that poor sod as a bed." As he mumbled something and turned onto his side I continued on to my dressing room so I could change out of the offensive garms and wash up before my next round with Dredmore.

I'd just stripped out of my jacket when the door opened and closed. "Well, it's about time you stopped lolling about, Harry. I'll be out in a few moments, so try to . . ." I smelled dark spice and anger and stopped unbuttoning my shirt. When I glanced over my shoulder at Dredmore, I thought of Harry, whom I'd never known to fall asleep while actively possessing a mortal. "What did you do to my grandfather?"

"Far less than I desired." Dredmore loomed over me. "Your back is bleeding. Take off the shirt."

All my thoughts of apologizing fled. "I can look after—"

"Take it off, Charmian," he said, very quietly. "Or I will."

I kept my back to him as I finished unfastening the placket and the cuffs. He eased it down from my shoulders and let it fall to the floor as he used something soft to blot my skin.

"It was my fault," I murmured. "I bumped into a mass

of claws surrounding some skull in the club. They went through my clothes."

"Some of the wounds have reopened. Be still," he added when I tried to look over my shoulder. "The White Lupine is a hellfire club."

"Doyle told me that, too."

He held my shoulder as he pressed a cloth firmly against my spine. "Did he advise you of what they do to women at such places?"

"He didn't have to," I admitted. "But I know who the Aramanthan is. He's possessed Louis Lykaon, the club manager. I recognized his eyes from my nightmare."

His hand tightened. "Did he touch you?"

"He grabbed me by the collar when I tried to leave, but that was all. The only thing that was molested was my opinion of certain gentlemen." I gathered up the shirt to cover my chemise before I faced him. "He wouldn't be creating the Wolfmen at the White Lupine; there's too much chance of discovery. If we watch the club and follow him when he leaves, he'll lead us to where he's keeping the men." When he said nothing, I looked up and saw his expression. "What?"

"Your blood is on my hands." He pulled me into his arms and held me close. "Before I kill him, I'm going to cut off his fingers, and shove them one by one down his throat."

"You can't kill an immortal," I said into his chest. "Mutilating the body he's stolen, while perhaps gratifying for you, won't hurt him, either. The spirit of the poor sod he stole it from may still be trapped inside."

"I don't care."

He truly was upset. "Nothing happened, Lucien. I'm

fine." I drew back and felt the air touch my bare breasts, which caused me to hastily cover myself. "I'm also half undressed and I'd really like not to be that with you while my grandfather is snoozing just down the hall. How did you make him go to sleep like that?"

"I used a spell as soon as you went outside." He touched the hollow at the base of my throat with one finger and watched my face intently. "He won't wake until I break it."

In another time Lucien and I had acted on our unreasonable passions and had become lovers. My trip through time had eliminated that event, but not my memory of it. I knew the pleasure he could give me and I wanted to feel it again—but surrendering once more to temptation would only lead to disastrous consequences. He would not be satisfied with a single dalliance and, I suspected, neither would I.

"I will not be seduced," I said as firmly as I could manage. "By you or any man."

His eyes darkened. "You would rather die a virgin than have me."

"Someone may offer me marriage one day." He didn't like hearing that any more than I cared to say it. "If I surrender to you now, what shall I tell him? I couldn't resist you? It seemed like a good idea at the time? *You didn't want me to die a virgin?*"

He smiled a little. "If that is your resolve, then why are you shouting at me?"

"Because you're not helping, you nummox. We're supposed to be friends this—" I clamped my mouth shut.

"This time?" Other fingers joined the one beneath

my chin and drifted lower. "We were lovers. I knew it."

"It never happened—"

"I dreamed it," he said, stunning me. "I chased you through the garden maze at Morehaven. You injured your hand." He grasped my wrist and brought my palm to his mouth, pressing a kiss in the center. "We made love by the reflecting pool." When I tried to pull my hand away he held on to it. "And you, madam, were *most* willing."

"In your dreams." But how could Dredmore dream of what to him had never happened? "Did I also stand on my head and recite the Territorial Settlement Acts in Talian?"

Someone knocked at the door, and I brushed past him to open it. "It's time you woke—" I was talking to an empty hall, and glanced down it toward the front entry. "Harry?"

Something cold and heavy latched on to my trouser leg, making me jump, and when I looked down I saw a gleaming brass rat wrapped round my ankle and gnawing at the tweed.

I tried at once to kick off the horrid little mech, but its paws stabbed through my trousers and curled to hold tight. *"Lucien."*

Without a word he came to me and began unfastening my trousers.

"What are you doing?" I demanded, slapping at his hands before I realized what he was about and tore at the fastenings with him. I yelped as I felt something like tiny daggers scrape against my shin. "It's biting me."

Dredmore yanked down the trousers as I braced myself with a hand on his arm and jerked my leg up. The rat began whirring furiously as it tried to hold on, and I yelped again as it bit me a second time. It felt ridiculous, being attacked by an animech no bigger than my foot, but the memory of the one that had been sent to my office and the very real pain this one was inflicting didn't entice me to laughter. "Get it off, Lucien. Hurry, please."

A blade flashed, and with a few swipes Dredmore cut away the trouser cuff, freeing my ankle. I stepped out of the pants as he wadded them round the rat, bundling it inside the tweed.

"It's another bomb," I said, but he shook his head and carried the writhing bundle out of the dressing room.

I grabbed my night robe as I followed him across the house to the back entry. "Where are you going with that?"

"Stay in the damned house," he ordered over his shoulder before he kicked the door open and rushed outside.

I went to my kitchen window and watched as he strode across my small patch of yard and into the street. There he dropped the bundle and backed away, removing something from his coat and tossing it up into the air.

A shower of iridescent crystals fell over the bundle, piling atop it and solidifying into a sparkling faceted globe. I could see the bundle of tweed inside the beautiful thing, but it wasn't moving. Streaks of frost rayed out from the globe, shooting across the cobblestones and grass in every direction.

I opened the window. "Why are you freezing it? If it's a bomb you have to put it in water."

"The ice will preserve the mech and the magic," he said, crouching down to examine the globe. "I'll take it to Morehaven so I can examine it." He glanced my way. "Don't come out here."

What he meant was, don't come out and ruin his

spell. "I wasn't planning to. Do enjoy the bomb." I slammed the window shut, thought for a moment, and then reopened it. "Will you be needing your driver back?"

"Yes." He gave me one of his brooding looks. "But not with your grandfather in him." His cloak swirled as he stalked off into the shadows.

Mrs. Cartwright, my neighbor to the right, came trundling out onto her back stairs. "Miss Kittredge, do you mind? I'm trying to get our little Oscar down for his nap, and . . ." She stared at her frost-covered flowerpots. "Sweet Mary, what's all this?"

"Spell gone wrong, Mrs. C. Sorry about your geraniums." I shut the window and went directly to Connell, who lay snoozing peacefully on my chaise. The moment I touched his shoulder he blinked, yawned, and then scowled.

"Charm." My grandfather sat up quickly. "That black-hearted demon—"

"—spelled you to sleep," I finished for him. "He's ready to leave now, so you have to give up the body."

He squinted up at me. "Do you think that's wise? I could hang on to this one until dark without any worries. You can tell him I've gone, he'll never know—"

"Dredmore will know," I assured him. "Get out of the man's driver, Harry."

"Oh, very well." Harry got up and frowned at the floor. "If that evil sod did nothing to you, why is your foot bleeding?"

"I stubbed my toe," I lied. "Time to be a ghost again, Harry."

"I never stopped," he muttered, closing his eyes and separating himself from Connell in a shimmering mist.

As my grandfather's spirit evaporated, Connell staggered, nearly falling over the chaise.

"Careful." I caught his elbow to steady him. "His lordship is waiting in the back for you, Mr. Connell. You'll need to drive the carri round the block."

The driver turned his head toward the front entry. "I was just standing over there, and then . . ." He shook his head. "Can't remember."

"Probably for the best." I handed him his cap. "Thank you for looking after me, Mr. Connell."

"My pleasure, miss." Still frowning he walked out.

I sat down on the chaise and lifted my robe, grimacing at the bite marks the rat had inflicted, one of which was still bleeding. I hobbled into the kitchen to wash the wounds and bind them with some of the clean rags I kept for wiping dishes. There I saw something floating in my tube port, and opened it to retrieve a cream-colored envelope marked with a scrolled B.

The handwriting was unfamiliar, but the message was short and to the point:

My Dear Charmian,

I have news of great urgency to impart. Please call on me at Bestly House as soon as possible.

Yours Faithfully,
Eugenia

I read the note twice more before I decided it was a forgery. Lady Bestly would never address me by my proper given name; I doubted she even knew what it was. Nor would she refer to herself by her own. Whoever had written this must have seen her calling on me and assumed we were friends—and that I would drop everything to rush to her side.

"So an idiot wrote it." I crumpled the note in my fist. "But not the same one who sent the rat."

CHAPTER ELEVEN

Borrowing Mr. Cartwright's horse to ride to the Hill required me to bargain with his wife. Already annoyed by the ice spell that had frozen over most of her garden, she extracted as much as she could from me without physically removing any of my teeth.

"So you'll replace all me flowers, sit with the children for our anniversary dinner next month, and run me market errands for a fortnight." She switched her drooling little Oscar from one broad hip to the other as she frowned. "I don't know, Miss Kittredge. Women aren't supposed to go riding about, particularly after dark. If anything happens to that horse me husband'll kill me after you. He might be a foreman but he's not all that clever, so they'll catch him and he'll hang for the murders, and then who'll raise our little Oscar?"

"If it comes to that you can always say I stole Daisy," I suggested. "You'll live, I'll go to prison, and your husband won't kill anyone. Little Oscar keeps both his parents."

That seemed to mollify her. "I suppose." She held out the stable key. "You'll have to go and saddle her yourself; I've got to put me boy in the tub now—and you'll bring her back before midnight, when my husband's shift at the factory ends, promise."

"He'll never know I borrowed it," I assured her.

I walked to the end of the block where the neighborhood horses were stabled, and walked back to the community stalls. Daisy gave me a placid look as I unlocked the latch and took down her saddle and bridle.

"I brought you a bribe, too," I told her as I took the oatcake from my reticule and fed it to her. "Don't mind my skirts, and I won't make you gallop."

Once I had her saddled I gathered up my gown and used the slats of the stall to climb up high enough to mount her. The old mare swung her head round to eye me but didn't object, and I led her out at a slow walk through the back of the stable.

The cool night air seemed to perk up Daisy, who shuffled into a lazy trot as I guided her down the back streets. Not having the weight of the Cartwrights and their brood and buggy to pull might have cheered her, too. It was only as we approached the road to the Hill that she slowed; the Cartwrights had never driven her near it.

I gave her some encouraging pats. "No worries, my gel, we've an old friend of mine to call on tonight."

I deliberately rode past the avenue leading to Bestly House and continued on until I reached a sparkling pink manor. On the walkway at the side of the great house a slim figure dressed in a dark cloak waved for me to follow, and led us back to the matching carriage house where a servant waited.

"Good evening, Miss Kittredge." Lady Diana Walsh pulled back her hood to nod at the footman, who opened the door and helped me to dismount before taking Daisy inside. "I confess, as soon as I received your note I was most intrigued. Shall I have Jones escort you to your ultimate destination?"

"That won't be necessary, milady." I glanced at the nobber striding quickly toward us. Riding Daisy to Lady Bestly's would have drawn too much attention, and it would still be a trick to get to her without attracting the notice of her neighbors' servants. "I'd much rather walk there with the patrolman, if you wouldn't mind having a word with him."

Diana nodded and intercepted the nobber, who listened and agreed to accompany me there and back.

"Jones will attend to your mare until you return," Diana said, smiling a little. "While I will look forward to hearing all about the matter when we next meet for tea in town. Good luck, Miss Kittredge."

"Thank you, Lady Diana." I bobbed a curtsey before joining the nobber on the walkway.

All of the Hill's private patrolmen were sizable fellows, but this one moved with the speed and surety of an experienced chaser. Whoever wrote the note to lure me to Lady Bestly's home would not easily escape him.

Once we turned the corner he gave me a sideways look. "Ask you a question, miss?"

"No one can hear us," I said, peering down the empty street. "Have at it."

He grinned. "You're the spell-breaker gel what saved Lord Walsh and his from the Talians, aren't you?"

The intelligent thing to do would be to deny it; the Walshes had gone to considerable trouble to keep the matter private. On the other hand he already knew almost everything about it. "It was my honor to be of assistance to his lordship and the family during a difficult time."

"Aye, that it was." He rolled his eyes. "You been doing business regular on the Hill, then."

"I've tried to stay away," I admitted, "but they keep getting into trouble and offering me money. Is it a problem for you and your men?"

"Not at all, miss. Way I see it, after a fashion we're doing the same job." He sounded as if he approved, too. "I'll put out the word to the boys, let them know. From now on no one'll give you any grief."

I didn't know any common people who were given free access to the Hill by the nobbers. "That's very decent of you."

"I expect you won't abuse it." His eyes narrowed and his smile disappeared. "Seems Lady B's right popular tonight."

I followed the direction of his gaze to a large, grand coach and four waiting at the curb in front of Bestly House. The driver wore the ornate gold-and-red livery of a city official's household, but I didn't recognize the elaborate crest adorning the coach's doors. "I'm guessing that's not the undertaker."

"Almost as bad," he muttered. "That's Lady Raynard, his honor's wife."

The tip of a fan emerged from the coach's window and rapped sharply on its side, which brought a footman who hurried to open it and help down the passenger.

Lady Raynard stepped out like a queen, standing serenely as a maid appeared and shook out the folds of her mistress's voluminous gown. I took in what must have been fifty yards of ruched lace fluttering from seven tiers of glossy satin skirts and crawling up a pearl-encrusted bodice to encircle a thin neck and drape along sleeves of lace buttoned with gleaming cabochons of polished shell from wrist to elbow. To make matters worse, the entire ensemble—including the pearls—had been dyed a particularly livid shade of yellow-green.

The lady snapped open the fan she held, which sent the maid back into the coach, and then held out one hand. The footman positioned his arm beneath her lady-ship's and escorted her as she approached us.

I couldn't take my eyes off her wig, the whitened curls of which had been fashioned into the shape of a swan. A real swan's head sprang from the powdered nest and bobbed regally with every step she took.

"Is that a bird on her head?" I murmured to the nobber as I watched her closing the gap between us.

"Aye," he muttered back as he surreptitiously straightened the line of his sleeves by tugging on the cuffs. "It matches her brains."

"Good evening, citizens." Lady Raynard halted with the languid elegance of kind condescension, her move-ments sending a thick waft of French perfume to roll over me and the patrolman. As we both tried not to breathe it in, she dismissed her footman with an elegant flutter of her fan. "It is a pleasant night, is it not?"

As the nobber bowed I bobbed, but after his per-functory, "Yes, madam" I had to say something. "Very pleasant, milady."

She turned her gaze on me. "You are not a resident here, I think."

She knew I wasn't. "I have been summoned here, milady." And since I doubted she had ever once personally addressed ordinary citizens on the street, she almost certainly had to be the author of the note I'd received. "If you'll excuse me."

"I most certainly will not." She softened the snappish words with a patronizing smile. "The welfare of my dear friend Lady Bestly is my every concern now that she has suffered the unthinkable." She eyed the nobber. "This is nothing to do with you, Patrolman. You may go."

The nobber nodded, bowed again, and leaned his head down to mine. "Back in a trice. Mind your mouth."

Once he departed, Lady Raynard minced closer, inspecting me as she might a confection she wished to devour. "You smell of horse, and your skirts are in an atrocious state. What are you doing here, Miss Kittredge?"

She'd need more than a fan to get me to jump. "Why, milady, I wasn't aware that we had been introduced."

"One does not require introductions to those in service." She didn't bother to make that sound pretty. "Indeed, I have been made aware of your association with our poor, dear Eugenia, and your calls upon each other. As there is always some unsavory sort willing to take advantage of a grieving widow, and my dear friend struggles so with her social responsibilities, I should like to know how I may aid her. Now."

She'd brought me to the Hill to find out why Eugenia had hired me or why she wasn't properly mourning. Probably both. "You must discuss that with Lady Bestly, madam."

The swan's head bobbed as she drew back a step. "Do you know who I am? My husband is the mayor of this city."

"Forgive me, milady." I heard something rustling in the hedgerow, and glanced in that direction before I added, "It is not my place to discuss Lady Bestly or her affairs with anyone, even you."

"Hawkins." She fairly screeched the name, and the footman came running. When he flanked her she pointed at me. "Put this ungrateful chit in the coach. We shall continue this discussion at Raynard Manor."

The footman reached out to grab my arm, and I tensed as I readied to shove him off, but before he touched me something nearby growled, low and with deep menace.

"What is that?" Lady Raynard exclaimed. "A dog? Hawkins—"

I heard the sound of windings and gears and seized Lady Raynard. "You must leave now, milady."

The swan on her head thrashed as if trying to escape the nest of her hair while Lady Raynard sputtered several genteel variations of "How dare you" and "Unhand me at once." I ignored her protestations and forced her to march along with me back to her coach. She resisted further by backpeddling her steps, only to lose one silk slipper, which her footman bent and scooped up as he trotted along after us.

I would have liked nothing better than to jump into her fairiestale wagon and ride far, far away from the thing behind us, but I couldn't abandon Lady Bestly or the nobber. I reached for the passenger door's gilded handle, jerking it open so quickly it slammed back against the gold-scrolled back panel of the coach.

A howl of fury made Hawkins glance back. "Miss, what is that?"

Trying to push Lady Raynard into the coach was proving more of an obstacle, as she had now latched onto both sides of the door frame. I looked over at Hawkins. "It's a Wolfman."

His eyes widened, and he rushed to help me. Together we pried off the now-screeching Lady Raynard's grip from the frame, and once Hawkins had lifted her off her feet I gave her a quick push that sent her tumbling inside, her face and the swan disappearing behind a billow of skirts.

"You, too, gel," the footman said, offering me his gloved hand.

I shook my head. "Get her out of here."

I intended to make a mad dash for the house but never got the chance. As soon as the driver raced away the beast came barreling out of the hedge at me.

A shot rang out, and the Wolfman fell and skidded across the lawn to stop in a heap of hair and shredded garms almost at my feet. Behind him I saw Lady Bestly standing at an open window, smoke still curling from the rifle she held.

I glanced down at the beast, who was rapidly transforming back into a man. He twitched several times before he went still, and when I nudged him over with my boot I saw a fist-sized hole in his chest sprouting springs and gears.

Another vicious growl made me look up to see a second Wolfman hulking toward me.

"She'll shoot you, too," I called to it, and as if it understood me it looked back at Lady Bestly, who had trained her rifle on his chest. "You have been bespelled by magic that will kill you, sir, but I can stop it."

The Wolfman began to revert to his mortal state, lowered his head, and whined.

"Kittredge." That was Lady Bestly, and she sounded furious. "What are you doing?"

"Talking to it." I kept my voice soothing as I edged along the walkway and spoke to the creature again. "There's still a man inside you, and despite his deplorable taste in clubs I expect he's a good man at heart. You must resist the urges you feel and let him guide you."

Gears ground together, making his limbs jerk, and the Wolfman's eyes glittered as he lifted his head. He bared his teeth, snapping at the air.

"Or not," I said, reaching down with my hands to take hold of my skirts. "Milady, close the window and lock it."

"Kittredge, you'll never make the door."

"I know." I spun on my heel and ran.

The Wolfman came at me from the side, impossibly fast, and knocked me flat a foot from her ladyship's front entry. I rolled to the side, banging into the cage of mourning doves, which fell over me and opened, releasing the frantic occupants in a flutter of gray wings. I seized the cage as I scrambled up, holding it before me like a shield. The Wolfman tore it apart with two swipes of his claws before they disappeared.

I drew the dagger from my sleeve and held it ready. "I don't think you were a good chap after all," I told the snarling man. "Come on, then."

As he grabbed at me I slashed his arm almost down to the bone, but the wound did nothing to slow him. Blood spattered me as he tossed me out onto the lawn and came after, straddling me as he went down on his knees. I gave up trying to spare him and drove the blade into the center of his chest, but the hard metal beneath the flesh deflected the blow. Fire blazed up my arm as he clamped on to my wrist, shaking it like a dog with a bone until I lost my grip on the dagger.

A strong arm latched round the Wolfman's throat, hauling him backward and laying him out on his back. I watched as a native wearing a cape of blue feathers planted his bare foot in the beast's now-mortal face, pinning his thrashing body down as he drew an ancient pistol and fired point-blank into his heart. He removed his foot and produced a second pistol, firing again into the beast's head.

I turned my head to see the remains only inches from my face, and felt bile rise in my throat. When I looked up to see if the native meant to shoot me as well, he had disappeared.

The nobber came rushing up, bending to check the dead man before reaching to help me up.

"Check the hedges," I told him. "There may be more of them."

He nodded and trotted off to have a look. I stared up at the night sky until Lady Bestly appeared over me, rifle still in hand. "It's not safe for you out here, milady."

"Nor you, Kittredge." She got me up and supported me with her arm. "Come inside."

She helped me into the house and steered me into the

receiving room, where she led me to a crackling hearth. As soon as I saw the fine tapestry covering the chair there I grimaced. "I can't. I've blood and dirt all over me."

"I expect that is not a new experience." Lady Bestly gave me a gentle shove into the chair and covered me with her own silk shawl. "I must go and collect some things from the kitchens. You will not move from this spot."

I glanced at the windows. "But milady—"

"I still have my husband's rifle, Kittredge," she informed me in her snootiest tone, "and I quite enjoyed firing it. Do not tempt me to shoot you in the leg."

She hurried out and I rested my aching head against the pillowy wing of the chair back. My arm felt like lead, and when I tried to move my hand the resulting pain made me bite back a groan. A second attempt assured me that my wrist was only badly sprained, not broken. I pulled back the shawl to check for bite marks, but all I spied was something gleaming in my flesh.

I sank my teeth into my bottom lip as I used a corner of the shawl to grasp the slippery shard of metal and tug it free. As fresh blood welled up in its place I held up the sharply pointed brass to examine it. It appeared to be the tip of a broken tooth. The inside hollow still held a bit of jointed mech and a tiny gear.

Animechs were fashioned to behave like the real animals they imitated: owls hooted, rabbits hopped, butterflies fluttered. I recalled the duchess I'd watched from the tram perambulating with her animech cheetah; along with blinking its topaz eyes it had sauntered, flicked its ears, and switched its tail.

I closed my fist round the broken claw. Just before the Wolfman had attacked me I'd heard its windings and gears working. We'd assumed the mech being put inside these men was to make them stronger and faster, which it certainly did. But just as animechs were fashioned to behave like their living counterparts, perhaps the Wolfmen had been designed to do more? Could the beast-maker have designed his creatures to do some other evil while on rampage?

Lady Bestly reappeared with a basin of water, a pile of linen strips, and a jar of salve on a tray, which she set on the table beside me. "What is that in your hand?"

I opened my fist to show her. "I think it's a piece of brass tooth. It was lodged in my arm." I yelped as she plucked it from my palm and tossed it into the fire. "Milady."

"This unseemly curiosity of yours will get you killed someday," she informed me as she drew back the shawl and studied my arm. "That beast looked as if he meant to tear your arm from your shoulder. I hope it is not broken." She retrieved a pair of scissors from the tray. "I must cut away your sleeve. Who was that native in all the blue feathers?"

"I don't know him," I said. "I think I saw him once, in town. Could he be in service to one of your neighbors?"

"If he was, he would be dressed very differently," she said as she began to snip. "It was very good of him to dispatch that other beast."

"I thought so, too." What plagued me was why he had bothered.

"I saw you also met Lady Raynard." Her lips thinned as she asked, "What manner of ham-handed scheme did she employ to lure you here?"

"She penned a note from you begging my immediate presence." As the sleeve fell away I grimaced at the dark marks mottling my forearm. By morning I'd be a walking bruise, but I no longer saw the wound from the broken tooth. "On your stationery, no less."

"Likely she stole it out of my writing desk. Hartley left her alone the last time she called." She gently blotted away the blood. "You knew the message was a forgery and still you came. Why?"

"I thought you might be in danger." I took in a hissing breath as she applied the salve. "Your reputation is, certainly. She tried to question me as to the reasons behind your lack of mourning."

"Infernal woman." She turned my arm from side to side before taking hold of my hand and carefully prodding my wrist. "I cannot feel any fractures, but you will need to keep it bound and in a sling until the swelling abates." She saw how I was looking at her. "My father was a country physick before his uncle died without issue and he inherited the title and the estate. Terrance liked to remind me of that whenever we quarreled."

I wondered what else he'd thrown in her face. "He must have forgotten that marrying you saved him and his title from ruin. Is Lady Raynard a particular friend of yours?"

"Not by even the greatest stretch of the imagination," she said as she began to wrap my wrist. "Caroline and I came out in the same season, and she instantly lost her heart to Raynard. She also behaved quite foolishly attempting to attract his attention. He would have none of her, and instead offered for me."

"He fell for you."

"Like a headsman's axe." Her mouth tightened. "I had no feelings for him, and after a proper interval intended to refuse him. When Caroline learned of his offer it sent her into a panic. She deliberately compromised Raynard, who thankfully for her sake was honorable enough to marry her. It was a most unhappy match, and she has not improved it by clinging to the belief that her husband still pines for me. But I cannot imagine that would compel her to see me ruined, not after all these years."

"You're a widow now," I reminded her. "Everyone is expecting you to remarry immediately. Ruining your reputation is probably the only way she believes she can prevent you from stealing her husband."

"Only Caroline Raynard could be so ridiculous." She tied off the linen strip round my wrist. "You did not inform her that I am expecting Bestly's heir, I hope?"

I smiled. "Milady, I didn't breathe a word."

"Excellent. She will stew in her own bile." As the front door bell chimed, she rose and went over to the window to look out. "It is the patrolman. The Yard inspector is with him."

"How convenient." I sank down a little in the chair.

"It is not a crime to call on a client," I informed Inspector Doyle as I was marched into the station house. "Nor is it against the law to be the victim of an unprovoked attack."

Doyle said nothing in response to me; he muttered something to his driver, who trotted off in another direction.

"Two unprovoked attacks, to be precise." I ignored the other cops staring at me as we passed their desks and tried instead to look righteously piteous. Since my arm hung in a sling, and my rumpled gown was covered with dirt and blood- and grass stains, I thought I must look convincing. "The patrolman must have explained what happened."

"Aye, he did." Doyle stopped in front of a locked door and removed a ring of keys. "He told me how you rode to the Hill on horseback, how you concealed your mount several blocks from your destination, and how you sent him away just before these unprovoked attacks."

I smiled with relief. "So you understand it was absolutely none of my doing and you have no reason to arrest me." I frowned. "So why have you dragged me down here?"

"You've been a very busy gel." He opened the door, pushed me inside, relocked it, and pointed to one of two chairs flanking a bare desk. "Take a seat."

"Inspector, I'm not—"

"Sit. Down."

I sat.

He did not do the same, but elected to pace round the table, over to the window, back to the table, and then made a complete turn round the room.

The only way to handle this was with wounded dignity. I even had the wounds. "You cannot detain me because you're annoyed with me."

THE CLOCKWORK WOLF

"Annoyed." He regarded the cracked base of the lamp hanging over the table. "I have received three complaints tonight. One from your neighbor, Mr. Cartwright, about his horse, Daisy that, according to his wife, you stole."

"I told her to say that," I corrected, "if he found out. She lent the mare to me."

He took a folded paper from his pocket and tossed it onto the desk. "Did you tell the mayor of Rumsen to issue an arrest warrant charging you with assaulting his wife?"

"What?" I shot to my feet. "That's absolute rubbish. I didn't assault her, I saved her from the first Wolfman."

Doyle regarded me. "So it was the Wolfman who dragged her to her carriage and bodily threw her inside."

"Yes. No." I had to think. "It was her footman. Chap named Hawkins." I thought again. "I may have assisted him. A very little. One push at the most."

"Of course." Doyle closed his eyes and pinched the bridge of his nose.

"You said there were three complaints," I reminded him. "So what's the third bit of nonsense?"

He opened his eyes. "Lord Lucien Dredmore has accused you of bespelling and abducting his driver."

"Did he." A faint red haze seemed to cloud my vision, but my face had turned burning hot. "I presume he has witnesses?"

"Several." He sat down. "They're coming in to give their statements in the morning." He tossed the key ring onto the table. "There's more to it."

I bared my teeth. "With Dredmore, there generally is."

"His lordship is willing to drop all charges," Doyle said, "on one condition."

I was going to kill Lucien again, and this time I wasn't going to bring him back. No, this time, I'd dance on his grave. "What does he want?"

He watched my eyes. "For you to personally apologize to the driver."

I nodded and rolled my good hand, encouraging him to tell me the rest of Dredmore's nonsense.

He looked away. "You must do this at Morehaven, before tomorrow dawn."

I started to laugh. I couldn't help it; it was that or explode. My face went red, my eyes blurred, my sides ached, and still I couldn't stop.

"All right, that's enough of that." Doyle crouched down in front of me, taking hold of my shoulders and giving me a firm shake. "I'll slap you if I must."

I clamped my mouth shut and shook a few times before I finally controlled my mirth. "Sorry," I gasped out, almost strangling on the word.

"Let me look at this." He untied the sling Lady Bestly had fashioned for me. As he unfolded he asked, "How did you hurt your arm?"

"I was bitten by the second one, who had brass fangs. Do you know what that means? The bastard who has been making them, he knew I'd break the transformation spell." I let out one desperate giggle before dragging in a deep breath. "So this time he pulled out all the poor sod's teeth and replaced them with mech."

Doyle met my watery gaze. "Tell me the bastard's name, Kit. Tell me and I'll bring him in, tonight."

He'd try to, and Lykaon would have his own chuckle before he ordered his ghastly soldiers to tear Tommy to pieces. "I don't know."

"Damn you, Kit." He took hold of my face, his fingers tight on my jaw. "You can't fight this man on your own. Help me put an end to the madness before you do get your throat torn out."

Looking into his blue eyes, so clear and true, made my heart shrivel. "I've told you everything I know, Inspector."

He released me, rose, and walked to the door. I watched his back tense as he turned and strode back to drag me to my feet, and then his mouth was on mine.

I didn't resist the kiss; I didn't want to. Being in Doyle's arms made me feel safe and protected, two sensations I didn't often enjoy. Then what he did to my mouth made my whole body wake up and take notice. My childhood friend no more—Tommy was a man of ferocious passions, hidden away beneath the mask of the cop, but now turned loose.

He ended it with a wrench of his head that made us both gasp. "I shouldn't have done that."

"Terribly unprofessional of you." I pressed against him, wanting more. "But then I'm wrinkling your jacket."

"It'll press." He ran one hand over my head, looking all over my face. "I know how it's been for you. You've had to rely on yourself for so long you've forgotten how to trust. But you can trust in me, Kit. I won't abandon you."

"I'm not your responsibility, Tommy." I then demonstrated my unshakable independence by resting my head against his shoulder. In my defense, it was beginning to spin. "Even if I was, you wouldn't want me. I'm a forfeit, not a prize."

"You don't know what I want."

"I know what I need. A new arm." Mine was beginning to burn as if it were on fire. "Do you have a physick on staff?"

Someone hammered on the door, making me push away from him, but Doyle held on to me as he turned his head. "Not now."

"Get stuffed," a familiar voice replied as the door slammed open. "Kit? Are you all right?"

I peeked over his shoulder at Rina and felt my legs wobble. "I don't know."

Darkness filled my eyes so abruptly that I thought I'd fainted again. Only when Doyle muttered something about the lights and moved away from me did I realize they'd all gone out at the same time; the entire station had gone dark.

Voices went as still as the air, and I smelled the sea, damp and salty, coming into the room. A glimmer of rainbow-shot blue flashed, and a feather brushed my cheek.

"Who are you?" I asked, turning my head and squinting, but unable to make out more. "What are you doing here?"

"Kit?" That was Rina, and she sounded furious—and very far away.

A cape of blue feathers enveloped me, and hard, cold hands wrapped something long and prickly round my wrenched arm. I should have pulled away, but I couldn't stop looking at the pale eyes in that dark face.

"The tree-man stole the War Heart from us," the native murmured as he tightened the thing round my arm. "You return this to the Alone."

I didn't understand most of what he was saying, but I knew one thing. "I don't have it."

"You will." He drew his thumb across my brow, sending some powder to shower down my face. "Now you sleep."

Since I didn't have enough sense to hold my breath that was exactly what I did.

CHAPTER TWELVE

"I can't wake her," Rina said somewhere near me. "I think that native at the station must have slipped her something."

"How long has she been like this?" That was Dredmore, and he sounded even angrier than Rina.

"Since I took her from the cops." Footsteps came close. "You'll be gentle."

"Always."

I opened one eye to a slit. The bed I occupied was large, sheeted, and canopied by gray silk, and smelled of sandalwood. The spike-and-fist crest embroidered on the pillowcase's hem confirmed my location.

Somehow I'd gone from police custody to Lucien's bed—but why would Rina deliver me to him?

"Why did you bring her to Morehaven?" Dredmore asked, as if he could hear my thoughts.

"So she could apologize to your bloody driver, what do you think?" My best friend's hand gently touched my brow. "I know Kit doesn't believe in magic, but with all that's happened to her it has to be a curse or something evil. I don't like you, but you're a deathmage, and you fancy her. To my mind you're the best chance she's got."

"I am the only chance she has." The bed dipped on

my right, and larger, stronger hands took hold of my arm. "Did you see the native who did this?"

Rina made a disgusted sound. "No one did. That shaman put out all the lights and used some sort of confounding spell on the rest of us before he went to work on Kit. We found her on the floor."

Dredmore was still touching me. "I will have to remove this."

Now I opened my eyes. "You're not taking off my arm. I'm rather attached to it." I glanced down and saw that he was unwrapping a gray and white fur from the offending appendage. "Father and Son, what is this?"

"A native dressing, I believe." Dredmore caught my hand and pushed it away. "No, let me see what was done."

As he did, I glared at Rina over his head. "Perhaps he should look at your head next. The shaman must have nicked your brains."

"Without some help you're going to die, you daft twit." She leaned over Dredmore's shoulder, nodding as he bared my arm. "She's not bleeding. Maybe he meant only to heal her."

"Then why would he do it in the dark?" I demanded. All I could see were bits of bone strung on some sort of vine that had been wrapped from my elbow to wrist. "Cut them off," I told Dredmore.

"Calm yourself." He took out a blade and sliced through the vine. As soon as he freed me I sat up and pushed aside the coverlet. "You're too weak to get up."

"Piss off." I swung my legs over, stood, and wobbled for a moment before I took a step. Then I fell on purpose into Rina's arms. "Whatever you do," I muttered to her, "don't leave me here with him."

"You're better off, love," Rina murmured, patting my back. "I can't look after you in the city, not with those things chasing about after you. Besides, he's so besotted he'll do anything to keep you alive."

"That's not exactly reassuring," I told her.

"You know I'd stay if I could, but I'm needed at the Nest. We've an epidemic of belly gripe. Felicity won't eat, and Janice, poor gel, hasn't kept down a meal in days." She gave Dredmore a narrow look. "I'll be back to look in on you tomorrow."

"Your faith in me is most gratifying, madam." Dredmore took me from her, lifting me like a child to put me back in bed. "I must have a word with your friend. You are to rest, and not to get up." He leaned down to say the rest for my ears alone. "If you do again, I'll shackle you to the posts."

"How kind you are." I suddenly understood why the Wolfmen were so fond of biting. "I feel better already."

Dredmore left with Rina, giving me an opportunity to examine my arm closely. The burning had stopped, but the flesh was still tender and the entire limb ached like a tooth going bad. My hand proved nearly useless; I could hardly bear to twitch my fingers.

With my good hand I picked up a piece of the bones the shaman had knotted round me, which bore saw marks on either end and thin vertical markings scored all round the outer edges. In the marrow hollow I found a bit of green leaf, folded tightly, and removed it. Inside the folds was a fragment of feather in the same vivid blue as the shaman's cape. The rest of the bones held the same odd stuffing.

For the first time I felt frustrated by my ignorance of native magic. If the shaman had meant to harm me, he might have easily cut my throat in the dark. The tribes preferred that manner of attack, for it silenced the victim and put an end to him quickly. Binding my arm with this gruesome business might well have been an attempt to heal me; the shaman had killed the second Wolfman.

Why save my life and risk his own again to attend to me at the station? Did he really believe I could give back to the tribe whatever had been taken from them?

As I brooded over the night's events, Dredmore returned, this time alone and carrying a tray of tea. He set it down and poured a cup, bringing it to me. "You must be thirsty."

Absently I blew on the surface of the steaming brew before I took a sip and sighed. "I've decided to steal Winslow from you. Will he work in far more congenial surroundings for almost nothing, or should I first rob a bank and buy a better house?"

"There is no better house," he assured me as he peered down at my face. "Your color is a little improved. Mrs. Eagle said she heard the shaman speaking to you, but could not make out the words. What did he say?"

I set down my cup. "I've been thinking on it, but it made no sense to me." I repeated the native's instructions before I added, "The tree-man, that could be Lykaon. The spirits of the Aramanthan were imprisoned in that oak grove by the Druuds, and he is using native magic.

Perhaps this War Heart the shaman wants back was the spell he stole."

"A spell cannot be cast by words alone," Dredmore told me. "Something must be paired with them to provide the necessary power. We use stones and runes, as the Aramanthan once did, but the natives use blood ritual."

I made a disgusted face. "You mean animal sacrifice."

He inclined his head. "They are fiercely protective of their magic. The shamans educate their apprentices only by words spoken in a place of complete isolation. No Torian has ever been permitted any real knowledge of their practices."

I gave him an ironic look. "Yet somehow you know the manner in which they teach it."

"I like to take long walks in the hills." He picked up one of the bones. "This is a piece of a small animal's leg bone. Fox, perhaps."

"Blue fox." My head ached as I said the words. "He chanted those words when he was binding me. He also said little fox."

"The natives often take animal names." Dredmore unfolded one of the leaves and held up another bit of blue feather. "The shaman wore this color?"

I nodded. "A cap covered with those feathers. Foxes are little, I suppose, but they're not feathered or blue."

"Blue Fox is a name, and given his penchant for the color, probably his." He produced a small leather bag and carefully put all the vines and bones into it before tying it. "And, if I am interpreting his works correctly, you are Little Fox."

I scowled. "I certainly am not."

He seemed amused. "As you like. The manner in which he bound you suggests a healing ritual, but the leaves and feathers inside the bones appear to be a different sort of invocation."

"Regret for slaughtering a small animal for no bloody good reason?" I suggested.

"No. One does not relinquish bits of a medicine cloak out of regret." He tucked the leather bag under my pillow. "I think he meant to extend his powers to cloak you. To protect you, Charmian."

"Magic doesn't work on me," I reminded him as I removed the bag and tossed it over the side of the bed. "The Aramanthan knows it now, too."

"Mrs. Eagle said one of the Wolfmen had managed to bite you this time." He touched the back of his hand to my brow. "No fever. Do you feel any nausea?"

I didn't like how solicitous Dredmore was being; it wasn't in his nature to fuss like a worried mother. "No, and why do you ask?"

He took a charred bit of metal from his pocket. "Lady Bestly sent this to me by tube with a note explaining what had happened at her home." He turned it. "It's hollow-tipped, and there is part of a valve inside."

"I'm sure Docket would understand that," I said, "but my knowledge of mech is limited to things like steam-dogs and carri controls."

"Lykaon mechanized the teeth to do more than bite." Holding the charred metal over the tea tray, Dredmore poured a few drops from the pot into the tooth. When he touched the hollow tip with his finger, the tea dribbled onto his skin. "Whatever is put in the teeth is transferred by the bite."

Now I understood why he was worried. "Poison?"

He used a napkin to dry his hand. "That, or perhaps blood. It is an important component of native rituals."

"Yes, and now I *am* nauseated," I informed him, but my mind was working away at what he'd told me. "Lady Bestly was bitten by her husband, and so were Rina's girls when they were attacked in the park. All of the Wolfmen tried to bite me, too, but this was the first one who succeeded, and only because he had mechanized teeth." I looked at him. "Lucien, were any of the men who were attacked bitten?"

He shook his head. "The Wolfmen use their claws on them."

"The market tram was filled with women." And the Wolfman had gone berserk trying to get inside. Only I had been able to lure him away . . .

Felicity won't eat, Rina had said. *And Janice, poor gel, hasn't kept down a meal in days.*

"Me. Lady Bestly. Rina's girls and the lady in the park." I looked at Dredmore. "The men are being attacked only because they're getting in the way."

His dark eyes narrowed. "In the way of what?"

"I think Lykaon is sending the Wolfmen out to find women. To hunt them." I yanked the coverlet aside. "We have to go to the morgue and see the bodies from the Hill."

"Not until after sunrise." When I tried to argue he nodded at the bedposts. "Shackles will make your slumber very uncomfortable."

"I'm not sleeping here." If what I suspected was true, I would also need more help than Dredmore could provide. "I must summon Harry."

Dredmore's expression darkened. "To my home? I think not."

"Don't be tiresome—and don't try to bespell my grandfather again," I added. "It absolutely infuriated him."

He folded his arms. "That is hardly discouraging, Charmian."

"This is why you have no friends," I told him before I closed my eyes. "Come on, Harry. I need you here."

The air chilled as a patch of mist appeared at the foot of the bed. Instead of forming itself into my grandfather, it stretched upward and crackled with miniature streaks of lightning.

"I am Merlin, master of all mages," a terrible voice boomed, the sound causing the very windows to rattle. "Those who trifle with me and mine do not live to regret it."

"Dredmore is very sorry about casting that spell on you," I told him quickly. "Aren't you, Lucien?"

My host gave me an ironic look. "Decidedly."

The little bits of lightning stopped, and the mist took on more solid form. "Back in his clutches again, I see." Harry inspected me. "And now his bed. Haven't you an ounce of self-respect, gel?"

"It wasn't my idea." I told him about the Wolfmen attacking me at Lady Bestly's. "I need you to pop over to Rina's and check the two women there who were attacked in the park."

"I'm not a physick," Harry complained.

I nodded. "But you are the only one who can tell if they've been possessed by Aramanthan spirits."

Once Harry was dispatched to check on Felicity and Janice I finished my tea and regarded the sorry state of my gown. "Did Rina happen to leave a change of garms for me?"

"She did not." Dredmore went to the armoire and opened it to sort through the gowns hanging inside.

I joined him. "Should I ask why you have an armoire filled with women's clothing in your bedchamber?"

"This is not my bedchamber." He took out a rose-colored waterfall of organza and satin with gilt braiding and delicate embroidery of cascading amaryllis. "You can wear this."

I made a rude sound. "To an evening at the opera, perhaps."

I took the gown from him and put it back, selecting instead a dark blue paneled skirt with a green and neatly tailored plaid dress jacket. Although the silvery half-lace bodice and the handkerchief hemming were somewhat fripperish for my taste, and the entire ensemble probably cost more than I made in a year, at least I wouldn't look destined for the ballroom.

"This will do." And then, because I couldn't help myself, I said, "These are very fine. Your lady friends never came back to claim them?"

"None of them have ever been worn." He closed the doors to the armoire. "The other things you'll need are in the dresser there." He headed for the door.

"Lucien." I waited until he looked back at me. "Whose gowns are these?"

"Yours." His lips twisted. "I had them made for you," he said softly, and out he went.

After that admission I had to have another look in the armoire, which contained three dozen gowns made of the finest fabrics and tailoring and suitable for every possible occasion.

"But no wedding dress. How remiss." I stalked over to the dresser and began opening drawers. They were filled to near overflowing with chemises, waisters, petticoats, and tiny little under drawers made of linen, cambric, and Nihon silk in snow white and flowery pastels.

"Sweet Mary." I held up one evil-looking confection in jet black satin trimmed narrowly with scarlet velvet, also sized exactly for me. "Just because my best friend is a harlot doesn't mean *I* am."

I picked out the plainest undergarments I could find, scowling as I stripped and donned them. The scanty things were sinfully comfortable, naturally, and the gown fit as if the seamstress had been dressing me for years.

Before I put on the dress jacket I checked the gown-maker's label, and found the initials SD along with the hand-inked face of a smiling, sleeping maiden—the hallmark of the ton's favorite gown maker and the most exclusive dress shop in Rumsen, the Silken Dream.

"Bridget." I jerked on the jacket and did up the jet buttons, wondering how hard it had been for Dredmore to persuade my friend to make up the dreamy wardrobe for me. "I hope you got at least a thousand pounds out of him before you sewed up this lot, you traitor."

I tried to brush my hair into some order, but it was a tangle of hopeless snarls. I also found a thumb-size patch of too-short hairs on the side of my nape; someone had cut away a short tress.

My old boots looked dreadful beneath the silvery lace hem of the glowing paneled skirt, but I stubbornly buttoned them up before I stomped out of the bedchamber. Outside I found Winslow coming to intercept me.

"Welcome back to Morehaven, Miss Kittredge," he said, giving me a polite bow. "I am happy to see you have regained your senses."

"So I am, Mr. Winslow. Thank you for the tea." I peered down the hall. "Where is the Master of Connivance?"

"His lordship asked that I escort you to the viewing gallery," Winslow said.

"I have to go to the morgue—"

"So you will, miss, very shortly." The butler made a calming gesture. "The master wished me to say that the ice encasing your animech rodent has nearly melted, and you may want to observe his examination of it."

I pressed my palm to my brow. "Bloody hell, I forgot about the rat."

"It has been an eventful night." Winslow indicated the center stairwell. "This way, please."

I followed the butler up to the third floor of the house and into a corridor that had been recently renovated, judging by the smell of fresh paint and recently sawn wood. "Has Dredmore been redecorating?"

"The master had the gallery relocated from the second floor last month," Winslow said as he directed me into one of the rooms. "To provide a safer place of observation for a particular guest."

Inside the room I was astonished to see three of the four walls and the entire floor had been replaced by enormous sheets of glass, which stopped me in my tracks.

"The glass is very thick, miss," Winslow assured me. "It will not break."

I took a cautious step forward, feeling a bit disoriented as I glanced down into another, seven-sided chamber with a dark oak floor that had been precisely inscribed with hundreds of runes. In the center stood an obsidian pedestal upon which sat the ice-encrusted rat in a pool of melted water. It didn't move, so I assumed it was still partly frozen. Then the glitter of the walls drew my gaze, and I saw every surface had been covered in large tiles of orange rock that sparkled with millions of gold flecks.

I recognized the rock, of course. "Is that tangerstone on the walls?"

"It is, miss."

I blinked. "It's flawless."

"I believe so, miss."

I stared at the butler. "Winslow, in the city they charge fifty pounds an ounce for tangerstone, and that's for the cracked, damaged sort. I don't even *know* how much an ounce of perfect costs."

"Rather more than fifty pounds, miss," he said.

One of the stone panels opened into the chamber as Dredmore entered in a spell-casting cloak made of mirror weave. I'd seen less elaborate versions with a few of the tiny round looking glasses stitched onto gilded cloth, but every inch of Dredmore's sparkled.

Before I'd come to know magic was real I'd have thought it nothing more than flashy showmanship; now the glassy cloak alarmed me. Mirror weave was bespelled very specifically to deflect evil power away from the wearer, and Dredmore had covered himself from neck to ankle with it.

"Maybe he ought to just toss the rat into the furnace," I said to Winslow.

"That would waste the opportunity to discover the mage who enchanted it," Dredmore said in a voice so clear he might have been standing beside me instead of two floors beneath us.

"Can you hear me as well?" I asked, and when he nodded I gestured to the rat. "Just how dangerous is that thing?"

"I won't know until I rekindle it. As a precaution I've sent the staff out of the house." He approached the pedestal. "It will have no effect on you, of course, nor Winslow, as long as he remains beside you."

I put my arm through the butler's. "So we're not separated if the thing explodes and blows off your master's face," I said. "You see, the rat they sent before this one was a bomb. I expect he forgot to mention that."

Winslow went pale. "A small oversight on his part, miss."

Dredmore placed several blue stones on the edges of the pedestal until they encircled the animech. He then made a tugging gesture over the rat, from which the rest of the frost immediately melted and trickled away.

The rat's jointed legs twitched as Dredmore began murmuring in a language I couldn't fathom, and light rippled along the tangerstone walls.

I shuffled back a step as the rat belched out an oily smoke that rose in a narrow, swirling column. "That's not promising."

Spots of red glinted in the rat's eyes as it sat up, rather like a small dog, and regarded Dredmore. "Grand Master," it said in a horribly squeaky voice. "I was not sent for you."

"It smokes and talks," I said faintly. "I wonder if it does any tricks."

"Yet come you have into my sphere." Dredmore lifted his hands, from which came arcing slashes of bright, crackling blue. "Your work is undone. Reveal your maker."

Fragments of metal flew as the rat gnashed its pointy teeth.

"I command you, name he who made thee." Dredmore threw his hands out, caging the animech in a net of the blue light.

I almost felt sorry for the rat as it squealed and struggled beneath the constricting net. "Tell him," I muttered under my breath.

The rat uttered something that sounded like laughter, and then a very familiar name. "Fox hee," it finally shrilled. "Fox hee Fox hee Fox hee—"

More smoke burst from the animech, this time with such violence both Winslow and I flinched. The explosion we anticipated, however, never occurred, and after a final grinding clank and a large blat of smoke the rat fell onto its side and lay motionless.

"Well." I felt a cautious relief. "No bomb in this one."

"So it would seem, miss." The butler absently patted the hand I had clenched on his forearm. "My lord, shall I summon—"

The rat rattled, its parts falling away from a cracking glass orb filled with swirling black bloodbane.

It was worse than a bomb—an assassin's snuffball, ready to burst.

"Lucien, get out of there," I shouted as I pushed Winslow toward the door.

Dredmore did nothing of the kind, instead drawing up a fold of his cloak to shield his face an instant before the snuffball exploded. Its lethal contents doused everything within two yards and obscured my view entirely.

I knelt down and hammered on the glass floor. "Lucien? Lucien! I'm coming—don't move. Or breathe."

I ran past Winslow and to the stairs, nearly tumbling down them until I reached the first level. It took me a moment to work out which room was Dredmore's spell chamber, and when I pushed in the door a waft of smoke and black powdery bloodbane enveloped me.

The moment it touched me the bloodbane became no more dangerous than ordinary soot, but I didn't care to breathe it in, and covered my nose and mouth with my hand as I made my way in. I felt in the blackness until I found glassy fabric and wrapped my arms round Dredmore, who somehow was still standing.

"Stupid, worthless man," I sputtered, coughing as I pulled him along with me out into the hall and away from the smoke. Once we were clear I pushed him against the wall and frantically swatted the bloodbane from his hair.

"Charmian." He lowered the cloak and caught my hands. "I am not harmed."

"You should be. You should be whipped." I pushed the now-filthy cloak from his shoulders, kicking it away from him. "Sweet Jesu, it's all over you." I kept hold of him as I dragged him down the corridor and into the nearest bedchamber. "Where is the bloody damn bathing room?"

"Charmian, there is no . . ." Dredmore paused and then nodded at a door on the right. "In there."

"Don't let go of my hand," I told him as I hauled him into the smaller room. I knew that by touching the bloodbane I could see I'd rendered it useless, but particles of the lethal powder had likely fallen down in his collar and God knew where else. "We have to get you out of these clothes and cleaned off."

I looked at the bath, which was not a tub but something like a wide, shallow, flat-bottomed sieve, over which hung several large pipes fitted with broad spouts like garden watering tins. "Sweet Mary, Lucien. Do you bathe in here, or pan for gold?"

"I dislike being immersed in water." Dredmore released his necktie and began to unbutton his shirt, but using one hand made him slow. "But you already know that."

"I know you're an idiot." I placed his hand that I was holding on my neck and went to work on his shirt myself. "How could you do something so reckless and stupid?" I wrenched off his shirt and reached for his trouser bands. "You're supposed to be a grand master of the dark arts, not some fumbling fete teller." I realized I wasn't getting off the pants with his boots still on his feet and made a murderous sound as I dropped to my knees and jerked up his trouser cuffs. "You didn't enjoy dying the last time, I assure you."

"Charmian."

I stopped wrestling with his boot as I realized we were no longer touching, and he wasn't dying. "If you tell me you're immune to bloodbane, I'm going to hurt you. Somewhere significant and very personal."

Dredmore helped me to my feet. "I am not immune to bloodbane."

I drew in a short, trembling breath. "But you didn't run out of there." I looked up into his black eyes. "Why didn't you run, Lucien?"

He cupped my cheek with his long, cool hand. "I was warded. Protected, by you."

"Me? I haven't any magic." I shivered as his thumb strayed along the curve of my lower lip, leaving a trail of heat. "I was completely utterly bloody useless. Do you know how that felt, when I saw that thing explode in your face?" And suddenly I was a blink away from bursting into tears.

"Oh, yes." He bent his head, and touched his mouth to mine. "I know."

Little dark puffs of bloodbane drifted to the tiled floor as we embraced. I wanted to kill him, not kiss him, but once we started I couldn't stop. Not when I felt him at the buttons of my gown, or when my skirts slipped to pool round my feet. I clung to his bare shoulders, rubbing my hot face against the hard vault of his chest while his fingers unwound the tangles of my hair.

I had promised myself I would never again be naked with Lucien Dredmore, but after a few more moments I was, and he with me. I knew it was wicked to press my skin to his, and stroke his lovely long limbs with my palms, but I didn't care. Whatever nonsense he believed, I'd almost lost him—again.

A gentle cascade of warm water spilled down my back as Dredmore moved me onto the basin, and there stood holding me as his shower rained down on both our heads. I stood watching the drops bead on his dark lashes and run down the haughty bridge of his nose, but it was the rivulets that wet his lips that proved irresistible. I stood on tiptoe, my hands slipping behind his neck to bring them to me so I could lick them away.

"Why is it we can never do this without imminent danger or death looming over us?" I murmured, gripping the tight muscles in his arms with my wet hands.

"This has happened to me only in my dreams, Charmian." He nudged up my chin, and his expression was that of a starved man presented with a feast. "And that is your magic."

The water raining down on us washed away the final traces of the bloodbane from Lucien's body, and took the last of my doubts with them. I could not think or know or care about anything more than feeling his touch, and being in his gaze, and falling under the spell of his passion. It should have been an awkward business, the two of us standing, the water drenching and making every inch of us slick, but it became instead a very intimate dance. His strong arms lifted me, sliding me up and then settling me, my legs winding round about his as he forged between them.

Although I knew very well how it would be, the shock of feeling him pressing and penetrating me with his shaft made all of the air leave my lungs. I sank as he guided me, taking the full length of his shaft into my body, the heated flesh piercing me with a moment of sharp pain before pushing deep.

Dredmore held me there, one arm under my bottom, his other hand on my face. "You *are* a maiden." He sounded bemused.

"You mean, I was." I shifted a little, trying not to clench against the most intimate invasion of my person— for the second time. "Fate seems determined to have you as my ruin."

"To hell with Fate." His arm tightened as he stepped out of the basin. "What will you have, Charmian?"

"You." I linked my hands behind his neck and tucked my face into the crook of his shoulder. "I'll have you. And a bed, if you don't mind the ruin of your linens. Gravity might"—a laugh bubbled out of me as he carried me back into the bedchamber and fell onto the mattress with me—"ah, interrupt."

The weight of his big body atop mine felt more splendid as I cradled him, nudging his hips with mine in wanton encouragement. Lucien's wet hair formed a dripping curtain about our faces and he drew back and then surged forward, completing the smooth fit of our sexes. He kissed every drop from my face and throat, pausing only to regard me with intense scrutiny before carrying on.

Delight made my toes curl and my hands grow restless, and I clutched at him as our bodies moved together, orchestrated by a deep and almost frightening passion that removed every thought but him from my mind. Revisiting the carnal sensations of lovemaking made my face burn, but inside me grew an ache so intense that soon I was like a wild thing, arching up to meet his heavy thrusts, bearing down to clasp him within, wanting nothing more for it to end and for it to last forever, both urgencies setting my blood afire.

My pleasure trembled, just out of reach, when Lucien dragged me up with him, gripping my hips and working me over him as I held on, breathless and wide-eyed. "I did not dream this. You gave yourself to me once before, as you do now. Tell me the truth."

I shook my head, and then groaned as he used his teeth to catch my earlobe. "Why does it matter?"

He moved deep and held me fast, staring into my eyes as I squirmed, desperate for more. "Tell me, damn you."

I wanted to slap him, and then I saw something in his eyes, a longing so desperate that it melted my heart and my pride. "Yes. It happened, twice." I rested my hand over his heart, and felt the hammering beat of it throb against my palm. "And now again."

"Then you are mine." He put his mouth on mine for a kiss so deep I felt it in my bones, one that sent us both to shatter within an enormous burst of pleasure.

We collapsed together, bodies still enmeshed, and

I never wanted to move again, not from his bed or his arms. Once I could breathe I examined the handsome lines of his throat, and traced a finger along the black cord encircling it. I found the silver filigree pendant suspended by it hanging askew, and absently turned it to admire its odd design. "I've never seen you wear this." I frowned. "It's a woman's locket."

"My mother's." He pillowed his head on his arm and watched my face. "Open it."

I pressed the tiny clasp and it sprang open to reveal a small curl of brunette hair tied with silver thread. "So your mother was dark, like you."

He shook his head. "She was a blue-eyed blond."

"But then whose . . . " I peered at the curl again. "Just a minute. This looks like *my* hair." I reached back to touch the shortened patch on my nape. "It *is* my hair. *You* cut my hair."

"I snipped away one curl where it would not be noticed. Given the general state of your mop, I doubted even you would miss it."

"Why?" Before he could answer I knew. "You thought my hair would dispel the magic? This was how you were protected against the bloodbane?"

He closed the locket. "It was not the reason I took it, but the possibility did occur to me."

"You weren't sure?" I thumped my fist against his chest. "You could have died in there, you bloody stupid man."

"So much anger." He kissed my mouth so gently I hardly felt the touch of his lips. "So you do care for me."

"As a friend, yes, I do. I'm thinking about making

other friends who aren't as bloody stupid as you." I gave him another halfhearted thump before I presented my back to him. "You knew this, the entire time. But you let me make a fool of myself anyway."

"No." He turned me onto my back and rolled over me to hold me down. "I want you, and I will do anything to have you. I have never concealed that. And if for once you will cease pretending this indifference that you have never truly felt toward me, then you can admit that it is the same for you."

"If I did, how long would that satisfy you, Lucien? Five minutes? Ten? If I become your mistress, would you not then want me to give up my business? With no means to support myself, you would then demand I live with you. Soon my days would be reduced to nothing but dancing attendance on your every desire." I closed my eyes. "Is that what you believe will make *me* happy?"

He rolled away from me and flung his arm over his eyes. "I do not know what will make you happy."

"Fortunately I do." I got out of bed. "You can get dressed and take me down to the morgue."

Chapter Thirteen

After the unfortunate snuffball incident Connell drove us to Saint Albert's. Once Dredmore had helped me down, I looked up at the driver, who had taken pains not to look at me once.

"Mr. Connell, I had no warning of what my grandfather's spirit intended to do to you," I said formally. "But that is no excuse when one has a body-snatching spirit in the family. I take full responsibility for Harry's actions, which were completely reprehensible, and that I sincerely regret. I assure you, it will never happen again."

Connell glanced down at me. "You needn't apologize to me, miss. I've no memory of it, and I came to no harm."

"Nevertheless." I curtseyed as low as the curb would allow. "Please forgive me, sir."

"Stand by, Connell." Dredmore took my arm and led me down the walk toward the delivery platform at the side of the building. "That was quite considerate of you."

"I consider your driver a decent chap," I said. "By the way, now you'll definitely have to drop those charges you trumped up against me."

A guard stood leaning against a wall and picking at his fingernails by the platform, but as soon as he spied us approaching he straightened and adjusted the set of his hat. "Visitors go in the front, sir."

"The mayor summoned me to inspect two bodies," Dredmore told him. "It is a matter of some urgency."

"Aye, sir?" The guard eyed me. "Surely not with your lady."

"I'm milord's secretary," I informed him in my best Middy accent. "Come along to take notes for Himself. Look alive, then, lad. We've not all day."

The guard nodded and hurried to unlock the door, bobbing his head as we went in.

As we headed down the hall Dredmore gave me a sideways look. "I've never heard you speak in that fashion."

"Ta, sir, I ain't always hobbed with nobs. 'Sides, plain speaking opens more doors than your fancy talk." The smell of preservative made my nose wrinkle. "Hopefully Dez is on duty, or this might require the use of some of your particular talents."

Inside the examination chamber we did find Docket's friend wheeling a body into a back room. He didn't see us until he returned, and then he scowled at me.

"Not you again." His gaze moved to Dredmore. "Who's this?"

"My secretary, Lucien," I said as I inspected the shrouded bodies still in the room. "Where are the two Wolfmen that were brought in from the Hill?"

"No." Dez thrust out his jaw. "I'll not have any of your poking round here, ever again."

"And why not?"

"Sister Bailey came down after that other one ran amok and near tore my head off about it." He threw out his arms. "As if I'd known some bloody mage would reanimate the creature the minute I turned my back."

"No worries, then. You can tell her I barged in and found them myself." I went to the first table and drew back the shroud. The elderly man beneath it looked entirely mortal and quite yellow. "Liver rot," I guessed. "Too much wine, not enough women and song." I went to the next table.

Dez beat me to it and put an arm over the shroud. "You'll not want a look at this one."

I peeked anyway and grimaced. "Trampled by a horse, or hit by a carri?"

"Barnacle scrubber, got pinned between two boats." Dez started to say more and then jerked the edge of the shroud back into place. "That's enough. You need to see a vicar, and talk to him about this fascination of yours with the dead. It ain't natural."

"I have one over here, Charmian," Dredmore said from across the room, where he had uncovered a hairy body with an enormous chest wound. As I approached the hair began to recede into the man's body. "The spell is still active."

"Not anymore," I said as I joined him, at which point the body transformed into its natural mortal state. "Dez, I need to look in his mouth."

The morgue attendant muttered several more, vile words as he brought over a tray of instruments and thumped them down beside the body. "What do you think you'll see?" he said as he picked up a metal depressor and wedged it in between the body's snarling lips.

"That." I nodded at the double rows of gleaming brass teeth.

"Blind me," Dez breathed, peering at the Wolfman's ghastly choppers. "I never seen the like of it."

"Can you tilt his head back?" I asked, trying to look behind the top row of brass fangs.

"He's too stiff now, but . . ." The attendant gnawed at his lip before he pushed the body to the edge of the table until the head hung over. "That should be enough to see something."

I tilted my head to get a better angle. "There's something attached to the roof of his mouth." I reached for a pair of narrow tongs on the tray and used them to extract a flattened pocket of thin hide. When I placed it on the table, blood began to ooze from it.

"You were right." Dredmore regarded the extraction. "But why blood?"

I set down the tongs. "I don't know." I saw the blood from the hide pocket creeping toward the dead Wolfman's arm, where a wound made an ugly gash across the flesh. On impulse I picked up the pocket and emptied it onto the wound.

A few moments later the three of us stared at the arm, which now appeared whole.

"Blood that heals," I murmured, prodding the corpse's arm to be sure the wound had disappeared. "It can't be spelled to do it. It wouldn't work with me so close."

"It can't be mortal blood, Miss Kit," Dez said, and jerked his chin at Dredmore. "I wager he knows what it is."

"There are tales about the healing qualities of Aramanthan blood," Dredmore said. "But the bodies of all the immortals perished in the grove."

"We'll have to assume that one escaped." I regarded the arm. "Why would you attack women and then heal them with immortal blood?"

"To erase all evidence of the bite mark serves no purpose," Dredmore said. "The women remember they have been attacked. Perhaps to addle them, or discredit them?"

"That can't be all. He's gone to too much trouble. All right, they grab them, they bite them, and then they assault them." I studied the corpse for a moment before I took hold of the shroud and yanked it away from the lower half of the body. I expected to see the most private part of the Wolfman's body, but that lay covered by more metal and gears.

"Another one with a brass hat," Dez muttered, and when he saw my face he reddened. "The last two had the same mech in their laps. Bit ridiculous, if you ask me. No woman would let them . . . oh, bloody hell."

I refrained from commenting and walked round the end of the table to examine it from the other side. That was when I spotted an odd bulge in the Wolfman's jaw. "Lucien, come here." When he did I pointed to the protuberance. "What is that lump?"

"A contusion." He reached out and pressed his fingers over it. "No, it's solid. It feels as if there is something lodged inside his cheek."

"Could be one of them mech teeth got knocked askew," Dez said, and came with a smaller pair of tongs. "Here, I'll have it out."

The attendant rooted about in the mouth until he latched on to something and extracted it. "Just a rock."

"Don't touch it," I said when he reached to remove it from the tongs. "This one is my specialty."

I took the stone, which was a vile blackish green with patches of yellow, and turned it over in my palm. I hadn't held that many Aramanthan spirit stones, but I knew exactly what sort of power it contained—a sleeping monster, waiting to be placed inside a mortal body and awakened by a spell to take control of it.

Dez peered at it, and then took a step back. "That isn't just a rock."

I found a specimen box, in which I put the spirit stone before I placed it in my reticule. "Will you check the other body for the same, please?"

Dez moved to another table and examined the body. "Nothing in this one. Perhaps it fell out during the struggle." He gave me a troubled glance. "Miss, are you all right?"

"Yes, and I think I know where it landed." It took another moment for me to collect myself, and then I removed my jacket. "I'll need you to do a bit of cutting now, Dez."

"I can't remove those teeth. You've already seen the clockworks in the chest," he pointed out, frowning as I rolled up my sleeve. "Sweet Mary, miss. Why are you all bruised up like that?"

"I was bitten by the second Wolfman." I pulled a stool over to the table, sat down, and stretched out my arm. "Get a clean blade if you would, and something to bandage it after."

Dez recoiled. "I'm not cutting on you. I'd never hurt a woman, and you've had enough harm done to you."

"No, Charmian." Dredmore loomed over me. "I won't allow it."

I grabbed his hand and placed it over the spot where I'd been bitten, where the hard lump of an Aramanthan spirit stone now lay beneath my healed skin. "Either Dez takes it out, or I do."

Dredmore's mouth thinned. "I will summon a surgeon—"

"—who will never believe our explanation and refuse to operate." I shifted my gaze to the attendant's pale face. "I am immune to magic round me, not inside me. If the spirit is released from the stone while it's in my arm, it will possess me. It has to come out, now."

"Miss, I can't. I can't risk it. I've never operated on a living person." He swallowed. "'Sides that, I don't have nothing I can use to knock you out. The pain will be too much, you'll move, and then—"

"I won't. Lucien will help." I glanced up at Dredmore. "He will hold me fast."

His arm came round me, and he pressed my face against his chest for a moment before he released me. To Dez, he said, "Do you have what you'll need to clean and stitch up the wound?"

He nodded. "Carbolic and boiled thread. Miss Kit, you really can't move. Not an inch. And screaming won't be good, not while I'm at it. I'll lose me nerve."

"I won't make a peep," I promised.

Once Dez assembled the necessary items, Dredmore took hold of my wrist and elbow. "Look at me," he said, and when I did he smiled. "You may call me as many names as you wish, as long as you keep watching my face."

"That shouldn't be difficult." I felt the cold edge of the blade. "You have a handsome—" I caught my breath as Dez began the work. "Countenance." White-hot pain made me drag in my breath. "When you're not . . . glowering."

"I must endeavor to seek more satisfaction." As he felt me tremble he shifted the hand on my wrist, lacing his fingers through mine. "I have some suggestions as to how you might bring me to that happy state."

"Naturally you would. You're a scoundrel and a womanizer," I said through my teeth. "Far too wealthy and powerful. A rake incapable of reform. Lucien—"

"I know, love. Nearly there." His eyes stayed on mine as he said to Dez, "Do you have it?"

"Yes." Something bounced onto metal, and a cloth covered my blazing flesh. "A few stitches now, Miss Kit."

I felt the stab of the needle and let out my breath before I dropped my head against Lucien's chest. "Nothing fancy, Dez, please."

The pain eased, but I didn't look at my arm until he had finished. The size of the wound astonished me. "Hardly a scratch, when it felt like you were cutting me from palm to pit." My gaze shifted to the stone he'd removed, an unimpressive dark azure pebble. "I wonder who you were," I said to the rock. No doubt the spirit of some hateful immortal warmonger like Zarath, or perhaps someone even worse.

"We'll not pursue it," Dredmore told me.

Dez bandaged me and gave me instructions to snip and pull out the suture threads once the wound had fully closed. "Until it does, keep it clean and wrapped."

"We'll have to go for a drive by the bay later," I told Dredmore once I added the blue pebble to the box in my reticule. "At least this explains why Lykaon wants the bite wounds to heal immediately—to keep the stones in place."

"So that they might later possess the victims." Dredmore had never looked more disgusted. "That heartless bastard."

"I don't believe the women are the intended hosts. Lady Bestly wasn't possessed, and neither were Felicity or Janice." I tightened my grip on the reticule. "I think their unborn children are."

Dredmore gave me a bleak look. "They're all with child?"

"I shall have to check with Rina and see the other victims, but yes, I think they must be." I turned to Dez. "Thank you for your help."

"If that's what you're calling it." He went to a stool and sat down, resting his face in his hands. "I've got to find another job."

Dredmore directed Connell to take us to a remote hillside spot beside the bay, where I took great pleasure in emptying the box of spirit stones over the cliff and watching them plummet into the dark, cold water.

"Have a lovely nap for the rest of eternity." For good measure I tossed the empty box and my reticule after them. "So how do we tell these women that they are carrying immortal children? 'Sorry you were attacked, you're going to have a baby, and it's likely to take over the world'?"

"The unborn are not yet suitable for possession."

Dredmore took hold of my hand. "In order to take over a body, the spirit stone must be first awakened by a spell. Only then can the Aramanthan be freed to enter and seize control of the mind."

"That spell may have been cast already," I pointed out.

"Even if Lykaon has released the spirits, these children sired by the Wolfmen have only just been conceived," Dredmore said. "It will be several weeks before they develop enough to be overtaken."

"All the victims will have to be checked," I said as we walked back to the carri. "I have a list of their names and addresses at the office. I'll call on them and see how many have been used as vessels."

Inside the carri, Dredmore instructed Connell to take us to my office building before he said, "If Lykaon spelled the Aramanthan spirits to bond with the unborn, then it may not be possible to safely extract the stones from the women."

"Dez had no problem with mine . . . because the spell wouldn't work on me." I thumped my good fist against the seat. "Damn. If we can't get the stones out of them—"

"—then it must be the unborn," Dredmore finished for me.

Sometimes the secrets I knew gratified me; other times they only made me feel wretched. "There are herbalists in the city who know how to put a discreet end to unwanted pregnancies. Rina's gels will likely do that, but Lady Bestly." I shook my head. "She's waited her entire life to have a child, and her future hangs in the balance. She'll never agree to it."

"I will go to Eugenia and make her aware that the conception was forced upon her for reasons other than providing an heir," Dredmore said. "That may persuade her to make the difficult choice. We cannot permit Lykaon to breed a new army of immortals."

"He can't sire them without the Wolfmen, so they must be stopped, too." As the carri halted in front of my building I adjusted my sling. "I will likely be some time calling on the victims, but I will save Rina's gels for last. Can you meet me at the Eagle's Nest by four?"

"I will, but we will not long be there. Until this is finished you are spending your nights at Morehaven." Before I could tell him what I thought of that he pressed a finger to my lips. "I will hire a lady's maid to attend to you and play chaperone. As it is, your arm will be unusable for at least a week."

"I suppose I should accept, seeing as I have a new wardrobe there. But I can manage without a maid." As Connell opened the door to help me down, I glanced back at Dredmore. "If I'm to stay at Morehaven, I'll want a turning bolt lock on the door."

He inclined his head. "I'll have one installed tonight."

As Dredmore drove off I turned to see Docket hurrying out to meet me. Grease made black streaks on his grizzled face, and all of what little hair he possessed appeared to be standing on end. "Morning, Doc."

"Kit, I've been watching for you for hours." He surveyed me. "Heavens, what did you do to your arm?"

"Banged it up a bit." Explaining the rest would have to keep. "So why were you watching? Have the other tenants voted to have me evicted?"

"If they have, they didn't get my ballot." He took hold of my good arm. "Come down to the workshop. I need you for the final adjustments. It's looking very tidy, I must say. I'll have to tighten down most of the clamps—I loosened them when I donned it for the first trial—but all the levers are aligned and the gears lubed up proper."

He rattled on as he brought me down to the Dungeon and led me over to his wall rack, and only then I understood.

"You finished the harness." I tried to smile. "How fabulous it looks."

Docket beamed. "Right proud of it, I am. Beats everything the militia's got, that's for sure. Oh, let's have this sling off before I fit you."

"My arm is really sore, mate," I said. "Perhaps I could try it out when I'm feeling more the thing."

"That's the beauty of the levers. They're so sensitive you'll have only to twitch a muscle for them to respond." He untied the sling and patted my shoulder. "No worries, love. Once you have it on you'll fancy it like mad."

I didn't fancy another trip to hospital. "Can you shut it off at once if something goes wrong?"

"No, but you can." He pointed to a bracket with a brass button at the end of one appendage brace. "Press that and all the motors shut off. Press it again and they'll kick back on. Now stand in front of it here and we'll fit the clamps to you."

Docket hustled me into place and began strapping me into the harness. I tried a few more protests but he kept assuring me I'd be perfectly safe.

"I've been trying to decide on a name for it," he said as he adjusted the clamps round my limbs. "What do you think of Auto Armor or Battle Brace or perhaps The War Wager?"

"Names have never been your strong suit, mate." As I said that I chuckled. "Well, there you are. What about the strong suit?"

He repeated it and grinned. "Perfect." He released the harness from the wall rack and backed away. "Now, press the button, and take a few steps."

I didn't want to move in the awkward, heavy rig, but nothing else would satisfy him but a real test of it. "If I fall forward you'll catch me, right?"

"Won't need to," Docket said. "Go on, then."

I tapped the button and felt the humming vibration of the motors whirring up to full speed. My best option seemed to be shuffling forward one step and immediately declaring Doc's contraption a resounding success. If that didn't work, pleading a call of nature would have to do.

"Here I go." As I gingerly inched my right foot forward, the flat lever heads pressing against the side of my skirts shifted and my leg lifted and came back down in a neat step. I could feel the other levers on my other leg, abdomen, and arms responding as well, and when I took a second step the harness moved my arms with a slight jerk.

"Oy," Docket called, now across the room, and threw something at me. "Catch."

I brought up my arms to deflect the can hurtling toward my face, and the harness opened my hands to catch it. My eyes widened as the jointed braces over my fingers contracted, crushing the can as if it were fashioned of paper.

"You see? You'll not be bashed by anything thrown at you." Docket hurried back to me and spread his arms. "Now pick me up."

I looked at the can. "I've no wish to crumple you, mate."

"You won't. I've installed weight scales to kick in the safety inhibitors, and keep your gripping power at hold torque for anything over thirty pounds." He pointed to a spot on the chest plate. "You can override them by pressing that red switch there."

I tucked in my chin to see the switch. "Did you test this function, too?"

He gave an eager nod. "Mr. Gremley was kind enough to volunteer. I scooped him up as if he weighed no more than a feather."

Slowly I reached out to Docket, putting my hands on his waist. "Please, God, don't let fail whatever it is that keeps me from smashing his ribs."

The strong suit made a faint whining sound as I moved my arms up, and suddenly Docket was dangling above my head. I stared up at him, unwilling to believe it had been so simple. "I can't feel your weight at all."

"The counterweights inside redistribute it," he said. "It's why it feels so heavy when it's switched off. You can lift at least three or four men at once if you like."

I put Docket back down and examined the harness once more. "It really does work." I took a few more steps, growing accustomed to the slight jerks as the harness moved with me. "Can I hit something?"

"That's the best part." He gestured for me to follow him over to a tall stack of his crated parts. "All you have to do is make a fist and point it at what you want to punch."

"Not all that." I eyed the heavy wood slats and the motors sitting inside. "I'll break my only good hand."

"Then use the hurt one," he suggested. "You'll not feel a thing."

I lifted my hurt arm and aimed my fist at the crate. The harness sent my arm flying forward and my fist landed with what felt to me like a bare nudge. Wood cracked, metal groaned, and the crate flew twenty feet into the back wall, where it smashed apart.

I barely felt a twinge from my wound, and turned my hand over to see bits of the crate fall from the braces. Beneath them my hand didn't have a mark on it. "Sweet Mary."

"The shock compressors take all the force of the blow for you," Docket said, pointing out the tiny geared joints over my fingers. "I've put these on the maximum setting, so you'll not want to punch a regular chap—you could knock his head off. But if you tussle with one of them beasts, it should match his strength blow for blow."

I almost felt like running out and looking for one of the beasts. "What if he hits back?"

"No worries." Docket picked up a sledgehammer, and before I could do more than shriek he slung it at my chest plate. As the metal collided with it I felt a mild nudge, as if he'd prodded me with his elbow. "The stabilizers kick in on impact; you'll not tip over. But if you should get your feet tangled in something, like this"—he hooked his leg behind mine and gave me a shove, toppling me over—"just relax."

I lay on the floor looking up at him. Although the fall hadn't hurt me I felt ridiculous. "Relax like this?"

"Well, relax and press the green button on your left forearm." Docket bent over me to tap it. I turned my head as two struts emerged from the sides of the harness and began maneuvering me and it upright. Before I could blink I was standing again.

"I can't believe it." I held out my arms. "What else does it do?"

"That's all for right now, but I've a list of improvements to work out." He walked round me. "I haven't devised a helmet yet, so remember that your head is unprotected. Also, you'll not want to take it in water; the motors and the clamps will seize, and you'd sink to the bottom and drown from the weight anyway."

"No going for a swim, right." I extended my arm and turned it to watch the mech in motion. "What if I'm caught in the rain?"

"Cover it fast with a waterproof, or you'll become a very pretty statue until I can cut you out of it," he advised me. "You might also put a loose cloak over it when you wear it outside. Keeps people from staring."

"You're not really giving this to me," I said. "Doc, if you sold this design to the queen's army, you could make your fortune."

"I've already gone through several fortunes, my gel,

and I didn't make it for money or barter." His merry expression turned serious. "You're to wear it when you go out after dark. And if you come up against those beasts again, you give them what for."

"Doc," I said, smiling. "Thanks to you, I think I can."

CHAPTER FOURTEEN

Docket agreed to deliver the strong suit to the Eagle's Nest that afternoon, and I went up to the office. The pile of post waiting in the tube contained enough business to keep me busy until summer, and it hurt to set it all aside in favor of the list of the Wolfmen's victims.

I scanned the addresses first, and used my map of Rumsen's streets to work out a route for my calls. Nearly all the women lived in one of the least affluent quarters, which was conveniently located half a mile from the White Lupine.

I pushed aside the map and sat back in my chair. "So you have them attack harlots and poor women, and one lady." On one hand it made sense to target the unfortunate; they couldn't afford physicks or a hospital; they'd most likely keep their pregnancies secret until they gave birth at home. Lykaon could easily have them watched until they delivered and he could snatch the babies from them.

But Lady Bestly was hardly without resources, and could afford the very best of care during her confinement. How did she fit in with the other women?

A groaning sound drew my eyes to the closet, and when I went to open it I found Gert huddled inside. "Now how did you get in here? No place to sleep again?"

I saw a bruise on her temple and lost my smile. "Who hit you?"

"Well, I do have a place to sleep, and plenty of work, thanks to you telling me about that tinker. As for this, I was watching for you this morning, miss." She accepted my hand and struggled to her feet. "Down the end of the hall, like always. Only this old bloke comes up and waves a stick and strolls right in, bold as you please. Couldn't let him rifle through your things, could I?" She touched her temple and winced. "When I braced him he turn round and whacked me. That's all I remember." She gave me a surly glare. "Must have dragged me in the closet, the filthy heathen."

"Heathen." I helped her sit down in my visitor's chair. "You mean he was a native?"

She nodded. "He'd put on regular garms, and tucked his knotty under the collar, but I could tell straightaway. Dark as Lucifer himself, he was." She spied my tea cart. "Could you make us a brew, miss? My throat's like sand."

I put on the kettle and brought her some water and a pain powder. "Here, this will help with your head." I waited until she swallowed the bitter stuff before I sighed. "Gert, you shouldn't have come after him. He might have done much worse." Which puzzled me, now that I thought about it.

"I reckon I deserved it, for what I done to you." She took out a crumpled rag and blew her nose. "Some of the mages near me old place, they made up like friends to me, and said terrible things about you. Told me it would be a favor to them, me getting rid of you. Only I couldn't, and then when me luck turned, I went to them asking for paying work. They called me beggar and chased me out of their shops, all of them. I never begged in me life, miss."

"I know, Gert." Pity made my anger recede, and I heard the echo of what I'd said to Lady Bestly in her words. The reason I had always been kind to the old woman was because I'd been the same when I'd come to Rumsen—alone and without prospects, but determined to live with dignity. "I'm sorry."

"You've no reason to say that, or to help me find work, but you did. You've ever a kind word for me, no matter what I've said to you, and always handing me coin for tea and such when all I've done . . ." She shook her head before she looked up at me. "I don't know what you are, miss, but there's no evil to you. No evil at all."

I made her tea and found a tin of biscuits to go with it, and then asked her if she remembered anything more about the native intruder.

"That stick of his might have been some sort of wand, for how he used it to get in, waving it over the lock." She frowned as she thought. "Had some odd beads and feathers hanging from it."

"Blue feathers?" When she nodded, I perused the floor of the office and wondered if another rat bomb had been set loose. "Did he have anything else?"

"Just that stick. When I came after him he was already in here, rifling through your post." She turned her head to my tube port. "Took something out of there. A little parcel, I think."

"Excuse me." I got up and performed a quick search of my port and both rooms, but found no parcel at all. I had to assume the shaman had taken it with him. Since

Dredmore had forced the second rat to name him as its maker, that made the situation even more bewildering.

I returned to refill Gert's cup. "You've been very helpful, thank you. One more question: did the native say anything to you?"

"He did mutter some nonsense before he hit me." Gert took a sip of her tea. "Heathens never do speak the queen's English as they should."

"Did you understand any of it?" I pressed.

"He might have let loose an animal." She made a contemptuous sound. "He said to me, 'Where Little Fox?'"

I offered to take Gert to a physick to be checked, but she insisted she was fine. I was able to convince her to ride with me in my hired carri to her new room in a cheap but relatively clean boardinghouse a mile away.

"I've never ridden in one of these horseless contraptions," Gert confided in me, her eyes almost glowing with excitement. "You should buy one for yourself, miss, and save the cost of the fares."

"A recurring dream of mine, Gert. Unfortunately women are not allowed to purchase driving permits. Oh, that reminds me." I took the envelope of coins I usually kept in my desk and handed it to her. "This is for you."

"What for?" She glanced inside and shook her head. "Oh, no, I can't, miss. Really." She tried to give it back.

"It's compensation for your courage in defending my business establishment," I told her. "That native might have stolen everything I owned of value, if not for you scaring him off."

"Compensation." She pronounced the word the same way she might a disease, and gave me a suspicious look. "I didn't do much scaring from inside your closet."

"If you had been conscious, I've no doubt you would have chased him off smartly." I closed her hand over the envelope and patted it. "It will buy you a few days to rest and recuperate. You shouldn't be out scramming for the tinker until your head feels better. You truly did keep me from losing my valuables."

"In that case, I guess I've earned it." She tucked the envelope into her bodice before she climbed out of the carri. "While I'm recouping as such, I'll expect you to have that lock warded. Else that heathen comes back for more mischief. Good day, miss." She swept like a grand lady into the boardinghouse.

From there the driver took me to the working quarter where the Wolfmen's victims resided, and left me off in front of the first address on my route, one of a dozen narrow split-houses built of graying clopboards. As I walked up the sagging planked steps to the entry I heard a child screaming in a tantrum, and smelled fish and boiled cabbage. Since there was no bell, I knocked and stepped back enough that I could be seen from the side window.

The iron-haired woman who opened the door had the shrieking child on her hip and shouted to be heard over him. "What do you want?"

Although I'd planned to use my Middy accent while calling on the victims, something told me that speaking like a lady might serve better to give me an air of someone visiting in some official capacity.

"My name is Charmian Kittredge," I said, and at the

sound of my voice the little boy immediately fell silent. "I would like to speak with Mary Cauld—is that you, madam?"

"No, I'm her mother, and you can't." She began to shut the door in my face.

"Has she been ill?" I asked quickly. "Since she was hurt?"

Mrs. Cauld peered out at me. "What do you know about that?"

"I may be able to help," I said carefully, "but first I must speak with Mary."

Mrs. Cauld inspected me again. "She's got the belly gripe," she warned me. "And me with six more to look after, it's all I can do to keep her cleaned up. Come in then."

I followed Mrs. Cauld through a dank but tidy hall to the back rooms, where she nodded toward one that stood closed.

"In there." She jiggled the still-quiet boy, patting his back with an absent hand. "Mind your step. She don't always make the bucket every time."

I knocked and stepped into a windowless room lit by a blackened keroseel lamp. The smell of puke was so strong I had to breathe through my mouth. On the rumpled bed lay a young woman in a stained nightdress, who turned away from me as soon as I stepped into the flickering light.

I introduced myself quickly. "I am sorry to bother you, Miss Cauld, but I need a word."

"Mum shouldn't let you in here," Mary Cauld said in a fretful voice. "I'm dreadful sick."

I went round the bed and, finding no chair, knelt down beside it. "This won't take long. I must ask you about what happened last Tuesday night."

"What about it? I got rolled coming home from work," she said, closing her eyes. "I didn't have nothing to take, and I didn't see no one. Now go on."

"I know you were attacked by one of the Wolfmen." I nodded as she stared at me. "So was I."

She rose up on one elbow and turned her head to the door before she said in a furious whisper, "I told the police, I'm not married yet. If me lad knew what that thing did to me, he'd call it off. Me parents'd toss me out. You can't say nothing to Mum."

"I won't tell anyone," I promised her. "But I have to know, did the creature bite you?"

"I'm going to puke again," she said, her voice strangling on the words, and when I picked up the bucket on the floor she snatched it from me and wretched into it.

I held the bucket for her, and once she'd emptied her stomach found a rag and a basin of clean water. After I wiped her mouth and face, she fell back against the pillows and groaned.

I took the bucket to empty it in the loo, and when I came back Mary was sitting up, her pale face drawn. "How did you know it bit me, miss?"

I set the bucket next to the bed and considered how much I should tell her. "I was bitten, too, on the arm." I lifted my sling.

"I thought I was. I mean, I felt it here." She touched the side of her neck. "Bloody monster. I was sure he meant to tear me head off. Only when I got home, there weren't a mark on me. Just this bump."

I watched her run her fingers over the slight bulge beneath her skin. "Mary, are you and your beau planning to marry?"

"Sure, soon as I'm better. Can't wait much longer to be a proper wife and start a family." She met my gaze. "Neither should you, miss."

I didn't have to tell her she was pregnant; she already knew. "I'd like to leave my card with you. If things . . . don't go as you've planned, will you contact me? I may be able to help."

"If you like." She took the card. "Thanks for emptying me bucket. Fine lady like you shouldn't be doing that."

"I'm a working lass," I admitted. "Same as you, Mary."

"Not for long, miss." She pressed a hand over her midsection. "God help us."

Mrs. Cauld stood waiting at the other end of the hall, this time with a basket of folded garms instead of the boy. "Told you it were the belly gripe. She'll be all right in a few days, and then she'll be married."

I saw the same knowledge in the mother's guarded eyes as had been in her daughter's. "Your daughter is frightened, Mrs. Cauld, of things that I daresay you would never permit to happen. Perhaps you might ease her mind and tell her so."

Stepping out of the Caulds' home was like being able to breathe again; at least until I saw Chief Inspector Doyle waiting at the curb. "I did apologize to Dredmore's driver, Inspector."

"You must have done it by dream, then. His lordship dropped the charges last night." He surveyed me. "You're looking much smarter today."

"A new gown always boosts the spirits," I confided. "Matches my sling, too. So if you're not here to arrest me as a fugitive from justice, to what do I owe the pleasure?"

"You're in a terrible neighborhood, by yourself, on foot, wearing a dress that cost more than my carri." He took my good arm in his. "You're a crime waiting to happen."

"That's not why you're here," I guessed as I walked with him. "What have I done now? Embezzled millions? Abducted a crown prince? Started a war?"

"Lord Dredmore requested I accompany you on your visits." He nodded down the street. "The home of the next victim is one block that way. Did you buy the list from the desk sergeant, or one of the clerks?"

"Inspector, I should never bribe one of your staff." I stepped round a pile of trash. "Among other things, that would be illegal."

"You're sounding very honest again," Doyle said dryly. "Very well, why are you visiting the victims?"

"We need more information about the Wolfmen. Which I will not obtain if you're with me." I watched a boy sitting on the curb using a twig in a vain attempt to wind up a badly battered animech parrot. "The women aren't going to talk about the beast who assaulted them with a man in the room."

"I'll wait outside," he offered. "Is Mary Cauld pregnant?"

I stopped and turned to him. "Dredmore didn't tell you that."

"If that's what you're asking them, you can strike Lucy Ennis off your list. She's in hospital after a suicide attempt, and also with child." He cocked his head. "Are you pregnant?"

"Absolutely not." As we continued on, I asked, "Why did Lucy Ennis try to kill herself? The baby?"

He nodded. "The husband is a mariner, and he's been at sea for six months."

I could well imagine how Mr. Ennis would react when he arrived home from his lengthy voyage to find his wife expecting. "Will she recover?"

"She has." Doyle held up one hand to stop an approaching horse cart before guiding me across the street. "Lucy's neighbor found her hanging from a clothesline in her yard this morning. When he cut her down, she began to breathe again."

I grimaced. "She must not have been there long."

"She told the doctor she went out at midnight to do the deed. Something revived her, in the same way the Wolfmen at Saint Albert's were, even after they'd been cut open and their parts taken out." He gave the horse cart driver a wave. "Any theories?"

"Yes. Dredmore didn't send you to escort me. You came on your own to ferret out as much information from me as you can." I checked the houses until I found the number I needed. "You'll wait out here?"

"I'm not going anywhere," Doyle assured me.

I concluded my visits shortly before tea time, and accepted a ride from Doyle to the Eagle's Nest.

"My friend Gert thinks I should buy my own carri,"

I mentioned as I adjusted my sling and shifted into a more comfortable spot. "I might manage an older model. Can't afford a driver, though, so I'd need a permit of my own. Of course it's illegal to issue them to unmarried women . . ."

"You can save your hopeful hints. I've naught to do with permit regulations or carri licenses." Doyle checked his watch. "We've less than two hours before dark, when more women will be hurt. Care to chat about that?"

"And relive my own unpleasant experiences? No, thank you." I kept my expression bland. "Can you announce a curfew? No women in the city to go out after sunset, or something of that sort?"

"Kit."

I couldn't keep him in the dark any longer. "With the exception of me, all the Wolfman victims are pregnant. Their children were conceived to serve as hosts for Aramanthan immortals, which the women also carry in their bodies at present. Lucy Ennis survived hanging because, like the others, she has a spirit stone in her body. It wouldn't let her die."

"All right." Doyle leaned forward. "How do we save them?"

"Dredmore believes the stones are spelled so they can't be removed. The same spell kept Lucy alive, and will probably defeat any attempt to end the pregnancies. I think as soon as the babies have grown enough, the spirits will be released from the stones in order to possess them." Saying it like that made me feel even more hopeless. "Tommy, these women are only the victims who came forward."

"You think there are more."

"I know there are." I glanced out the window. "On the Hill. Most of the men who have disappeared came from there. Like Lord Bestly."

"Bloody hell." He sat back. "No. We'd have had reports from the physicks—"

"Lord Bestly attacked his wife in their home before he went into the city," I said flatly. "She did not report it. You know the law as well as I do."

He looked disgusted. "A wife cannot be violated by her own husband. How many more do you think there are?"

"Without examining every woman on the Hill, there's no way to tell. Lady Bestly was one of the first to be attacked, and she will deliver in the fall. By Christmas the Aramanthan will have made their grand return." I watched his face. "So you see, Tommy, they won't be invading Rumsen. They already have."

Doyle started to say something, and then frowned. "That old chap out there with the dolly; isn't he from your building?"

I glanced out to see the old mech wheeling a shrouded pallet down the alley. "Yes, that's Mr. Docket. I asked him to deliver something for me. Tommy, what I've told you, you can't repeat to anyone."

"Oh, I've no desire to be tossed in the loony bin." He got out and helped me down, and then eyed Docket, who gave us a merry wave. "What is that he's carting?"

"My birthday present." I smiled. "Thank you for the police escort."

"Don't go traipsing about after dark, Kit." He touched my cheek. "Please, for my sake."

I nodded and started down the alley after Docket, who presented me with a grin and the dolly handle.

"I've fashioned a sleeved cloak to cover the works," he told me. "Made it out of an old waterproof, so you needn't worry about rain." He glanced past me. "That copper a friend of yours?"

I nodded. "I know him from when we were kids in Middy. Doc, how long will the strong suit work?"

"As long as you keep moving, love, the autowinders'll keep the motors going." He patted the top of the dolly. "She's built to be perpetual."

"You're amazing, mate." I gave my old friend a kiss on the cheek. "Truly you are."

I had Wrecker take charge of the dolly, and went to find Rina, who was tending to Janice.

"I thought I told you to stay with the deathmage," my friend said as she coaxed her gel to take a spoonful of broth. "Or do you plan to spend all day and night casting up your accounts, too?"

I closed the door and leaned back against it. "Janice isn't sick. Neither is Felicity."

"They can't keep down so much as a cracker, neither of them," Rina snapped. "If it's not sickness, then . . . oh, God, no."

"What is it?" Janice pushed the spoon away and sat up. "What?"

"You've been sloppy, is what." Rina dropped the spoon back into the bowl. "You're knocked up."

Janice laughed. "I don't think so. I never take a john without a hat on, and I tidy myself after with the herbal, every time. Besides, I ain't had me menses in a year and better. I'm on the change."

Rina regarded her and then me. "I doubt the angels were involved. So how can she be pregnant?"

I walked over to the bed. "Janice, when the Wolfman attacked you in the park, where did he bite you?"

She shrugged her left shoulder out of her nightdress. "Felt like he sank his fangs down to the bone, but when I got back to the house there was only a bruise, and that's gone."

I touched her shoulder, felt a hard spot beneath her skin, and drew back. "You should rest now. Rina, may I see Felicity?"

The other harlot was in much the same state as Janice, and grew hysterical when I asked her if she'd been bitten. Rina sent me from the room, and emerged a short time later.

"She's a bit of a priss," she said after she closed the door. "Got her on the hip before he took her from the back. No wound, but something hard under her skin. It's a stone, isn't it?"

I knew Rina's gels were experts at eavesdropping, so I touched a finger to my lips before I said, "Likely a bit of swelling. You look as if you could use some air. Can Almira sit with the gels so we can have a walk?"

Rina accompanied me downstairs to the kitchens and instructed her cook to take over nursing Felicity and Janice. "Make them some dry toast and sweet tea," she advised her. "That should settle their bellies."

We walked down to the tavern, where Rina ordered a pitcher of hot cider and cakes to be served in a private room. Once the waitress left my friend set down her mug. "Right. Let's have it."

I told her what Dredmore and I had discovered at the morgue, how Dez had removed the spirit stone from my arm, and about my visits to the other victims. "Dredmore is trying to find a spell that will stop the possession of the unborn, but it doesn't look promising."

"Then we take the gels to the herbalist." Rina drank down her cider. "She can give them a purgative."

"That may not work—"

"It always works." Rina met my gaze. "I got knocked up on my maiden night. I couldn't look after myself, much less an infant. One drink, bit of night cramps, and then it was over. Doesn't damage anything. I can even have more kids, if I ever lose my mind and decide to."

"Carina." I moved to sit beside her, and put my arm round her shoulders. "I'm so sorry you had to endure that."

"I don't think about it much. Only every other time I see a mother with a pram." She gave me a wan look. "What about you?"

"I was bitten, but the Wolfmen never had a chance to finish." I glanced down at my belly. "So no bun to bake."

"I don't mean them," she said. "What about you and the deathmage?"

I decided to lie. "He's not tossed up my skirts, if that's what you mean." No, I'd let them fall to my feet.

She nodded. "And Doyle?"

"Chief Inspector Doyle." I sighed. "He's also been a perfect gentleman."

"I must have imagined him bussing you at Rumsen Main, then." Rina poured more cider in our mugs. "Face it, love. They're both sinfully handsome, charming chaps with much to offer, and they both want you. Rather badly, from what I've seen. You being a gel alone and all, in time one of them will wear you down."

"Your confidence in me overwhelms," I told her. "I think I can resist their charms. I'm not made out to be a mistress."

"Dredmore has magic and money, and Doyle a decent heart and position. You'd do well with either of them." She made a face. "I can't believe I'm saying this, but you should consider guiding one of them to the altar."

Me, married to Dredmore or Doyle? I couldn't help but laugh. "I think not. Men like them do not make offers for gels like me."

"Why shouldn't they? You're a pretty, clever virgin who owns a business and a home. You may not have a pile in the bank, but you're trustworthy, fair, and a good friend." She moved her shoulders. "If I fancied the ladies I expect I'd be after you."

"Even if you did, you're the sister I never had, so it'd be incest." As the street window darkened I went to draw the curtains and then secured the door. "I have to summon Harry. If you'd rather go back to the Nest—"

"And miss the chance to meet your immortal grandda?" She settled back and sipped her cider. "I'm not budging an inch."

"You won't be able to see him," I advised her. "He only manifests to the spirit-born."

Rina reached for a cake and nibbled on it as she watched me go through the brief business of summoning Harry.

"He's driven you to drink I see. It'll be gambling next." He saw Rina and grinned. "Hello, my angel. At last we meet."

She smiled back. "Did you haunt me in another life?"

I gaped at her. "You can see him?"

"Course, he's right there." Rina's expression turned smug. "I guess that means I'm not so ordinary."

"No," I glared at my grandfather. "I suppose you're not. Someone might have mentioned that."

"Slipped me mind." He rolled his eyes at me before he sat down beside Rina. "Oh, no love, don't do that," he said as she tried to touch him. "I'm not exactly solid, and you'll only freeze your fingers. In fact you may want to wrap up."

"I guess there'll be no cider for you, then." Rina shivered and scooted away as she pulled on her shawl.

"Harry, we need you to work a spell," I said, and told him about the spirit stones placed in the pregnant women. "Can you protect the unborn from being possessed by the Aramanthan?"

"For a time." He eyed my middle. "You're not with child, you know."

"She hasn't done anything to make one," Rina advised him in a half whisper. "I think she's determined to die a virgin. Absolute waste if you ask me."

"Don't distract him," I warned her before I said to Harry, "How long can you protect the unborn?"

"Not for nine months." He thought about it and then his expression cleared. "But there is another way. I'll have to make individual visitations, but they'll never know I'm there." He stood up. "I'll be gone most the night. Mind you gels stay indoors."

Rina's eyes widened as Harry vanished. "He just pops in and out like that all the time?"

"Unfortunately." I turned my head as muffled shouts came from outside the door. "Rowdy place, this."

"Too early for the usual drunken rows." Rina hiked up her skirts and drew a blade from a sheath strapped to her calf. "You didn't bring a dagger, I suppose. You never think to bring a bloody dagger, and I was in too much of a hurry to grab a pistol."

"Not my fault this time. Dredmore nicked mine." I grabbed a fire iron from the hearth and went to stand behind the door, which burst open a moment later.

The natives who filed into the room were armed with pistols and dressed in fine livery of a dozen different houses. Rina didn't look at me as she backed away, holding her blade ready.

"This room's taken, gents," she said. "You'll want to have your libations somewhere else."

"We not here to drink." A short native dressed like a gentlemen stepped out of the crowd. "Where's Little Fox?"

"In the bloody little forest, I imagine," Rina snapped.

One of the natives raised his pistol and cocked the hammer.

"Tell me," the shaman said, "or die."

"I'm here." I stepped out from behind the door, ignoring Rina's swearing as I faced the natives. "You let my friend go, and I'm all yours."

As the shaman nodded, Rina swore. "Kit, damn you, no."

"If he wanted me dead, he'd have cut my throat at the station," I reminded her as I watched his pale, chilling eyes. "Now drop the blade and get the hell out of here, Rina."

CHAPTER FIFTEEN

I was cloaked and led out the back of the tavern by the shaman's livery party, which hustled me into the back of a straw-lined horse cart.

I pulled off the cloak and struggled to my feet. "Where are you taking me?" No one answered me. The doors slammed shut and I heard the bolt drop before the cart jerked. I landed in the straw, fell back, and looked up at a coil of rope. "Away, right."

I tried kicking the doors to dislodge the bolt bar, which didn't move, and pounded on the sides of the cart and shouted for help. None came. After an hour of that I lost my voice and occupied myself by picking an assortment of splinters out of my good hand with my teeth.

By my reckoning and sense of direction we were out of the city and headed into native country. As a child I'd heard the usual gruesome tales of what happened to citizens who strayed into the pact territories; they all ended up in a cooking pot or buried to the neck in sand for the delight of the vultures.

I couldn't see myself making much of a meal for the shaman, but the thought of having my eyes pecked out before I could expire of brain boil under the burning sun did needle a bit.

"To think, I could be wheedling tea and biscuits

out of Winslow right now." The inside of the cart was growing dark; the little bit of sunlight shining through the chinks was rapidly dwindling. At least the Wolfmen wouldn't have another go at me, not out here.

I closed my eyes to summon Harry, and then stopped. While my straits were rather dire, I hadn't been harmed yet. "I'd better save you for when they start digging the pit."

A silver mist formed over the straw. "What pit?" Harry materialized and fell down. After rubbing his hip he frowned at me. "What are you doing all the way out here in the wilderness?"

"Oh, I thought I'd tour a village or two." I fought back the urge to fling my arms round him and sob with gratitude. "What about you? Were you able to bespell the unborn?"

"About half done. I should have the rest seen to before dawn." He glanced round the cart. "What are you doing in this thing?"

I sighed. "I've been abducted. Again."

"You do make it a habit, gel." He picked a piece of straw off his sleeve. "By natives, too, and that's not good at all. What have you done to infuriate this lot?"

"The shaman never said. A heathen of few words." I felt the cart beginning to slow. "Any suggestions?"

"Be polite. They still fancy scalps." As the back of the cart opened he vanished.

I ignored the native offering me a hand and jumped down into knee-high grass. Firelight glowed from a large pit some distance away, illuminating dozens of round huts made of bundled twigs and branches, and painted with large, curving designs. From the pointed roofs fluttered strips of twinkling beads, and curtains of feathers hung over the arched entries.

I scanned the unfriendly faces round me, but didn't see the shaman. I did notice some of the locals had come out of their huts to have a look at me, and they hadn't bothered to dress. I kept my eyes on their faces. "Lovely village. Very colorful."

A native woman wearing a hide cape over very little else pushed past the men and beckoned to me. "You, come."

I followed her, trying not to flinch as some of the men reached out to touch my hair and my sleeves. They didn't hurt, and seemed only curious, but the experience was decidedly unnerving.

The caped Godiva led me through the village to a smaller hut on the other side, where she pushed aside the curtain of feathers and motioned for me to go in.

I hesitated. "Could I speak with someone in charge, please? Or perhaps you could send for a bureau agent, to speak on my behalf?"

"In," she said with a jab of her finger.

I walked through the arched opening and turned as the curtain fell back in place. Beyond it I could see the native woman standing with her back toward me as if guarding the hut.

More hides covered the dirt floor, and while there were no proper furnishings, I noted a bed made of woven blankets covering a mound of straw, and several dried gourds and strings of smoked fish. Seashells, most polished, hung on strings from the woven-branch ceiling.

I looked for scalps but didn't see any, nor a shovel for any pit digging. "Harry," I whispered. "What's happening outside?"

My grandfather appeared on the blanketed straw and reclined. "They've gathered about the fire to talk. Some of them look important." He pointed to his head.

"I know almost nothing about natives," I advised him. "And I've not time for charades."

"It's the gull feathers," he said. "They're white and gray, and only chiefs wear them. There are ten blokes out there with gull feathers in their hair."

"That's utterly fascinating." I folded my arms. "And completely useless."

"You youngsters never bother to study your Torian history." He sighed. "There's only one reason so many chiefs would gather like this in one village. They're holding a war council."

"I've started a war?" I sat down with a thump. "How? I've never done anything to offend the natives." That I knew of, anyway.

"I don't think it's you." He frowned. "Dredmore is summoning me, the cheeky bastard."

I could imagine the deathmage riding out to lay waste to the village. "Go, but don't tell him where I am, not yet. And don't stay long with him. You have to finish bespelling the unborn."

"I've hardly a moment to myself anymore." He started to turn transparent, and then said, "They bury you in the desert only if you break one of their laws. So don't do anything unlawful."

Shortly after Harry disappeared I heard the native

woman and a man talking in low, hostile voices. I got up and moved to the back of the hut, picking up one of the gourds, which was harder and heavier than I'd expected. When the feathered curtain moved I hid it behind my back.

The native man was younger, and dressed in the working clothes of a stable hand. "You are the one brought from the city?" he asked in flat-toned but flawless English.

"I am, unless your people stopped along the way to take some other unsuspecting citizens hostage." I didn't bother to hide my contempt. "You obviously work in Rumsen. Are you acquainted with the punishment for kidnapping a Torian woman? I believe it includes public flogging, loss of your pact lands, and spending the rest of your life in prison."

"I did not take you," he said.

"Yet here you are, aware of my circumstances but doing nothing to release me." I made a tsking sound. "That makes you an accessory to the crime, which carries much the same punishment, including the flogging."

He stiffened. "I am not afraid of your people."

But he wasn't happy about my abduction, either, I could see that. "What's going to happen to me?"

"It has not been decided." He approached me, halted, and gestured at me. "Please put down the gourd. I will not hurt you."

I carefully set down the gourd and then straightened. "Can you at least tell me your name, and why I was brought here?"

"Your people call me Trainer." He looked uncomfortable now. "I think you are to be traded."

I tried to fathom that. "I am not merchandise to be taken by or offered to anyone."

"Those of us who work in the city know your laws," he assured me. "We are against the trade."

So Trainer was an ally. "Well, then, perhaps you could speak for me to the others who are in favor of it."

"The others who are against the trade," he continued, "want you killed so no revenge will be taken against the tribes."

I shouldn't have put down the gourd. "You know, now that I think about it, I wouldn't mind being traded at all."

"I do not wish you dead or used as barter, miss." He glanced at the feathered curtain and lowered his voice. "You were brought here because a sacred object of great power was stolen from our holy man."

"The War Heart." I nodded as Trainer gave me a shocked look. "Blue Fox spoke of it to me when I met him in the city." I touched my sling. "He tried to help me."

"He has been in the city watching over you for weeks." He sounded grim. "He did not say that he had approached you."

So I'd been right about that, too. "Does he understand that I didn't steal the War Heart?"

"Blue Fox knows you did not take it." He seemed to silently debate whether to say more, and then told me, "He calls you the daughter of his spirit, and claims you have great magic in you. But what he has said, it frightens our people. No woman of the tribe has even been shaman, and you . . ."

"I'm not of the tribe." I heard more voices outside,

and sensed things were coming to a head. "If you really want to help me, Trainer, tell them that I am willing to be traded, and that I will say nothing about this to the authorities. Say I give my word, out of respect for what Blue Fox did for me."

He looked skeptical, but finally gave me a curt nod and ducked back outside.

The next to enter was the shaman, two men with many gull feathers in their hair, and the stable hand. Remembering Harry's warning, I dropped into a deep curtsey and remained there.

One of the chiefs spoke, and Trainer said, "You may rise, miss."

I remembered not to look directly at the shaman or the chiefs. Since the stable hand was acting as translator, I kept my gaze on him.

Blue Fox began to speak, and as he did the younger man repeated his words in English. "The tree-man has been using the War Heart to make beasts of men. We cannot allow this to go on. He has said if we bring you to him, he will return it to the tribe."

"I understand," I told him, "and I am willing to be traded."

Blue Fox held up one gnarled hand to silence the stable hand, and in broken English said, "Tree-man think you fix spell, make beasts not die. I know you break all spell. You break *his*."

I nodded. "You are very smart, and I will. But I must know how he is using your magic, and why it doesn't work."

As soon as Trainer translated what I'd said both

chiefs made furious protests, but Blue Fox only looked at one and then the other to silence them. He then said something that sent them both stalking out of the hut.

"Our holy man will tell you what you wish," Trainer said. "But first you must agree to become his daughter."

"He wants to adopt me?" I glanced quickly at Blue Fox's impassive features. "Why?"

"As daughter of Blue Fox you become one of the people, and you must follow our laws." The stable hand looked weary now. "You cannot speak of the magic he teaches you. If you do that, or break any of our laws, you will be hunted by our warriors. You will be brought before the tribe and tortured for many days, and buried alive in the desert."

I swallowed. "Then your shaman had better teach me all of the laws, too."

We left the small hut and moved to the largest in the village. During the next hour there I was adopted by the shaman, and learned more than I ever wanted to know about hunting magic and native law. Because Blue Fox knew only basic words in English, Trainer (who grudgingly revealed his tribal name, Night Snow) remained to translate for us. He watched with jaded eyes as Blue Fox first presented me with a leather thong from which hung an abalone pendant.

"Once he has performed the naming ritual you will be known as Little Fox, daughter of Blue Fox," Night Snow said as the shaman hung carved and polished shell round my neck. "This is your tribe name. It is to be spoken only among the people."

I admired the abalone, which had been etched with the image of my namesake. "I'm called Kit in English. It also means little fox."

The shaman spoke again as he touched my cheeks with his hands in a fond manner.

"Hearing your English name is how Blue Fox knew you were the daughter of his spirit." Night Snow gestured for me to sit down beside a large, rounded piece of slate in the center of the shaman's hut. Shells had been arranged in strange circling designs atop the slate, which first appeared speckled. A closer look revealed the slate had been meticulously inlaid with hundreds of pearls.

"Blue Fox will now instruct you," Night Snow said. "You are the only invader ever to know the secrets of our magic."

I could see he was still feeling a bit put out by that. "I'm honored."

Through Night Snow, my new father described how the magic of the tribe had been practiced since the earliest times, when the first Alone crossed a bridge of ice to come to Toriana.

I wasn't especially enthralled by his tale of how the tribes learned to borrow the life force and talents of the animals through sacrifice and blood ritual, but it soon became obvious that such measures were not frequently taken. Minor spells and charms were most often worked from the bones the tribe saved from the game hunted to provide food. Rats, skunks, and other unpleasant vermin were reserved for sacrificial rites, as only their blood had value.

"When the tribes fought the redcoats who came to our land, the shamans were called to council," Night

Snow said. "Our warriors could not fight against muskets and sabers, and died along with their villages. It was decided to create the War Heart, to aid them in battle. One shaman went into the hills and there fought a white wolf of great strength and cunning. The shaman cast a spell to take from the wolf its spirit and contain it until he could send it to walk the land again within our warriors. This made our men change, and hair covered their bodies like pelts. Their teeth grew long and sharp, and from their fingers came claws."

"They became Wolfmen." I leaned forward. "That's the same spell Lykaon is using on the men in the city."

Blue Fox spoke sharply. "Not same." He reeled off more in his own language.

"Our warriors walked with the white wolf spirit only on nights of the round moon," Night Snow said. "By dawn the spirit always returned to the War Heart."

"They wouldn't have had much time to battle, then." I felt confused. "What *is* the War Heart, exactly?"

The men exchanged a look. "The spirit of the white wolf resides in its skull," Night Snow said.

"I think I've seen it." I recalled the strange bone fetish I'd spotted at the White Lupine. "If Lykaon is changing his men in the same way your warriors were, then why is it killing them?"

As Blue Fox answered he made a fist with one hand, and then extended the other as if he wanted to shake mine.

"Tree-man sends the spirit into his warriors, but he does not release them," Night Snow explained. "White wolf's spirit will not be trapped so. He will hunt for a time, but then he grows weary. He kills the warriors so that he may be free to return to the War Heart and sleep."

"But why doesn't he release the spirit?" I covered my mouth. "Oh, my God. He doesn't know he has to. He's the one who's killing them."

Now I suspected exactly why Blue Fox had chosen me to trade for the War Heart. There was more to discuss, but I would have to be alone with the shaman.

"Night Snow," I asked, "may I have a moment in private with Blue Fox?"

The younger man scowled. "You would speak without me?"

"Make daughter," the shaman said suddenly, and gestured for Night Snow to leave us.

Something like envy shone from the younger man's eyes as he turned away. "He will perform the naming ritual now."

I waited until he stomped out of the hut before I regarded Blue Fox. "I cannot allow you to adopt me, sir. I would make a very bad native woman. Also, I had a father, and I cherish his memory. He was also a very clever man, like you. I'm sure you understand."

"I see him." He touched one corner of my eye. "You see with his spirit here."

That hadn't offended him, so I pushed on. "You know that the thief—the tree-man—will never give you back the real War Heart. Not even for me. All you will get is the skull of another wolf."

"Tree-man think Blue Fox fool. Blue Fox let him." He reached across the slate to take my hands in his. "I send you, Little Fox."

"I want to be sure of what you wish me to do." I told

him what I suspected, and when he confirmed it, I was compelled to ask if what I described was really what he wanted.

"Yes." He clenched his fist. "Make him fool."

"I will, sir." That much I could promise. "But what will your people say?"

He tapped his chest. "I know." He nudged my shoulder. "You know." He glanced over his shoulder at the hut's curtain. "They not shaman. They never know."

"All right." I touched my abalone pendant, and for the first time noticed it seemed to be glittering. I held it up and saw what was causing the sparkle. To the shaman I said, "Do you know what this is?"

Blue Fox grinned. "Big magic."

The shaman escorted me personally through the village back to the horse cart. While the tribe followed us, and seemed even more curious about than before, Blue Fox's presence kept them at a respectful distance. Shocked murmurs erupted from them as he placed his hand on my head and chanted at length before handing me up into the cart.

"Daughter." He inclined his head before turning about, scattering the nearest gawkers before he strode like a king back to his hut.

Night Snow climbed in with me and closed the doors before he produced a bundle of cord. "I have to tie your hands, miss. The thief will expect it."

I carefully removed my sling and extended both wrists. "When we meet him should I fuss and resist, or can I simply go quietly?"

His dark brows arched. "Do you *know* how to be quiet?"

"Ha-ha." As the cart began to move I sat down and propped my bound hands on my knee. "I'm sorry if it upset you to be sent from the hut. You've been very kind."

"I am not offended. Naming is sacred." He settled down beside me. "Blue Fox is glad to be your father. He has waited a long time for you."

That seemed an odd thing to say. "Surely he has other children?"

"Shamans do not take wives. When they grow old they choose a man from the village to be their son. When they die, the son becomes shaman." He rested his head against the cart's wall and closed his eyes. "It is a great honor to be chosen."

I would never fathom native customs. "Perhaps he'll choose you."

He glared at me. "You are his child now. You are his choice."

I couldn't let the poor chap go on thinking his chances were ruined; being named Blue Fox's son must have meant everything to him. "Tell me, Night Snow, does it break tribal law to tell a lie?"

"We do not lie," he snapped. "That is what *your* people do."

"Very well. What if you say you're adopting an English gel as your daughter simply to keep the unruly members of the tribe from killing her so that she can help you recover a sacred relic?" I smiled at his astonishment. "Law broken then?"

"If the father never admits it, and the English girl says nothing, and the relic is recovered . . ." His mouth quirked. "No law is broken."

"In that case, I'm delighted with my very real adoption that no one actually witnessed. This is all purely conjecture, so that I might better understand tribal law." I winked at him.

He gave me a flashing grin. "You have a very good grasp of it already, miss."

The cart drove on for another half hour before coming to a stop.

"You should struggle a bit," Night Snow advised me as he helped me to my feet. He paused. "And I must make you appear more . . . unwilling."

"Very well." I sighed and braced myself against the wall. "No hitting."

He didn't strike me, but he did remove my dress jacket, tousle my hair, tear my right sleeve almost completely away from the shoulder seam, and rent my skirts in several places.

He stood back to inspect me. "That's better. Sorry about your garms."

"So am I." I lifted my bound wrists. "No jostling the hurt arm, please."

He knelt down, slung me over his shoulder, and jumped out of the cart with me.

Although my helpless position caused me to see everything upside-down, as Night Snow strode from the cart I noted our destination: toward a group of men on horses, gathered round a gleaming white carri. The vehicle, which looked as immaculate as if it belonged to a Duke, had been outfitted in polished bone instead of the usual brass. None of the men surrounding the ghastly monstrosity looked especially happy, and more than a few drew out daggers and pistols as Night Snow drew nearer.

Lykaon climbed out of the white carri, his gloved hands holding a neatly wrapped bundle. "How good of you gents to be on time."

Night Snow placed me on my feet and held a blade to my neck. "Don't struggle now," he whispered before he called out, "Show us the War Heart, or she dies."

The Aramanthan unwrapped the relic, which was simply the bleached skull of a very large wolf. "As you see. Now bring her to me and we will make the trade."

Night Snow lowered the blade and marched me forward, at which point I thought it prudent to begin my resistance.

"You can't trade me for some old bones," I protested loudly. "I am a free citizen, not a hank of beads."

"Calm yourself, Miss Kittredge," Lykaon said as I was presented to him. "I am here to rescue you."

"Please, sir." I gave him an ironic look. "I know you had them abduct me precisely to make this exchange."

"Nothing is free, Miss Kittredge. It is a rule of commerce." He handed the skull to Night Snow and then took hold of my wrists. "This concludes our transaction. Do give my best wishes to the rest of the heathen hordes."

He shoved me into the carri and climbed in after me, catching the back of my bodice as I stumbled and pushing me onto the rear-facing bench.

"Really, sir, must you manhandle me?" I tried to shrug my sagging sleeve back into place.

"That voice." He tapped his chin before snapping his fingers. "You were the courier who was arrested at the club."

"You are mistaken," I said, and realized Doyle was correct; I did sound very sincere when I was lying. "I have never been a courier."

"I know exactly what you are, spell breaker." His full lips stretched wide. "You think your playacting back there deceived me? I have walked among your kind for millennia. I know what the old shaman has planned. He thinks you can dispel my soldiers and dismantle my army."

"You have an army?" I feigned surprise. "What a coincidence, so does Rumsen. But I expect very soon you'll become acquainted with them."

He leaned forward, his eyes burning with a disagreeable yellow light. "While you will become very intimately acquainted with mine."

"As it happens, I've already met several of them," I advised him. "I don't believe they will wish to repeat the experience. But then, the others are all going to die soon anyway, aren't they? Thanks to you and your bungling the magic."

"Insolent insect." He slapped me for good measure, sending me careening into the side of the carri. "You know nothing of me. I could kill you with a thought."

It would have been to my advantage to stay huddled and silent in the corner, but no one ever accused me of being especially prudent under duress.

I pushed myself up, squinting at him as I wiped the blood from my mouth on my ruined sleeve. "So where am I to meet to this most unpleasant of fates? In Rosings Park? In a hospital bed? Surely not on another market tram; that didn't work at all well the last time."

"My soldiers are waiting for you at the club," Lykaon said. "Where you'll be the main entertainment for my esteemed membership. You do remember the romping room."

I didn't say anything more to him, for he'd told me everything I needed to know. I could also feel my eye beginning to swell shut, and I'd need the other to carry out Blue Fox's plan.

If I lived that long.

CHAPTER SIXTEEN

Lykaon's driver stopped in the alley behind the club, where I was unceremoniously dragged out by two footmen and carried inside.

"I'll be a much livelier victim if you'll stop crushing my limbs," I told the men, who did not respond or ease their grip. "I never imagined natives would be superior captors, but compared to you they were practically gentlemen."

I was taken directly to what Lykaon called his romping room, which appeared filled to capacity with new club members. They applauded me as I was led through them toward some sort of platform made of black-painted wood. Heavy shackles had been fixed to all four corners, and one of the men released me to unlock them.

A tall, thin man got up and walked past me without so much as a glance. "We need more champagne. Where the devil is that butler?" He sauntered out of the room.

I regarded the leering faces round me. "Is there not a decent man among you who will put a stop to this now?" I was answered by raucously laughing and several of the most lewd and lascivious suggestions ever to pollute my ears. "I see."

I looked at the footman still holding on to me. Fortunately he was rather young and looked somewhat green. "I'm a helpless woman, and they won't stop until I'm dead, you know. You'll be an accessory to murder. Or you may end up on that thing."

He gave me an incredulous look. "Can't do that to a man, miss."

"They didn't tell you? Oh, dear." I leaned forward as if to whisper more, and then drove my knee into his groin. As he dropped I slipped my hands out of the cord Night Snow had merely wrapped round my wrists, picked up a full bottle of champagne, and smashed it over the skull of the other footman. "Seems I'm not so helpless after all."

I ran, dodging the hands that snatched at me, and made it out into the hall before more footmen appeared. I feinted going for the stairs before I ducked under grabbing arms and fled to the front foyer.

Lykaon stood waiting for me just outside on the steps, and climbed them as he brought with him a young, writhing boy he was holding by the throat.

"Take another step," he said, "and I'll snap his neck."

As I retreated, he carried the gasping urchin inside and set him on his feet. The butler appeared, and hurried to lock the entry.

"I won't try to run again," I said quietly. "You don't have to hurt the boy."

"I knew what you would do before you did it. That is how simple you are to me." The Aramanthan stroked the matted hair of the sobbing child. "Now we have a dilemma. Should I give them the boy first? He won't last very long, but you'll gain a few more precious minutes of life. And you may have some wine and watch with the others."

This was the last straw. "I had thought I had met the worst scum of your lot, but I was in error." I closed my eyes, summoning Harry with every ounce of my will.

Lykaon made a satisfied sound before he murmured, "At last."

Something felt wrong, and my eyes snapped open to see the Aramanthan holding aloft a glittering stone. At the same time Harry materialized, looking from me to the boy, and then at Lykaon.

"Wait— Harry, it's a trap!" I shouted, but by then the power of the stone was dragging at him. When I tried to fling myself at Lykaon someone caught me from behind and held me.

"He is mine now," the Aramanthan said.

The mist that had been my grandfather was pulled into the stone, vanishing into its core. As soon as Harry was imprisoned, Lykaon pulled the street urchin closer and forced the stone into his mouth.

"Swallow it," he told the child, shaking him until he did.

The boy staggered away, his eyes rolling up in his head before he dropped to his knees. When he lifted his face again his eyes had filled with a cold, relentless fury.

"You would imprison me in this babe?" the boy said in Harry's voice. "He is an innocent mortal."

"Where is your gratitude, old friend?" Lykaon picked up the boy like a doll. "You shall have a long and interesting life in this body—once it matures. Until then, you will be like a son to me. A very faithful, obedient son."

With a quick movement, Harry latched on to Lykaon's nose with his teeth, viciously clamping down as blood streamed to the Aramanthan's chin. Using his hand to squeeze the boy's jaw mercilessly until Harry released him, Lykaon handed the boy to the butler. "But for that, you will be whipped. Take him away."

I watched Harry struggling to free himself from the butler's viselike grip, and when they vanished down the hall I regarded the Aramanthan. "This is why you traded the skull for me. So that I'd bring him to you."

"It isn't cleverness if you realize it after the fact." Lykaon mopped the blood from his face and felt his nose, which had already healed. "But thank you just the same."

I stared at him. "You think I'm going to give up, just like that?"

"Merlin—or what is it you call him? Harry? Names are so tedious." He went to a mirror to examine his reflection. "Your Harry will be whipped for injuring me. As he now possesses a mortal body, his skin will come apart. He will bleed and scream and feel every lash, just as the boy would."

"He was only defending himself."

"So am I. Do you know, in my time among you mortals I have witnessed punishments so painful and cruel that they are only spoken of in whispers. So while it is true that I cannot kill Harry, Miss Kittredge, I can make him wish for death. I daresay in time I can even make the old meddler beg for it."

The pleasure in his voice turned my spine to ice. "You really are a beast."

"Once I was called the Wolf King. Soon I will be king of Rumsen, and then Toriana, and then the world. I much prefer that." He turned round and nodded to the footman holding me. "The men will be growing restless, and they deserve some special entertainment tonight. Take her back to them now."

No one applauded this time as I was dragged kicking and screaming back to the altar. The men sat as if bespelled by the sight of me being strapped down, their hands holding goblets with wine they weren't drinking, and ash falling from the cigars they weren't smoking. I fell silent, too, as heavy thuds sounded from outside in the hall.

At least two Wolfmen, coming to make my acquaintance.

I turned my head and addressed the man nearest to me. "You know that Lykaon has been taking men from the club and turning them into monsters. But what he hasn't told you is that the magic is lethal—it kills every man it's used on. He means to do the same to you, and because the spell is wrong it will turn out the same as all the others." I turned my head to the other side of the room. "He will sacrifice every one of you."

Some of the men paled, and several began muttering to each other. Yet not one of them moved to help me or made any protest.

They were nothing but sheep, all of them. "Every Wolfman has died, you simpletons. You know this—and the same will happen to you. All of you will run amok and then die horrible deaths."

One of the spectators took a quick gulp of his wine before he said to footman, "Can't you gag her, man?"

The Wolfmen were in full, hairy transformation as they burst in the room. I saw men scrambling out of the way as they stalked toward me, their beastly countenances filled with hatred and lust. Dredmore could not save me, and Harry had been rendered helpless. In my heart I knew there would be no escape from them this time.

I closed my eyes and thought of the gardens at Morehaven. Whatever was done to me now, I would be there in my heart.

The sound of another Wolfmen came thumping into the room, but instead of growling he spoke. "Get away from her."

I opened my eyes to see Chief Inspector Doyle standing just behind the Wolfmen, his body encased in Docket's strong suit. My relief was so massive that I screamed his name.

"Tommy!"

The Wolfmen both attacked him in tandem, snapping and clawing as they set on him. I cringed and then craned my head as Doyle knocked both of the beasts away into the spectators, causing furnishings to smash, crystal to shatter and men to shout in terror.

Motors whirred as Doyle thumped over to me, his determined features a sight even lovelier to behold than my memory of Dredmore's flowers.

"They're getting up," I told him as he hooked his hand brace over one shackle and tore it free. "When you have another go at them, hit them square in the chest; that's where the clockworks are."

Doyle didn't have the opportunity to hit anything, as he was dragged away from the altar by one beast and clawed by the other. Sparks flew from the strong suit as he returned the mauling by catching the Wolfman's hand and crushing it to a mangled pulp. I went to work on my other shackle, yanking at it furiously as Doyle fought off the beasts.

Lykaon's servants and the club members began piling out of the room as the battle raged on. I alternated between watching and cringing and trying to work myself free. One Wolfman went hurtling into a wall, disappearing through the hole created by the impact. Plaster dust and shattered brick billowed out from the ruined wall, clouding the air and making me cough.

The other stayed on Doyle, savagely snapping and clawing at him from every direction until he barreled into him and knocked him flat. I saw the Wolfman fling himself atop Doyle and screamed.

Several shots rang out, sending the Wolfman tottering backward until he fell on his back, the smoking ruin of his clockworks giving a few final, slowing ticks before they went still.

The inspector was levered back upright by the suit, and had his pistol ready as the other Wolfman clawed his wall out of the wall. He fired, and the third shot took him down.

He had defeated them, one man against two monsters, thanks to the strong suit. As soon as I saw Docket again I planned to kiss him into a swoon.

"I do like your birthday present," Doyle said as he came to me and went to work on the rest of my shackles. "Can I borrow it again sometime?"

I wrapped my arms round his neck and sobbed something female and ridiculous before I could compose myself. "You're insane. Thank you." As my heartbeat stopped trying to bang its way out of my chest I took in a steadying breath. "Tom, we must find Harry—my grandfather," I added. "Lykaon has him trapped in the body of a child."

He drew back. "Sorry, what?"

The strong suit was making such a racket I didn't bother to repeat it. "Never mind." Once he'd removed the last shackle round my ankle I sat up and braced my good hand against his shoulder to climb down.

"Here." He pressed the power switch, and the noise stopped along with the motors. "You said your grandfather has a child?"

Three more Wolfmen appeared behind Doyle and seized him by the arms and neck, dragging him back from me.

"Switch it back on, Tommy," I said, but before Doyle could press the button on his palm one of the Wolfmen clouted him on the back of the head, knocking him out.

I lunged toward Doyle, but was hauled back by one of the club members. As I struggled to free myself I saw a strange little man in a doctor's coat walk in front of Doyle and pause to study him. "I have an admirer, it seems. The device is rather primitive, milord, and made to serve more as body armor than augmentation. The output delivery is tolerable, I suppose."

Lykaon joined him. "He defeated two of my soldiers, Mr. Desney."

"By shooting them," Desney said, sounding like a sulky child. "Still, I would like to meet its maker."

"It's mine," I said, drawing their attention. "The inspector only borrowed from me."

"A female did not build this, milord," Desney said, as if I were invisible. "Women have no head for engineering."

"Take it to the testing area," Lykaon told the Wolfmen, who dragged Doyle from the room.

"Tommy," I shrieked, yanking my arms free and stumbling as I tried to follow.

"No, Miss Kittredge," Lykaon said as he blocked my path and took out a long, thin blade. "You have caused quite enough annoyance for one night. It's time you—" He stopped and frowned as a gleaming brass rat scurried between his feet. "Mr. Desney, I thought we agreed, no vermin."

"It is not mine, milord." Desney reached down to capture the rat, but as soon as he touched it the rat squealed—and then exploded into a billowing cloud of white crystals.

The ice spell had no effect on me, but instantly froze Desney and Lykaon into frosty statues. I ran past them into Dredmore's arms. "Lucien, I will never complain about your timing again. We have to save Tommy; did you see where they took him?"

Behind me ice began to crack.

"He's disrupting the spell. Come." Dredmore lifted me off my feet and carried me with rapid strides down the hall, where he stopped at the wall. With one kick of his boot he opened a door concealed in the bricks, which swung inward.

"I can walk." When he didn't put me down, I wriggled. "Really, Lucien, I'm fine."

Reluctantly he set me on my feet. "I am never letting

you out of my sight again." He pushed the wall-door back into place. "Now, be quiet."

I nodded, and followed him down a dark hall that led to an enormous chamber that looked at first glance like a larger version of Docket's Dungeon. Then I saw the operating table and racks of gleaming surgical instruments, and the long rows of giant cages filled with Wolfmen.

Tommy was being hung by the three Wolfmen on a pair of hooks dangling from a rafter. He was also still unconscious.

Dredmore motioned for me to follow him into a narrow recess between some cabinets and the side wall. We edged through the space by walking sideways, until we were directly behind the operating tables.

"As soon as they go, I will free him," Dredmore said in the barest of murmurs.

I nodded, feeling slightly more confident. My hopes, however, were immediately dashed by the sight of Lykaon entering the chamber.

"Come along, Desney," he said as he approached Doyle's dangling figure. There wasn't a speck of ice on the immortal now. "It's only a spot of frostbite."

"What about the two that escaped?" the rude little man said as he appeared, his reddened hands rubbing at his still-icy ears.

"The men will find them and bring them back, and then you may have them," Lykaon said. "But first we will attend to this fellow."

"Yes, milord." Desney glanced up at Doyle. "I can cut the man out of the rig, but to avoid damaging it he will have to be dismembered."

I surged forward, but Dredmore pulled me back and clamped a hand over my mouth, shaking his head as he looked down into my furious eyes.

"Killing him will only waste an excellent opportunity," Lykaon said. "We have never attempted the transformation spell with such mech as this."

Desney looked indignant. "This design is decidedly inferior, milord."

"Are you questioning me again?" Lykaon drew out a dagger and regarded him. "I thought not. The last time was so very painful for you."

Before I could blink the Aramanthan sliced open the palms of his hands and flung them at Doyle, spattering him with blood. Lykaon began to chant as he walked round Doyle.

I struggled against Dredmore, who refused to release me. Only when the chains suspending Doyle's body began to shake did I go still.

The gouts of blood covering Doyle began to shrink and disappear into his body, absorbed as if he were a sponge. The fabric of Doyle's garms rippled and then began to tear as the mech fitted on his body seemed to contract. I didn't understand what was happening as his body jerked and writhed, and then I saw the shreds of one sleeve fall away, baring Doyle's muscular arm. The braces clamped to his flesh tightened so much his skin bulged out and then tore just as his clothes had. The mech grew bloody as it burrowed into the horrible wounds, which I knew would be the death of him in only a few seconds.

Doyle did not die, however, and the terrible injuries inflicted by the shrinking of mech did not bleed. Instead, his flesh began to stretch, closing over the gaping wounds and the mech inside them.

Dredmore caught his breath, and I blinked madly through the tears in my eyes, frozen with disbelief as I watched Doyle's body heal itself over the mech, the flesh rejoining and knitting itself back together. Each horrible scar then began to fade, smoothly out until no trace of the wound or the mech appeared on Doyle's skin. By the time all the blood disappeared, so had the mech, and Doyle's limbs bulged and writhed.

"He will not survive the bonding, milord," Desney said, looking satisfied now. "The device was not meant to function internally."

Doyle did look as if he were dying, his face contorting as his body jerked. Dredmore's hand came away from my mouth, and he turned me to him, trying to hide my face against him. Only then did I realize I was silently weeping, and I clutched at him in despair.

The chains stopped rattling, and when I looked again Doyle hung in garments reduced to rags, his body ominously still.

"I think he is dead now." Desney went to release the chains, and let Doyle drop to the floor. "Shall I burn the body like the other failures?"

"Not just yet." Lykaon walked over to Doyle and crouched beside him. "This one has a switch, remember?" He pressed Doyle's palm.

I nearly screamed as Doyle's eyes opened, and two struts shot out of his sides to push him upright. When they contracted, he stood, swaying as he stared at the floor.

"It still functions." Desney bent to peer at Doyle's

face. "The device will animate him, of course, but the flesh will soon rot—"

Before he could finish Doyle lashed out at him, sending him sprawling, before he lifted his head and eyed Lykaon.

"I am your master now," the Aramanthan said. "You will not attack until I command you." As Doyle took a step toward him, he frowned. "Desney, it does not obey. Desney?"

Doyle lunged, seizing Lykaon and tossing him into the cages, where the Wolfmen howled and clawed at the bars. He followed, his hands bulging with the mech inside as he reached for the immortal's throat. At the last minute he faltered, looking down at his hand and then turning away. His steps shuffled, and then lengthened, and when he reached a wall he punched a hole through it, stepped out, and was gone.

Lykaon went to Desney, lifting him up to shake him. "Why doesn't it obey me?"

The rude little man's head lolled to one side, revealing the gruesome angle of his broken neck.

The Aramanthan made a disgusted sound, dropping the dead man before opening several cages. "Come, my soldiers. We have a new recruit to tame."

Dredmore would not listen to me as he led me out through the back of Lykaon's ghastly Wolfmen factory. "The inspector is still alive, and has a far better chance than we of prevailing over Lykaon, or of escaping on his own."

"We have to find him and bring him to Docket," I insisted. "He'll know what to do to get the mech out of him."

Dredmore stopped. "Charmian, you saw the transformation. That device is now inside Doyle's body. Removing it without killing the inspector is impossible."

"Not if we obtain some of Lykaon's blood. Its healing powers will restore him, I know it will." What I didn't know was how we would manage taking it. "Isn't there some spell you can use to put him to sleep, or freeze him again, long enough for us to funnel some blood out of him?"

"The only reason the first freezing spell worked was because he was not expecting it. He will be on his guard now, and counter any magic I attempt to use against him." Dredmore marched me out into the alley, where Connell and a carri were waiting for us. "We will consult with Harry as to what may be done for the inspector."

"Harry, oh, God." I tugged at him. "Lykaon trapped him in the body of a street boy. He's still somewhere inside."

"I will go and retrieve him." Dredmore lifted me into the carri. "You will stay here."

I was exhausted, frightened, and angry, but I wasn't going back in that club ever again. "I'll wait."

Dredmore said something to Connell before he went back into the building. The minutes seemed to drag as I watched for him, and then saw him emerge alone.

I jumped out of the carri. "Where is he?"

"Not in the club. He escaped during the commotion." Dredmore glanced down the street. "He will not have gotten far. We will find him."

"He won't walk about in the open; he'll look for someplace he can hide until daybreak." I thought for a moment. "The park."

Dredmore had Connell drive us round the block and make a circuit of the park's borders, but it was too dark see anything from the street.

"Connell, stop. I'm getting out." When Dredmore frowned, I said, "He can't see me in the carri." I reached for the door handle.

He stopped me. "May I remind you that Lykaon and the Wolfmen are out there as well?"

"Sod them," I said flatly. "Harry is stuck inside a helpless little boy. I'm not leaving him here."

"I'll go with you." Dredmore removed his cloak and draped it over my shoulders. "Don't argue, Charmian. You're white as chalk and ready to drop."

I did take his arm as we started into the park, and peered at every shrub and flower bed we passed. "Lykaon imprisoned Harry in a stone and made the boy swallow it. As soon as we find him, we have to get the stone out."

"That can be done with a finger down the throat, or a spell to prompt Nature to take its course." Dredmore stopped at the fountain in the center of the park and turned. "Try summoning him."

I closed my eyes, sending out my thoughts, but felt no response. "Maybe he can't hear me inside the stone."

"You are too impatient." He guided me to a bench. "Harry heard and watched you all the years he was imprisoned in your nightstone pendant."

I hadn't told him that, now or in the time before Zarath had possessed him. "You didn't discover that in your dreams. Who told you?"

"Harry did." Dredmore chafed my cold hands between his. "He also said you were captured and taken to a native village, where you were adopted by the shaman who has been attacking you. I assume they traded you to Lykaon for their sacred relic."

"He didn't give them the real War Heart." I scanned the perimeter of the fountain. "It's not in the club, either. I looked for it."

"I expect the Aramanthan will have moved it to a safer location." Something rustled behind us. "You may come out now, Harry. It's safe."

"Safe my tiny ass." The street urchin climbed out from under the bench and stood up to brush some leaves from his garms. "I saw that wretch running after that cop with a herd of his beasts. I'd have stopped him"—he gazed down at his body in disgust—"if I weren't the size of a blasted monkey."

"You're perfect." I picked up the boy and hugged him tightly before I sat him on my lap. "But you have to come out of there before the possession becomes permanent, and then we need to help Doyle." I explained what had happened to the inspector.

"That's not good news." Harry clambered down and paced in a small circle. "If I dispossess the boy now, dawn will render me powerless. We may not find Doyle before sunrise." He skipped a few steps and stopped in surprise. "It seems my host has no objection to sharing his body a bit longer."

"In a day his spirit will begin to wither and fade," Dredmore warned. "I believe he will mind that."

"Do you think I want to be a helpless child again?" Harry demanded. "I'd rather spend the next fifty years driving *you* about town."

"Boys." I smiled brightly at both of them. "There's a beater coming toward us."

The patrolman walked up with his trunch in hand, but as soon as he saw us he tucked it into his belt loop. "Sir, madam. Bit late to be in the park, don't you think?"

"We'll be departing shortly," Dredmore said. "You can be on your way."

"Now don't be cross with the nice officer, dear." I drew Dredmore's cloak round me as if I were cold to better hide the state of my gown. "It's our little boy, sir. You see, he begged to take a turn in the park. Had quite a fit about it, in fact. I told my husband it was an indulgence, but he insisted the boy will sleep better." I turned to Dredmore. "Didn't you, darling?"

"I suppose I spoil him now and then." Playing along, Dredmore seized Harry and sat him on his knee.

"You're a lucky lad, then," the beater told Harry. "Every time I threw a tantrum as a boy me da would only give me a thrashing."

"Mortals," Harry muttered, and yelped as I gave him a surreptitious pinch. In a higher, sweeter voice he said, "I am, sir, thank you."

I saw the beater frown and realized Harry's grimy face didn't fit his part. "We'll go home and put him straight to bed now, Officer, after I give him a good scrub." I held out my hand to Harry, who grabbed it and leapt down. "I don't know how my boy manages to get himself and his garms in such a dreadful, dirty state. Why, to look at him you'd think he was nothing more than a street urchin."

"Aye, he does look the part." The beater eyed Dredmore. "It'd be best if you abide by the curfew, sir, and keep your wife and boy home. Until the hostilities are done the militia'll be patrolling the streets with us, but we'll be occupied with rounding up the heathen population and carting them off to detainment."

"What hostilities?" Dredmore asked at the same time I said, "Why are you arresting natives?"

The beater looked incredulous. "Everyone was notified by tube. Didn't you get the curfew order?"

"Our port is being repaired," I said quickly. "What has happened, Officer?"

"Well, the tribes have surrounded the city, madam." He gestured toward the east. "They've blocked all the roads and set up camps."

Dredmore also looked to the east and then at me. "For what purpose?"

"I don't know all the particulars, but my sergeant said they're wanting something that was stolen from them," he said, scratching the back of his neck. "They've told the mayor he has until tomorrow night to send it back."

"And if he doesn't?" Dredmore asked.

The beater eyed me. "Begging your pardon, madam, but you might want to take the boy for one last turn round the fountain."

I nodded, taking Harry's hand and walking slowly about the fountain. When I returned the beater had gone, and Dredmore looked grim.

"Well?" Harry said. "What do the heathens say?"

"If their relic is not returned, the tribes will march on the city." Dredmore looked to the east. "At which time they've promised to kill us all and burn Rumsen to the ground."

CHAPTER SEVENTEEN

The curfew prevented us from searching for Doyle, and the tribal blockade made a successful retreat to Morehaven improbable. Since Lykaon had discovered my identity, I could not go to the office or my goldstone, which left only one safe haven for the three of us.

"You can't bring a little one in here, Miss Kit," Wrecker said from the door slot. "Some of the gels are still engaged, and the rest are lolling about half dressed."

"I'm not a child, you idiot," Harry said before I could persuade Wrecker. "Nor is there anything in there I haven't seen a thousand times over in the flesh and spirit. Now open the bloody damned door."

"He's my grandfather," I put in. "And he is—only temporarily—trapped in this body. The boy he's possessing won't actually see anything. I know how mad this all sounds, but please, Wreck. We need help."

Wrecker eyed Harry. "Can't pick your family, more's the pity."

Rina's man took us to an unoccupied parlor, where I dropped in a numb heap onto a chaise while Dredmore checked the windows and Harry began eating from a box of bonbons.

"The natives must have somehow discovered the relic was fake." I covered my eyes with my hand. "Blue Fox knew, and so did Night Snow, but they wouldn't have told them. Everything hinged on them believing they had the real skull."

"He is not the only shaman to the tribes," Dredmore said as he came to cover me with a velvet throw. "I daresay another exposed him."

I lowered my arm. "We have to find Doyle, the real War Heart, and stop Lykaon and the Wolfmen. How are we going to do it?"

Rina came in and slammed the door. "I can't believe you're back again. Do you people have no other place to congregate?" Her gaze dropped. "A child. In my brothel? *Kit.*"

I didn't bother to get up. "Rina, you remember my grandfather. Harry, say something unchildlike, please, before she tosses us all out the door."

"You needn't shout at her," Harry said. "Gel's had a very trying night."

"He looks nothing like your grandfather," my friend said, glowering. "What he looks like is a kid."

"Well, I'm not. I don't know exactly how old I am; I came into my prime round when that young messiah chap you mortals fuss over so much was born. His mum did deliver in a manger—poor gel, no money at all—but the bit about the star and the three kings?" Harry grimaced before he shook his head slightly.

"You knew Jesus Christ?" Dredmore seemed amused.

"Not personally," Harry admitted. "Although I did bump into him when I left Egypt. Nice fellow, lots of friends. Decent carpenter."

"I need a drink." Rina headed for the libations cart.

I sat up and made myself focus. "Right, let's have at this. Lykaon is using the War Heart to bespell the Wolfmen and Tommy. We have to find it first, and once I break the spell we can attend to everything else." I looked at Harry. "You know Lykaon. Where would he have moved it?"

"I don't know him that well, but I can track the magic back to the source," he said. "I'll need to begin at the spell's end." When he saw my face he added, "One of his Wolfmen will do."

Rina thumped down her brandy decanter. "You are *not* bringing one of those beasts into my house."

"We don't have to." I regarded Harry. "Could you track the magic from a child sired by a Wolfman?"

He thought about it. "I can try."

After some bickering Rina took us to Janice's room, where I explained what was needed.

"I don't know how my bun can help, but as long as it won't harm him . . ." She pushed back her covers.

I boosted Harry up to sit beside her, and watched as he placed his small hand on her bulging belly. "I don't remember her being so, ah, plump," I murmured to Rina.

"She's been swelling up like a balloon ever since she stopped puking," Rina muttered back. "I thought it might be bloat, but she says it's the baby. Claims you can even feel it kicking now."

"It is the baby," Harry told her, and smiled at Janice. "The ward I placed on the unborn speeds growth, so we can have it out of there quickly, before the protection wears off. Won't harm the babe." He moved his hand and his brows rose. "Make that very quickly."

"Can't wait to see the little rabbit," Janice confessed. "Kicks so much, has to be a boy."

A glow rayed out from Harry's short fingers, and then he removed his hand and nodded. "He's moved it to a house at the top of the Hill. Big, fancy place with white columns and a circular drive. Lots of red and blue flowers about it."

"Is there a bronze statue of a portly man with no chin in the center of that drive?" Dredmore asked. When Harry nodded he turned to me. "I'll have to go and retrieve it."

"If you try carting it about Lykaon will know," Harry warned. "Take Charm with you. She can break the spell there."

"I don't think I'll be admitted to the house," I said. "But Lucien, you can open a window, surely."

"Unless the militia has been sent to guard the household," Dredmore warned. "Then even I may not be permitted access."

"Why should you have to climb through a window?" Rina demanded.

"Because Lykaon hid the skull in the Lord Mayor's manor," I told her.

Before we set out for the Hill I had to tidy myself up. This also required the loan of a gown from Rina, who after seeing my arm volunteered to play lady's maid. She also rebandaged my arm and fashioned a new sling for me.

As she replaced my boots with a pair of more ladylike slippers, she glanced up at me. "How long has it been since you've slept, or had a meal?"

"I don't know." I let my head fall back on the backrest of the dressing chair. "I don't care."

"You're blaming yourself for Doyle. Don't look at me like that, I know how you are." She put down one foot and started on the other. "The fact is you didn't put him in that contraption, and you didn't magic it inside him. So leave off the self-flagellation. You didn't ask him to go in that club after you."

"That's because you did." As her hands faltered I smiled a little. "You also told Dredmore where I was. How else could they have known I was there?"

"One's a copper, the other's a mage," she scoffed. "Probably just came to them through the usual routes."

"What I can't fathom is how *you* found out I was there. None of your girls service that club"—I paused as she muttered something filthy—"and the servants are too afraid to be bought. I'd say one of your johnnies must be a member. Who is he?"

She gave me a defiant look. "Doesn't matter who he is. He owed me a debt, so I cashed it in." She went back to fussing with the slippers. "Wouldn't fancy him turning into a beast anyway. Doesn't get any from the wife, so he'd probably bash in here, hurt my gels, and wreck the place."

"I think when I break the spell Doyle's going to die." I sat up and inspected my slippered feet. "That will be on both of us. You for sending him, and me for killing him."

"Aye, but he's a tough one, our inspector. He may surprise you." She stood up and helped me to my feet. "You look very good in my gown. Try not to rip this one to pieces. Wait." She plunked an enormous hat on my head and secured it with a ruby pin. "Keep your head down and maybe her ladyship won't know it's you."

I wasn't too tired to tell her how I felt. "You are the sister I should have had."

"I love you, too." She gave me a brief, hard hug. "Go on with you. The deathmage is waiting, and he's making everyone jumpy."

I went downstairs to meet Dredmore, who gave me a nod of approval before leading me out to the carri. Connell took the back roads to avoid the curfew patrols on the mains but was stopped on the service road to the Hill by a band of militia.

"Turn it back, lad," one of the sentries said. "There'll be no deliveries tonight."

"Wait, Connell." Dredmore got out and had a few words with the soldier.

I watched the suspicion gradually fade from the sentry's broad features and then the dazed smile appear before he waved back the other men.

"No worries," he called out, "this one's got clearance."

As we went through the roadblock I brushed an ostrich feather out of my eyes. "When this is all done, I may need you to have a chat with my neighbor about a borrowed horse."

He took my hand in his. "Charmian, the spell Lykaon cast will be more pure and powerful than any you've encountered before now. If there is a backlash—"

"It will do nothing to me," I said. "You, on the other hand, had better stand clear."

Raynard Manor stood at the peak of the Hill, a very large jewel in the crown of the grandest houses ever built for Rumsen's ton. I knew the governor was a frequent guest, as were most of the minor royals who came over from the queensland. Balls held by the mayor were rumored to be the most expensive and exclusive on the Hill, and were known to last as long as a week.

We were not permitted to drive up to the house, but instead were braced by a quartet of heavily armed nobbers guarding the gates.

"I have this," I said to Dredmore, and leaned out the window. "I am Charmian Kittredge. My companion and I have been summoned to attend to the mayor's wife."

"I heard about you from Jimmy." One of the nobbers pushed back his cap. "You're the one what kept Herself from being attacked, he said." He eyed Connell. "You and your friend can go up, but the carri and driver stay here."

I nodded. "That's fine."

He opened the door for Dredmore and then helped me down himself. "Sorry about the walk, but Herself don't like any mech near the house. Says the noise gives her the headache."

"I wish I could blame mine on that." I took Dredmore's arm and started up the drive. Two footman with stony faces stood flanking the entry, from which the most elegant butler I'd ever beheld emerged to greet us.

"Good evening, milord, milady." He sketched a perfect bow. "I regret to say the family has retired for the evening."

Dredmore drew a stone from his pocket, murmured something low and then reached out his other hand. When the butler took it said, "Who is inside the house?"

The spell he cast caused the butler blinked once before his face cleared and relaxed. "Her ladyship, the household staff, and several men with guns."

"Keep your head down," Dredmore told me before he asked the butler, "You were told by these men to turn away anyone who came to the house?"

"Yes, sir." The man beamed. "If I do not, they will shoot her ladyship and the servants."

"Guards for the skull," I murmured. "Where are they?"

When Dredmore asked him, the butler confirmed that two men were with the servants in the dining hall, and a third was watching Lady Raynard in her bed-chamber, where she had retreated in hysterics and bolted herself in. "The rest are in his lordship's study with the animal bones they brought to the house."

Five men were going to be difficult to lure out of the room. "Did you happen to bring an extra rat?"

"I have better." He removed his coat and vest, and rolled up his sleeves. He then unwound his neckcloth from his throat and tied it over the lower half of his face. Brandishing a pistol, he took hold of my arm. "A pretty new hostage to deliver."

Dredmore told me his plan before having the butler lead us through the house to the mayor's study.

At a nod from Dredmore, the butler knocked once, opened the door, and bowed. "Gentleman, another ruffian has arrived. He has a hostage." He bowed a second time and stepped out of the way.

By now I was an old hand at playing the abducted wench, and added to my repertoire by wrenching away from Dredmore and running straight at one of the men inside.

"Please, don't hurt me," I begged, sagging against him.

"What's all this then?" he said over my head.

Dredmore shot him in the leg. "You've been relieved." He turned and fired four more times, dropping each man before he could react.

I played helpful hostage by collecting all the weapons they dropped and placing them on the tray brought in by the butler. "Lucien, the others will have heard the gunfire. You might take a strategic position in the hall. Take some of these ruffians with you." I smiled at the butler. "Could you assist with the wounded, sir? And summon those nice lads guarding your drive."

"Right away, milady."

Once the butler and Dredmore were out I secured the door and looked over at the War Heart. I knew wolves had heads approximately equal to that of mortals, but this skull had to be twice that size. Otherwise it was simply an ancient, brittle dry thing that made my skin crawl a bit.

I steadied myself. As soon as I placed my hands on the bones, the spell would be broken. Doyle would be freed of the wolf's spirit, but he could not survive the stress of the mech inside his body. The strong suit would kill him from the inside out.

Could I do this? Could I end the life of such a man as Tommy Doyle? My head was sure, but my heart wanted none of it.

A shadow passed across the window behind the desk, drawing my eye an instant before the glass shattered round a bulging fist. Motors whirred as Doyle smashed his way through and stepped over the windowsill.

I saw no reason in his eyes, and when I called his name he did not react. I tried to get to the skull, but he blocked me. "Tommy, please. It's the only way I can help you now. I'm sorry."

He looked past me at the door, and then grabbed me and jumped back out through the window.

CHAPTER EIGHTEEN

Doyle ran down the hill in giant, terrifying leaps, holding me against his chest as he descended. Beneath his skin I could feel the mech flexing and stretching with every movement, and it only made him stronger and faster. Soon the world blurred round us as he ran into the streets, jumping over carris and at times to the tops of buildings. I closed my eyes, too frightened to watch any longer.

We came to a stop, and leaves brushed against my hair. I looked to see the White Lupine beneath us, as well as the thick bough of a tree.

Doyle set me down and crouched in front of me, his eyes searching my face.

I turned my back on the club and gripped the branch to keep from tumbling to the ground. "Did he send you to bring me back?"

His lips peeled away from his teeth as he uttered a low growl, and then reached for my hand, which he jammed against his cheek.

"All right." I wasn't sure what he was trying to do, but I'd take that as a gesture of friendship. Then I saw some of the wildness leave his gaze and realized why he wanted the contact. "You can't feel the wolf spirit when I touch you."

What started as a growl became a word. "Y-yes." He pulled me closer. "Kit."

"You're all right." I wrapped my arms round him. "Oh, Tommy."

He shook his head as he drew back. "Too. Hard. Master." He stared at the club. "Calls. Me."

"You don't have to obey. You can resist him. You did before, remember?" I brought his hand to my cheek. "You got out of there."

His features grew tormented. "Kit. Don't run." He gathered me up and dropped down to the ground, rolling with me into the bushes.

Branches snapped and scratched me, and a shower of leaves pelted me as Doyle pressed me against the hard, cold ground. The sound of quick, heavy footfalls and a faint grind of gears turning made me squint through the patches of shrubbery until I could see the walkway, and the two beasts trotting toward us. As Doyle covered me with his heavy body, I held my breath and prayed they wouldn't discover us.

I went as still as Tommy when they drew near, holding my breath as I stared at their monstrous faces. Both were panting, sending great clouds of breath through their snouts out to whiten the cold air, and the spell that had transformed them had been completed, arming them with nightmarish brass teeth and long, gleaming scythe-like claws.

One paused and sniffed the air, causing the other to growl and snap at him. They collided in a brief, vicious tussle before their bodies began to shake and they tottered apart again.

Lykaon had done something to prevent them from fighting each other—improved on the mechanism inside them, perhaps. That did not enhance our chances of escape.

After another minute of lingering and sniffing, the Wolfmen headed in the direction of the Hill. I almost groaned with relief; they'd picked up the scent Tommy had left carrying me off but were following it backward.

Once the beasts had disappeared from sight, Doyle rolled onto his back, bringing me to rest atop him. "He hunts me. You."

I cradled his face between my hands. "I won't let him have you. I'm going to fix this, do you understand?"

He used a clumsy caress to brush the hair out of my face, and said in an almost normal voice, "You can't fix me."

I didn't want to hear any more of that, so I kissed him. His mouth hadn't changed; it still tasted as hot and darkly delicious as the first time. He was still Tom Doyle, my childhood friend, my reluctant ally . . . but that wasn't enough for me now.

I wanted to bring him back to the man he had been. The man he still was. The strong suit had not been changed by Lykaon's magic, or programmed by that horrid man Desney, but the Aramanthan's blood and spell had taken away Tom's humanity. I needed to disenchant him, inside and out.

He brought his arms up round me, gripping handfuls of the back of my borrowed gown, and I lifted my head when I heard it tear.

"No." He brought one hand round to rest it over my breast. "I am not. A beast."

So he wanted me, too. The more he touched me, the more human he became. If I pushed him away now, he would fall once more under Lykaon's spell. I had to bind him to me in ways that the immortal never could, with chains of love and delight—that much magic Dredmore had taught me.

I knew what I was about to do was a betrayal of my feelings for Lucien. But I loved Tommy as well, and I was responsible for what had happened to him. I had to make this right. I knew the risk I was taking; it could very well end in disaster for me. But losing Tom to madness, to Lykaon, would be far worse than anything that could happen to me.

"You are a man," I told him, putting my hand over his. "My man. And tonight I am your woman."

He pulled my head down to his, and I gave in to my own desire. His mouth ravished mine so sweetly I had to feel more where I ached most, and pulled down my bodice to bare my breasts for him.

He nuzzled me, soothing his hot face against my cooler skin, latching on to suck gently. I reached down to pull my skirts up so I could straddle him, and he helped by tearing open the front of his trousers.

"Oh, yes." My eyes fluttered at the press of his body between my thighs. My drawers parted as he stroked against me, and he went still as he felt the slickness of me touching his shaft.

There was nothing so human as lovemaking, I thought, and smiled at him. "I want to feel you inside me." When his features took on a desperate tightness, I shifted forward, catching the distended bulb where it needed to go. "Come into me, Tommy. I need you."

He pushed, pausing to close his eyes and savor it before he pressed in. The lovely satisfaction of being filled made my fears dwindle to nothing, and I kissed his mouth as I sank down to his root.

Sweat trickled from his brow as he eased back and forth within me, the gentle friction causing me to shudder and grip his shoulders. He was watching me, his eyes once more that clear, heavenly blue, and as my excitement built I felt completely naked to his gaze, bared in every sense and feeling.

His hands gripped my bottom as he began to work me over him, going harder and deeper into me, and I writhed like a mad thing, clamping down on him as the pleasure rushed over me. He drove into the center of it, bringing me a release so bright and strong I thought I would shatter like a glass dropped on stone.

He went rigid, pressing his face against my breasts as his seed pulsed into me, and then cradled me, his breath rasping in and out as I let myself go limp. I'd brought him back to me, I knew it instinctively, and that made the slow waves of satisfaction spread through my heart as well as my limbs.

Once I could find the strength to lift my head, I rested my chin on his chest and watched his face. He wore an expression of utter contentment, his eyes drowsy, his mouth curved slightly.

"I was right about you," I whispered, and brushed a kiss across his throat. "You are quite the man."

"You are shivering." He sat up slowly, holding me as he pulled my bodice up over my breasts. He then rubbed a hand over his face in such a human gesture that I grinned, and he smiled back. His expression turned dark as he saw the bandages protruding from my cuff, and he pulled back the sleeve before giving me a direct look.

I wanted to tell him it was nothing, but that would be like saying we hadn't a care in the world. "I had a spirit stone cut out of my arm. Another gift from Lykaon."

His eyes took on a different light now. "It will be the last."

"Not just yet, Tommy," I said. "I have one left to give him."

Doyle took me back to the Hill at the same reckless, effortless pace, demonstrating that the strong suit was still working perfectly, but when we reached Raynard Manor he refused to come inside.

"I must stop the Wolfmen." He glanced down at the city. "They have caused enough suffering."

"Wait." I tugged some hairs from my head and tucked them into his shirt pocket. "For luck."

He brought my hand to his lips. "Thank you, love."

As I watched him speed down toward the city I heard the door open behind me. "I found Doyle," I said, "and broke the spell binding him to Lykaon. He's going after the Wolfmen." I didn't know how to say we'd become lovers behind a bush in the park. "Lucien—"

"I beg your pardon," an indignant voice said. "What are you doing here?"

I turned to face Lady Raynard, who was dressed in a

green gown with so many flounces she resembled a walking cabbage. "I'm sorry, milady, I thought you were . . . never mind." I glanced past her. "Is Lord Dredmore still here?"

"No, he is in jail. You will kindly leave the premises at once, or I will have you join him there." She marched back into the house.

The butler caught the door and looked out at me. "I'm sorry, milady, but her ladyship summoned the authorities. Your companion was taken along with the ruffians. I will be happy to attest to his innocence as soon as the house is restored to order."

"Thank you, sir," I said, clenching my teeth to keep from relating my real opinion. "What happened to the skull?"

"Her ladyship had one of the stable hands remove it from the house." The butler glanced over his shoulder before he added, "Unfortunately the man was also arrested when the police saw him leaving. I believe they are detaining all the natives in the city."

Dredmore would have to be bailed out later. "Does the stable hand's name happen to be Night Snow?"

The butler looked uneasy. "Her ladyship does not approve of non-Christian names and insists we call the natives by their position."

Of course she did. "Was he called Trainer?"

He smiled. "Yes, that's it."

I walked down the drive and greeted the nobbers, all of whom looked as if they'd gotten an earful from her ladyship. "Lads, do any of you know where they're detaining the natives?"

"I'm not sure, miss." He nodded past me. "Maybe you should ask that one."

I turned to see Night Snow driving Dredmore's carri, and grinned as I hurried over to him. "You got away from the police."

"He had some assistance, my dear." The door opened, and Lykaon stepped out and leveled a pistol at me. "If you run or call for help or do anything besides getting in the vehicle, I will shoot you."

A blanket-wrapped bundle the size of the War Heart sat on the bench next to Night Snow. "He's been using you all along, hasn't he?"

The native didn't speak or look at me, but once I got into the carri Lykaon was happy to gloat.

"You shouldn't feel any bitterness toward the heathen," he said. "It took only a flick of my power to have him steal the War Heart and the wolf spirit spell along with it. He doesn't remember anything I've made him do."

I kept my tone pleasant. "You had him bring the skull to Raynard Manor for safekeeping."

"That did not require a spell," Lykaon admitted. "I had only to tell him what he'd already done, and promise to tell his tribe if he did not obey me."

I regarded him. "I wonder, what will you do when the other Aramanthan are reborn? I daresay you won't be able to bespell or blackmail any of *them*."

He smirked. "I will have restored them to the world. For that they will worship me."

"I should think they'll all want to be in charge," I said. "None of your lot are especially subservient. It is why your race was destroyed, isn't it? Too many chiefs, not enough stable hands?"

Instead of hitting me, Lykaon chuckled. "Merlin would have told you such tales of us. It is not entirely unexpected. He has ever been a hypocrite, and now he is quite powerless."

"Yet he escaped you," I pointed out, "and he did that in the body of a helpless child. Kings are not usually so easily defeated. If fact I can't think of a single one who has been outwitted by a small boy."

The Aramanthan's mouth distorted into a sneer. "You will not provoke me into anger, hell child. I know the shaman adopted you as his daughter, and told you how to bring the wolf spirit under my control. The young heathen confessed it all."

"Now you need *me* to secure your kingdom. I see." I closed my eyes. "You really should rethink these plans."

I needed to conserve what was left of my strength, so I allowed the sway of the carri to lull me into a doze. I'd never been one to wallow in regrets, and while I'd acted on impulse with Tommy in the park, I was not sorry for it. Nor for my time with Dredmore before I'd destroyed that. Both men had their place in my heart, and I'd cherish each memory for as long as I could.

My nap ended with the abrupt braking of the carri, and I looked out to see the road leading into the city filled with natives dressed for battle, each carrying a flaming torch. On the opposite side of the road, a man in a tweed suit stood by a carri and seemed to be watching the advance of the natives through a short telescope.

Lykaon climbed down and offered me a hand. "It is time for you to do your work, Miss Kittredge."

I ignored his hand and got out. From here I could see the Wolfmen pouring out of the city a mile beyond, their jaws snapping and their claws slashing. Night Snow came down from his bench carrying the bundle, which Lykaon took from him.

The native warriors closed ranks and gave a terrifying shout as they raised their spears and bows. The approaching Wolfmen answered them with savage howls.

"My soldiers will fight until the death," Lykaon said, "but without the proper spell they stand no chance against the heathens. Once they have been defeated, the tribes will attack the city."

"We have a militia," I told him, measuring the shrinking gap between the two armies as intently as the man in the tweed suit was. "They will defend the citizens."

"My Wolfmen have been hunting your soldiers all night," Lykaon said. "Their bodies already litter the streets. You cannot save Rumsen unless you have my Wolfmen to protect it—and that I will not do until you give me the spell."

Blue Fox and the tribal chiefs were riding at the front of the attacking warriors, I saw, and closed my eyes. "I gave my word to the old shaman. I can't betray him like this."

"Do you think that heathen cares anything for you, Miss Kittredge?" Lykaon leaned close. "He gave you to me to get the skull. He knew I'd kill you before you could work the spell. He wanted you dead."

I shook my head. "He wouldn't use me like that. He was kind."

"It was all a ruse, to manipulate you and me," Lykaon assured me. "All that old man has ever wanted is the skull. It's the only real power he has left—and you are handing it over along with the lives of everyone you care for."

"If you give him the skull, he won't attack the city," I insisted.

"Then why does he need the skull now? Why did he bring all these warriors to surround Rumsen, if he sent you to defeat me?" Lykaon shook his head. "You have been a fool, my dear. I am the only one who can save you and your people now, and you know my price."

I gnawed at my lower lip. "If I tell you how to work the spell, will you promise to spare the city?"

"I give you my solemn vow," he said. "Only the natives will die. As they should, for their treachery."

Slowly I reached for the carved shell pendant Blue Fox had given me, and removed it from my neck.

"You must wear this," I told him. I waited until Lykaon slipped it over his head before I said to Night Snow, "Put the War Heart on the ground and uncover it."

The young native gave me a bleak look before he set down the bundle and removed the blanket.

I started to walk off, but Lykaon latched on to my arm. "You are not running away."

"I am *moving* away from you," I told him, "so that I won't disrupt the ritual. As soon as I do, wait until you see the first rays of sunlight, and then cast the binding spell again. Oh, and you must hold the pendant high above your head, to send the spirit where it belongs."

He scowled. "My soldiers are already bound to me."

"You're not binding them to you," I said, pointing at the pendant. "You're binding the spirit to that. Then whoever wears it controls the spirit. Forever."

"Go with her," Lykaon told Night Snow, and tossed a dagger to him. "If she tries to escape, slit her throat."

As we walked away the young native stuck the dagger in his belt. "You are very brave, miss. Very . . . convincing."

I gave him a nudge with my elbow. "You did rather well, too, I must say."

CHAPTER NINETEEN

We stopped and turned as the sun began to rise, and Lykaon raised the pendant and began to chant. As the Wolfmen reached their master they encircled him, howling with delight as War Heart became illuminated by bloodred power. One by one they fell silent as the pendant began to glow.

Night Snow cringed a little. "I have never seen this done."

"I have," I said. "Lykaon did it to my grandfather just the other night. Pity he didn't look closer at the pendant." I nodded at the man in the tweed suit, who had turned his telescope on us. "Friend of yours?"

"Bureau man," Night Snow said. "He reports to the mayor."

"Oh, how convenient," I said. "I'll have to give him a note of apology for Lady Raynard."

Yellow light shone out from the carved shell in Lykaon's hand, and fell round him in a vivid swirl. It also cast a glow on the young native warrior who came up behind the immortal and thrust a spear through his body.

Lykaon staggered, but the light held him like a cage. The end of the spear impaling him caught fire as the pendant fell from his hand. He spun about until his gaze caught mine.

"What have you done to me?" he roared.

"I forgot to mention," I called back. "The spirit that is being bound isn't the wolf's. It's actually yours."

The Wolfmen began to drop in their tracks, one by one, their bodies going limp as a scarlet mist rose from their chests and flew toward the War Heart. The approaching tribal warriors also halted, their faces growing solemn as they watched the wolf spirit returning to their relic.

Lykaon's body began to shake. The color of his flesh dulled to gray, and began to flake off like ash, bit by bit. When he tried to grasp the spear, his arms fell away from his shoulders, and hung from it like ghastly trophies. The morning breeze caught the ash and set it adrift.

"It cannot end this way," the Aramanthan howled. "It cannot—"

I felt certain he would have said more, but his jaw chose that moment to fall from of his face and disintegrate. I looked away and saw a familiar figure emerge from the native ranks, the wind dancing along the feathered edge of his blue cape.

As Lykaon's body deteriorated, his spirit rose from his ashen remains, battering the cage of light, which began to shrink, smaller and tighter until he was trapped in a terrible bright light no bigger than a pebble.

Beside me Night Snow tensed, and I patted his shoulder. "This is the best part."

The light danced for a moment before it was sucked into the shell pendant, which fell to the ground at the feet of Blue Fox.

With great dignity the shaman bent and picked up the pendant by the strip of leather and held it up to show the warriors, who let out a tremendous cry of victory.

The sunlight warmed my face as I walked over to the Wolfmen. Some had already died, but many were still breathing. I suspected the mech in their bodies would slowly poison their blood; without Lykaon's magic they could not survive. The only true relief I felt was not finding Tom Doyle's face among them.

I turned to see the red glow of the War Heart fade away, until all that remained was an old, brittle wolf skull. It still made my skin crawl, but then, most bones did. It made me glad I hadn't let Blue Fox adopt me. I really would have made a terrible native woman.

Night Snow escorted me back to where Blue Fox stood waiting, and the shaman held out the pendant to me. "My thanks, Miss Kittredge."

I put the pendant round my neck before I walked over to the skull. I gave Blue Fox a final glance—he nodded at me—before I picked it up and carried it back to present to him.

"The people of Rumsen are very sorry this was stolen from your tribe, Blue Fox," I said for the benefit of the chiefs watching us. "Please accept it with our apologies."

He bowed to me before he carried the skull off to the waiting chiefs.

The now very pale man in the tweed suit rushed up to us, stopped short, and then gave me a little wave. "Excuse me, miss, but is this, ah, settled, then?"

I eyed him. "And you are?"

"Toby Gervais, Bureau of Native Affairs." He

pointed to a group of other pale, nervous-looking men standing off in the distance. "We were sent to observe the, ah, whatever this was." He bobbed his head. "How do you do?"

"Very well, Mr. Gervais." I glanced at Blue Fox and Night Snow before I smiled at him. "And yes, I believe everything has been settled quite amicably." I noticed a familiar-looking carri racing out of the city and toward us at great speed. "At least with the natives."

Dredmore couldn't drive over the unconscious Wolfmen, now transformed into their mortal selves, so he walked round them to get to me. Then he snatched me up and kissed the breath out of me.

When our lips parted I looked up at him. "Who bailed you out of jail?"

"Mrs. Eagle." He glanced at the mess on the ground. "Lykaon?"

"All tucked away in here." I held up the pendant to my ear. "Do you know, I think he wants to go for a sea bathe."

Dredmore watched with me as Blue Fox and the tribal chiefs retreated eastward with the War Heart, followed by their warriors. "So you gave them back the skull."

"I promised the shaman I would." I yawned. "I don't think Blue Fox will be using it again, unless he needs a lampshade or something."

Dredmore turned to me. "What did you say?"

"I *gave* it to him, Lucien. I picked it up with my own hands and carried it to him. Just after the wolf spirit returned to it." Which had been for the very last time.

"Indeed." He examined me. "And no backlash."

"I told you." I brushed a bit of burned Lykaon from my sleeve. "There never is."

Dredmore wanted to take me to Morehaven, of course, but I wished to sleep in my own bed. I told him that several times as we drove back to the city before my eyelids refused to stay up and I slid into a deep and dreamless sleep.

I woke up in Rina's bed at the Eagle's Nest, with my friend fussing over me like an old hen. "Now this time you can't scold me. I told Lucien to take me home."

"You needed someone to look after you, love." Rina brought me a cup of tea. "You've been out for three days straight. Bringing you here was his way of compromising, I guess. Doyle's been by to look in on you, too."

I choked and nearly spilled the tea down my front. "Tommy's alive?"

"Bit banged up from fighting them Wolfmen, but nothing too serious." She frowned. "What?"

"He still has the strong suit inside him?" When she nodded I sat back. "If the wolf spirit isn't binding him, and Lykaon isn't controlling him, then what's keeping him alive?"

"Will to live, I'd say." She chucked me under the chin. "Told you the lad was a tough one."

Lad. I bolted upright. "God in Heaven— Harry. With all the madness I never gave him a single thought." I reached for her hand. "Please tell me he's not still trapped inside that child."

"He is not, and for that you may thank me and my bottle of gut-toss," Rina said. "Didn't hurt Harry or the kid. I sent the lad over to John Halter; he'll see to his schooling and keep until he's old enough to get work."

I wanted to sleep for another week, but I'd imposed on Rina long enough, and forced myself out of bed. Once I'd dressed and had an enormous breakfast with Rina, Wrecker drove me home. The last person I expected to see sitting on the steps of my goldstone was Annie. She stood up and peered at me as Wrecker helped me out of the carri. I smiled as I saw her absently reach to twist the apron she wasn't wearing.

"It seems I have company," I told Rina's man. "It's all right, I can take it from—oof." Suddenly I was being hugged like a rag doll.

"Milady told us what you done for the city. Getting caught between them natives and the Wolfmen was foolish, reckless, and shoulda got you killed dead, Miss Kit." Wrecker drew back and straightened my hat, his expression softening with fondness. "I don't know how you do it. You're like a cat with all them lives."

"Cat, fox, something." I shrugged. "Thanks for the ride, mate."

Annie didn't wait for me to reach the steps; she trotted over and bobbed quickly. "Milady said I was to watch for you and tell you straightaway when you come. I didn't want to leave her when it started, but that sister showed up and said she'd manage everything—"

I held up my hands. "Slow down, Annie. What's started?"

"It's the baby, miss," she said. "Herself is having it, right now." She grimaced. "Um, in your bed."

"Now?" I rushed past her, pausing only to toss my

hat and reticule on the hall table before running back to my bedchamber.

Sister James was coming out of the room with an armful of stained linens. "There you are. Milady was hoping you'd come home soon." She beamed. "Everything went very well—and very fast for a first child, too."

"The baby was born? How? It's hardly a minute old." I recalled Janice's swollen belly and Lady Bestly's age. "Is her ladyship going to be all right?"

"She did beautifully, and the baby's fine, too," the sister said. "You can go in and see them if you like."

I hardly knew what to expect when I stepped in, but it was not to see Lady Bestly sitting in my rocker chair and cooing to the small bundle in her arms. As soon as she spied me she gestured for me to come closer.

"I have delivered a son," she said with a touch of her old arrogance. "I was waiting for you to return when the pains started. I thought Hartley might have to deliver the boy when Sister James arrived." She held out her arms. "Go on, Kit. He doesn't bite."

With great reluctance I took the surprisingly heavy bundle from her, and looked down at the wee glowing face of the sleeping infant. Golden hair covered his little round head, and as I smiled he opened his eyes and stared up at me. "He has your eyes, milady."

"He has rather more than that," she said dryly.

A little arm worked its way out of the swaddling, and gears whirred as the tiny, golden mechanized hand attached to it swiveled, grasping the air.

"Oh, God." I sat down in the chair beside hers and opened the swaddling. His left foot was also made of mech, and in the center of his chest was a pocket watch–size medallion of gold.

"Sister James believes your grandfather's spell to protect the babe caused the unique fusion," his mother told me. "Christopher must have already been changing when it was cast. Harry saved my son, Kit."

I glanced at her. "Can the mech be removed?"

She shook her head. "Not without hurting and crippling him. Sister examined his differences with a magnifier and found they are all part flesh. She believes they will grow with him, although we shall have to keep close watch for any malfunctions."

I regarded the baby boy, who was watching my face with his solemn blue eyes. "I don't know what to say, milady. I know my grandfather never intended to do anything more than protect him. I'm so sorry."

"My son is alive, and so am I. As Terrance's heir he inherits the estate. We now have a future, thanks to you and your friends. Christopher will be a very unique young man, but no less adored because of his differences." She gave the baby a fond look. "Indeed, I think him superior in every way."

I wrapped the blanket over the baby before I carefully returned him to his mother. "Christopher was my father's name."

"As well as my own." She chuckled. "And you said we had absolutely nothing in common."

CHAPTER TWENTY

After assuring Eugenia that she would not be permitted to leave my bedchamber—or the premises—until she had fully recovered, I went to see to rooms for Sister James and Annie. Before I'd bought the goldstone it had been home to several other families, so I had enough rooms to house a dozen visitors.

Once I'd made up the beds I went in search of Annie, whom I found preparing a meal downstairs.

"I hope you don't mind me taking over your kitchen, miss," she said as she rushed from stirring a pot on the stove to punching down a crock of dough. "I didn't think Herself would be able to leave with the baby and all, so I figured I'd cobble up some morning tea and get a start on luncheon."

I peered at the pot. "I didn't think I had any food in the house."

"Oh, you didn't, miss," Annie assured me. "Sister James sent me with a list to the market right after the baby came." She smiled shyly at me. "Right handsome lad, isn't he? All that gorgeous hair, 'twas like spun gold."

I thought of the baby's more unique features. "He's quite exceptional."

"You needn't worry about his little gadgetry parts," Annie said, astonishing me. "There's gloves and shoes aplenty, for while he's little, so no one makes merry over them. World's gone so modern that by the time he's growed up I expect everyone will have them."

"Annie, I doubt any other babies will be born with . . ." I trailed off as I remembered Felicity and Janice, and all the other women who had been attacked by the Wolfmen. "Oh, Harry." I sat down on one of the kitchen stools and held my head in my hands.

"There, there, now, miss." A flour-dusted hand awkwardly patted my shoulder. "T'wasn't your doing, you know. You and Mr. Harry saved all them children from becoming monsters." She crouched down before me to look in my eyes. "Sister and me and the others, we'll look after them."

A terrible suspicion seized me. "You and Sister and what others?"

"She did tell you there were more of us," she said, standing and nodding at the stove, where the pot of soup was presently stirring itself.

"You're spirit-born." A giggle escaped me. "And you can cook with your mind."

"Here, now." Annie helped me up from the stool. "What you need, miss, is sleep and lots of it. Sister and I'll manage, and I'll wake you in time for dinner."

I nodded tiredly and trudged to the door. Before I stepped out, I glanced back at Annie. "Just how many others like us are there? Do you know?"

She made a face. "Can't count so good." She looked round the kitchen and pointed to the wall. "They stored grain in the walls here once, didn't they?" When I nodded, she said, "There are more of us than that."

My eyes widened. "You mean, more than the amount of grain it takes to fill the wall?"

"All the walls in the house, miss," she corrected. "And maybe some of your neighbors' walls."

I couldn't count that high, I thought as I trudged upstairs to make up one more room for myself. Although I meant to stay closer, my feet kept going until I was on the top floor in my old flat. My renovations hadn't reached this level, and aside from some furnishings I'd carried down to my new quarters, the flat was almost exactly as it had been when I'd lived in the building as a tenant.

I was too tired to strip the bed, so I pulled back the slightly dusty coverlet to air the sheets, and opened the hearth flue to let some of the heat from downstairs warm the room. In the dresser I found a threadbare sleeping gown to wear and draped it over the drying stand by the hearth as I undressed.

Lady Bestly had been the first woman Lykaon had used as a vessel; in the days to come dozens of women would be delivering the children Harry had bespelled.

"Sister James is going to be very busy," I muttered as I drew the old gown over my head. Something tickled my neck, and I reached to pull it out of my collar. The leather thong no longer held the carved shell pendant, but now sported a black feather with a deep blue sheen and three greenstone beads tied to its quill.

"Pretty pendant," a low voice said, making me jump. "I like it much better than the other one."

I closed my eyes for a moment. "Tommy Doyle, if you stood there and watched me undress without saying a word, I'm going to report you for a peeper." I took the feather over to the dresser and dropped it into the drawer before I turned round. "How are you?"

"Heavier than I was. I've broken six mugs and two chairs since I've gone back to work." He came into the room and inspected it before fixing his gaze on my face. "My memory is a bit fuzzy, but I know I owe you my life."

I batted the air. "Next time we're near a tea cart you can buy me a sticky bun."

"What about the park?"

"What about it?" I glided round the bed, putting it between us. "You were bespelled by Lykaon. Magic has a strange effect on the mind and the memory, and you're not believing a word of this. Right." I sat down on the bed and looked down at my hands. "Why couldn't you have been mindless? It would make things so much simpler."

"No, it wouldn't." He came and sat down beside me. "Kit, when that blood magic told hold of me I fought it with everything I had, everything I am. I've never been so angry or frightened or enraged in my life, but I could do nothing. It was horrifying to be so helpless, and then I was sent after you. I thought I would see you die at my hands—not feel you welcome me into your arms."

"I didn't know what else to do." I leaned against his shoulder. "I had to bring you back."

"I think you saved my sanity as well as my life." He took something out of his pocket and placed it in my hand, holding his palm over it. "I'm not the grandson of a duke. I'm a cop, and when I'm not being meddled with,

I'm a good one. I live simply in a house much like this one, no debts or obligations, no mistresses or bastards to support. I'll marry in the eyes of God and Church, which means no divorce." He took away his hand.

I stared at the plain gold wedding band on my palm. "Tommy, you don't have to do this just because we—"

He put two fingers against my lips. "What I'm asking is for you to think on it. Consider what your life would be like as my wife. You know I'd never lock you in a house or try to stop you from your work, any more than you'd keep me from mine. I'd trust in you and I'd never give me reason to doubt me. I swear to you, Charmian Kittredge, that I'd be a good and faithful husband to you until the day I die."

"Of course you would." My eyes stung, and I blinked back hot tears. "But . . . you don't have to do this."

"I want to. I want you to be my wife." He cupped my chin, raising it to place a gentle kiss at one corner of my mouth and then the other. "What happened between us in the park made me realize how much. You opened your heart and your body to me, Kit. Would it be so hard to let me in again, and have me stay?"

"No." I could see myself as Tommy's wife; as clear and true as if we'd already stood before the vicar and made our promises. He wouldn't be a good husband; he'd be the best of them.

He eased back and smiled at me. "Now go to sleep. You look as if you're ready to drop. I'll be back for an answer in a few days."

He kissed my brow before he left, and once he had I fell against the pillows and groaned. "A baby and now an offer of marriage. I am never getting out of this bed again."

I rested my cheek on the pillow as I looked at the ring Tommy had given me. It wasn't new, as I feared, and when I looked inside the band I saw a worn inscription in elegant script: *To B. from yr loving A.* It was his grandmother Beatrice's wedding ring, of course. Somewhere in Heaven Uncle Arthur was probably chuckling himself pink.

I placed it on the nightstand before I put out the lamp and stared up at the ceiling. Arthur Doyle had instilled a strict code of honor in Tommy; naturally he wanted to make an honest woman of me. We'd gotten along famously as children and I very much liked the man he'd become. He wouldn't expect me to stay home and have his children, not unless that was what I wanted. As his wife I'd come to want that. We'd probably make beautiful babies together.

I closed my burning eyes. Every bit of sense in my head said yes, marry him. I'd be loved, and I'd be safe.

Love isn't about being safe, Charmian.

I'd fallen asleep, and a fat lot of good that did me. *I'm tired*, I told the sparkling darkness swirling round me. *Go dazzle someone else.*

You listened to the inspector. Dredmore emerged from the whirlwind, raising his hand to release a burst of silver sparks. *Now you'll hear me.*

It's very rude to eavesdrop on private conversations. I turned my back on him. *And it's nothing to do with you.*

On the contrary. Doyle has an advantage over me now. Cool hands alighted on my shoulders. *But I have prior claim.*

Despite what the Crown thinks of women I'm not a piece of property to be squabbled over or seized. The way he was caressing my arms was making my knees weak. *Nor should you be coming to me in a dream.*

It's the only way I can get to you. Dredmore turned me round to face him. *Inspector Doyle is a very good man. He would make a fine husband for any woman.*

I glared up at him. *Really, Lucien, you're not helping.*

Allow me to finish. His hands cradled my face. *You're not just any woman, Charmian.*

I knew what was coming. *Don't say it. Once you do, you can never take it back.*

I know. He sounded as grumpy as I felt. *But it has to be said now, before you do something you'll regret for the rest of your days. Marry me, Charmian.*

No, no, no. I banged my head against his chest. *Bloody hell, why did you have to say it?*

You know you can't marry Doyle because you're not in love with him. He stroked the back of my head. *You haven't accepted it yet, but you're in love with me.*

Light flared between us as Lucien set me at arm's length and used his hands to capture the sparkling air. He shaped it, his long fingers spinning it smaller and smaller until it formed a ring.

This is my heart, he murmured, drawing back. *You've had it since that day in the market, and whatever you do, it will always be yours.*

The ring drifted toward me, and when I reached up it nestled onto my palm. I peered at him. *You're asking me to marry you only because Doyle proposed.*

I'm asking you to marry me because I love you, Charmian.

Miss.

Miss.

"Miss?"

I hurtled myself out of the dream by latching onto that voice, and opened my eyes to see Annie frowning over me, and the sunlight of dawn streaming into the room. "No. Yes. Sorry, I'm awake."

"Almost couldn't find you, miss." She gave me an unhappy smile. "Some gentlemen came to call on you. I've put them in your sitting room with a tray of tea."

I had an image of Doyle and Dredmore glowering at each other over my crockery. "Who are they?"

"Never seen them before, miss," Annie admitted. "But they look important."

I rolled off the bed. "Tell them I'll be down in a few minutes."

I had no clothes stored in my old flat so I was obliged to dress in my damp, soiled gown. I dragged my fingers through my curls to fluff them and checked my reflection. I looked as bedraggled as an alley cat after a rainstorm, but it couldn't be helped—everything I needed to restore an illusion of respectability lay in the room with Lady Bestly and her baby.

I heard the men talking as I came downstairs, and squared my shoulders as I entered the sitting room. There stood three nobs from the Hill, all in fancy evening dress.

I cleared my throat to interrupt what sounded like the beginnings of an argument. "Good morning, gentlemen. I'm Miss Kittredge. How may I be of service?"

The oldest gave me a hard look. "You're the dispeller who defeated the Wolfmen and struck peace with the natives?" Before I could answer he said to the youngest man, "This is nonsense, Dickie. She's hardly out of the schoolroom."

"Augustus." The middle of the trio, a quiet-looking chap with calm eyes, put a hand on the oldest man's arm before coming to me and bowing low. "I am Lord Raynard, Miss Kittredge. It is an honor to meet you."

"Lord Raynard, the mayor?" When he nodded, I dropped into a hasty bob. "Forgive me, my lord, I—I'm an idiot."

"I have had many reports about you, Miss Kittredge, and that is not how you were described to me." He gestured at the other men as he introduced them. "Allow me to introduce Lord Augustus Chapel, my city manager, and Viscount Richard Logen, the city treasurer."

Lord Chapel looked as if he were making the acquaintance of a skunk. "Kittredge."

I bobbed again, but not as deeply. "Milord." When I turned to do the same for the viscount he grinned like a boy and grabbed my hand before I could tuck my foot back again.

"Delighted to make your acquaintance, Miss Kittredge." He shook my hand, patted it, and seemed prepared to cover it with kisses before a harrumph from Chapel put a small damper on his enthusiasm. "Forgive me, I have heard so much about you, and none of it was exaggerated in the slightest. You are a scintillating vision."

"I try never to scintillate before tea, sir. It makes me queasy." I regarded the mayor. "To what do I owe the honor of this visitation from the city government?"

Raynard gestured for me to sit down, and Logen set about pouring me a cup of tea. Chapel wandered over to the window, peering out and frowning as if not quite sure where he was. I switched my attention to Raynard, who sat across from me and kept his expression pleasantly bland.

"Dickie, Augustus," the mayor said, "I think it best that I have this conversation with Miss Kittredge alone. Why don't the two of you take a turn in the garden?"

"There is no garden." Chapel glared at the back of the mayor's head and then at me. "Why should you be alone with the gel when we know all about it?"

"I should like a turn outside. I've never been in this part of the city. Oh, come on, Gus." Logen trotted over and ushered the old man out.

"That'll cost you an earful later." I drank some tea before I set aside the mug. "But now you have no witnesses."

The mayor inclined his head. "I am by nature a cautious man, Miss Kittredge. Most politicians are." He set his elbows on his knees and linked his hands. "Three nights ago the commander of the city militia reported to me that the native tribes had retreated back to their territories."

"That must have been a relief." I picked up a scone and nibbled off one corner.

"Indeed it was, as well as somewhat confusing," Raynard said. "A few hours before this report I received word that the tribal chiefs had declared war on Rumsen, and had sworn that they and their warriors intended to burn the city to the ground, or die every man trying."

I swallowed and coughed a little. "They must have thought better of it."

"Not according to a rather bedraggled agent from the Bureau of Native Affairs who arrived shortly after the commander," the mayor continued. "Mr. Gervais had witnessed everything, and reported that the hostilities had ended thanks to a young woman who had exterminated a small army of beasts, defeated their commander, and returned to the tribes some sort of sacred property. Thus the city is intact, peace has been restored, and evidently we owe this all to you. We came to officially express our gratitude, and we will, as soon as one matter is clarified." He leveled his gaze at me. "How did you do it?"

"It really wasn't an army of beasts," I said slowly. "Certainly there were a few of them, and I did break the spell that was controlling them, but it couldn't be helped."

He sat back. "And the sacred property was . . . ?"

"That? An old animal skull. Nothing you or I would call sacred, although I'm sure it has a great deal of sentimental value to the tribes." I smiled wanly. "You know how natives are with their animal bits."

His mouth thinned. "Is that all the explanation I'm to expect?"

I took another sip of tea. "It's all I can offer you, milord." I picked up one of the cake plates. "Unless you'd care for a crumpet?"

Over tea his lordship the mayor and I came to a swift and mutually amicable agreement: neither of us would explain to anyone how Lykaon's Wolfmen had been defeated or why the natives spared Rumsen and returned to their lands. Raynard would order to silence the commander, the Bureau of Native Affairs agent, and lords Chapel and Logen, while I would say nothing about the matter to anyone for as long as I lived.

"I sincerely wish I could present you with a key to the city or some other form of recognition for your courageous intervention, Miss Kittredge," Raynard said, choosing his words with great care. "There is no doubt in my mind you have earned that and more. However, questions would arise that would almost certainly compromise our agreement, particularly where the press is concerned. Indeed, I am rather relieved that I will be retiring at the end of my term in office."

I had no need of medals or keys, but the mayor wasn't getting off that easy. "I want something that is within your power to grant." I told him what I wanted, and when he frowned I added, "My name need never be mentioned in connection with the change in the regulation. You may present it as your own notion."

He gave me a sharp look. "You are aware that in doing this I will be reviled by every man in the city."

I nodded. "It is a good thing you are retiring."

"Considering what was demanded of you last night, perhaps it is fair compensation." He stood and held out his hand. "I shall see it done by the end of the week. You have my word."

"Thank you, milord." I tried not to look at the window where I spotted Lord Chapel peering in at us. "I believe your companions are ready to rejoin us."

"Let them sit on the stoop." Lady Bestly swept into the room wearing my best dressing gown. "Hello, Raynard. I might have known you'd make an appearance."

Raynard's jaw dropped. "Eugenia, what on earth—"

"Should you need an official excuse as to why you called on my young friend, you may use me," she continued. "Last night when I called on her my pains began and she very generously saw to my comfort. You may congratulate me, for I now have a son."

"I think I need to sit down." Raynard dropped back into his chair.

"Nor should you be scampering about the house, milady." I went to guide her to the chaise and pour a cup of tea for her. "The scones are very good. Annie is a fast learner."

"She's had to be, thanks to the ton." Lady Bestly regarded the mayor with impatience. "Oh, do collect yourself, Foxy. You are the mayor. Try to act like one."

Foxy. In my mind I heard it differently; squealed from the mouth of a rat. *Fox hee.* "How did you acquire such an interesting given name as Foxy, milord?"

"It's Foxworth, actually, after my mother's family." The mayor cleared his throat. "Eugenia, I should like to see this new boy of yours."

"That won't be possible, milord," I said before Lady Bestly could answer. "In fact, I must ask you to leave now."

Lady Bestly gave me a quick look before she said, "Yes, perhaps you should, Foxy."

I accompanied the mayor to the door, where he paused. "I do regret any disturbance I have caused you, Miss Kittredge. You understand in all that I do, I have only the best intentions for our great city."

"I know you were the one who sent the rats after me," I told him flatly. "I know you won't admit it, and

I'll never prove you did. But if it's the last thing I do, I'll find out why."

"I cannot claim responsibility for your vermin problem, but I am sorry for it." He pressed a card into my hand. "Should you ever need to contact me, this is my private tube number."

I crumpled the card in my fist. "You think I'd ask you for even the time of day?"

"Do you know the funny thing about intentions, my dear, is how easily they can be misguided? Such as being persuaded that an extraordinarily gifted person is using their talents for evil, and then discovering quite the opposite. Such as when that gifted person saves the life of a much beloved spouse. Twice." He doffed his hat. "Good day, Miss Kittredge."

I stood there long enough to compose myself before returning to the sitting room. I dropped the card onto the table, picked up a crumpet, and took a large bite.

"Foxy isn't a such a bad chap, you know," Lady Bestly said as she refilled my cup. "He could be very helpful to you in the future. Such as when he passes the change of regulation next week."

I set down my crumpet. "You were eavesdropping?"

"I did no such thing. I merely delayed joining you so you could finish bargaining with the mayor." She gave me a serene look. "Now what sort of carri are you considering buying once you are issued your new driving permit?"

Acknowledgments

The adventure of launching a new series brings with it a towering heap of work; while working on *The Clockwork Wolf* I was blessed to have these folks to provide invaluable and unstinting assistance:

My guy and my family, who always do whatever they can to make room for my writing life, bail me out of housework, make dinner, do laundry and still cheer me on. I suspect I will never love you as much as you deserve, but I'm going to try.

My editor, Adam Wilson, who by now probably needs a strong suit of his own. Thank you for being the kind of editor a writer dreams of working with, and for always being willing to help with anything no matter what I ask.

Author Jeff Somers, wicked marvel, superb writer and splendid chap, has my eternal gratitude for being so great, so talented, and so patient. This is the man whom you want to make a book trailer for you; trust me on this.

My loyal readers and regular visitors at my Paperback Writer and Disenchanted & Co. blog, who have always been so enthusiastic and supportive of my work, but never more so than with this series. I owe you more than you can imagine, thank you so much.

Finally, author Darlene Ryan should get combat pay for being there for me with this novel, especially during that moment with the pink thing (the dedication is not nearly enough, but for now it will have to do).

Torian Glossary

abstainers: religious agnostics

across the pond: When in Toriana, a reference to Great Britain or Europe; when in Great Britain or Europe a reference to Toriana ("pond" being the Atlantic Ocean)

aid-solicitor: legal representative provided by the Crown to defendants who can't afford to hire a barrister

ambrotype: photography that uses chemicals (silverblack) to etch images on glass plate negatives

animech: mechanized animals

annum: year

apothecary: pharmacy

Aramantha: the island homeland of the Aramanthan, destroyed by mysterious forces which caused it to break up and sink beneath the sea

Aramanthans: a race of superhuman magic practitioners who ruled the world before the rise of mankind

GLOSSARY

bacco: tobacco

barrister: attorney

bathboy: a male attendant/masseur who works at public baths for women

beater: a uniformed police officer who patrols the streets, usually on foot

believer: someone who believes in magic

belowground: beneath street level

binding: a stone or other object that can contain psychic energy until its release is triggered by touch or proximity

black: very strong, thrice-brewed tea

blackpot: a coal-fueled boiler

blacks: formal suit worn by high-class male servants

Blind my Cupid: an vulgar exclamation of amazement and disbelief

bloodbane: one of the highly toxic magic poisons used in snuffballs

blower: a chamber that uses air leeched from the city's tubes to dry wet items

blue ruin: gin

blues: people of aristocratic birth

bookmaker: printer

braves: warrior class of native Torian people

BrewsMaid: an automatic tea maker

brickie: a bricklayer

bronze, bronzen: a theatrical cosmetic that temporarily darkens the skin

brown: Talian currency

bruiser: a large or physically intimidating man; thug

bucks: clothing made of buckskin

bum: ass

calendula: an herbal tincture used as a topical disinfectant

care kit: first-aid kit

carri: steam-driven carriage

carriwright: maker of steam-driven carriages

cartlass: a girl or woman who sells food and/or beverages from a portable cart on the street

cashsafe: a hidden, locking recess in a private home where money and other valuables are kept

catchall: an extending/grasping device with a pinchers at one end

Church: the Torianglican Church, the only religion recognized and approved by the Crown; the Church of England

clearstone: quartz

clopboard: building siding made of planks recovered from abandoned horse barns

coal burner: engine that runs on coal

coddles: cod cut into chunks

coin: money

collar: vicar

commoner: an ordinary, untitled individual; someone of low birth

conciliator: mediator

cosh: bludgeon

crispie: potato chip

croke: croquet

Crown, the: the English monarchy as well as its authority over Toriana

crowswalk: a viewing deck that encircles the upper portion of a building

dear: costly

deathmage: magical practitioner licensed to kill

deb: debutante

detector: a magic practitioner (generally employed by the court) who uses touch to discern truthfulness

digger: miner

dink: a small or short man

dipper: strip of treated paper that changes color when exposed to poison or drugs

drawers: underwear

drips: syphilis

Druuds: mortal magic practitioners who captured and imprisoned the Aramanthans to end the mage wars

ducklings: children

echo: device used to detect hidden objects

elshy: hellchild

entitlement: inheritance of title and property

exormage: exorcist who nullifies curses and rids people and places of demon infestation

faeriestale: fantasy stories told to children

fete teller: the humblest of fortune-tellers who set up tents at village fetes to do many readings for very little money

fichu: a shoulder wrap, usually made of lace

firebrigader: firefighter

fishncrisp: a shop that sells fish fillets fried together with potatoes cut in various shapes

flat: apartment

GLOSSARY

flathouse: a building that has been divided up into flats

Fleers: remnant members of the American rebel forces who fled west after losing the war to England

flystick: a clear glass rod containing live lightning bugs, used like a flashlight or lantern

foundling: abandoned orphan

freeclaiming: a social practice caused by the shortage of women among the original colonies, which allowed men to kidnap and hold captive unprotected or abandoned women

freedman: ex-convict

fry bread: bread fried in bacon drippings

furrin, furriners: slang for *foreign, foreigners*

garms: garments

gaslamp: exterior lighting powered by natural gas

gel: girl (common, casual, generally used to refer to females of the merchant class)

get the sack: be fired

gildstone: marble

ginger: woman with red hair

glass: common term for ambrotype glass plate negative

glassed: photographed

glasshield: windshield

glassies, glassines: protective, preservative glass coatings applied to documents

glasslung: terminal respiratory disease caused by inhaling sparkglass; suffered by painters and construction workers

gogs: protective eyewear

goldstone: building made of blocks of pyrite-flecked granite

gone off: suffered a mental breakdown

gowners: dressmakers who specialize in creating gowns for wealthy society women

gravecart: hearse

Great Uprising, the: Toriana's name for the failed revolutionary war against England

Great War, the: Toriana's version of WWI

hair grips: bobby pins

hatch drop: manhole access to underground tunnels

hellchild: a child believed to be demon-possessed and therefore impervious to magic

Herself: slang term for the queen of England

hidey-holes: small, concealed places in houses for people to hide in or use to spy on someone

Hill, the: an area of Rumsen where most of the wealthy and titled reside

H.M.: abbreviation for Her Majesty

hothead: woman with red hair

illuminator: a device that works like a primitive film projector

Independence: freedom from English rule

johnnies: men who hire prostitutes

keep safe footing: to be cautious or conservative

keroseel: a combination of seal, whale, or fish oil and kerosene

keyfob: a chain-and-loop key ring, carried by men

keylace: a ribbon key ring, worn around a woman's wrist

kipbag: mesh tote

kneecappers: criminal enforcers who use clubs to shatter the knees of their victims

knickers: underwear

lampflies: fireflies

lass: girl (affectionate, proper)

lav: lavatory

loo: toilet

GLOSSARY

loomgel: a girl or woman who works in a menial position at a textile factory

loomworks: textile factory

loon: a mentally disturbed person

loon herder: an orderly at an asylum

loonhouse: asylum for the mentally disturbed

Lost Timers: brigades of English and Italian soldiers who became lost in the Bréchéliant forest and were there possessed by Aramanthari spirits

lungfever: slang for influenza

mage: magic practitioner

magis, magistrate: judge

maiden night: the first time a virginal woman has sex with her husband; term often used for betting purposes by men who want to break an engagement

mariners: sailors

matchit: a disposable, one-use lighter

mate: friend

mech: a mechanic; anything mechanical

mechworks: mechanical rooms

mercantile: a shop selling some variety of merchandise

GLOSSARY

Middleway: industrial Torian city located on the Great Lakes; also called Middy

mixpot: mixing bowl

mole: city underground worker

nappy: diaper, women's panties

navyman: a current or former member of H.M.'s naval forces

necktwister: assassin

negli: negligee

netherside: the spirit world, invisible to ordinary mortals; the source of magic power

new industry: the beginning of the industrial age in Toriana

New Parliament: governing body of Torian officials who petition the Crown and enforce the Queen's legislation; the Torian version of Congress

nightstone: a semiprecious mineral used to contain the spirits of long-dead mages and Aramanthan wizards

Nihon: Japan, Japanese

nits: head lice

nobber: private security guard hired by Hill residents to patrol their streets and keep out any undesirables

Norders: people from the North of England

nozzer: nose; a face mask used with a portable oxygen tank

nudie: a flesh-colored garment worn to give the illusion of nudity under a semitransparent gown or overgarment

Occupancy, the: a period of thirty years after the Rebellion failed during which Toriana was occupied by English troops and governed by martial law

on the stroll: working on the streets (said of prostitutes)

pain powder: a mild opiate or analgesic

partymage: a magic practitioner who uses his power to entertain

pasturelands: farmlands

penders: suspenders

physick: doctor

piesafe: kitchen cabinet where food is stored

pin minder: a dresser or vanity stand that holds hairpins and hat pins

piper: plumber

pong: stink

portents: predictions or signs of future events

portints: portraits made from ambrotype photographs that are hand-painted to colorize

posh, posher: wealthy aristocrat

poxbox: diseased prostitute

prayerhouse: the Fleers' religious gathering places

privy: restroom

prodder: iron fireplace poker

prommy: the promenade in the city's central park used by horseback riders and carris

pyre: crematorium

queensland, the: England

Queen's Voice, The: the Crown's official newspaper

questioning: police interrogation at New Scotland Yard

rasher: strip of bacon

Reapers: a secret society comprising important political, business, and social figures in Talia; enemies of the Tillers.

red joy, ruddy joy: opium

redcoats: English militia

redstone: brick

reticule: purse

rondella: an automated carousel-type apparatus

rotagears: gears that drive a rotational device

rounder: a rubber carri tire

rub: massage

Rumsen: major city on the west coast of Toriana, roughly equivalent to San Francisco in the United States

satchel: tote bag carried by women

scrabbler: a person who makes a living by scavenging

scram: salvage

seeing: an act by a fortune-teller of predicting a client's future

seeking: an act by a fortune-teller of finding someone or something

Settle: Seattle

shaman: a native Torian holy man

shelfairs: aerated shelving, usually for books

shopkeep: shop proprietor

short sheet: a hastily printed, illegal daily list of horse races and other events for the purpose of placing bets

silverblack: chemicals used to etch photographed images on ambrotype plates

skip: boat

Skirmish, the: a recent, brief naval conflict between England and Spain

GLOSSARY

slaterow: a row house with slate shingles

snuff: kill

snuffballs: hollow glass spheres filled with magically enhanced poisons like bloodbane that kill on contact, used like grenades

snuffmages: mage assassins who generally work in teams of two

Son, the: Jesus Christ

soother: chamomile herbal infusion, usually added to tea, to relax, relieve stress, and help with insomnia

Southern Church: a Baptist version of Church of England, begun in the southern provinces of Toriana, tolerated by traditionalists

sparkglass: a substance made of various minerals such as mica, galena, and silica that have been ground to a fine dust and mixed with exterior paint in order to create sparkle

spellcraft: the methods and materials used by magic practitioners to cast spells

squawks: slur for native Torian females

stones: testicles

streaky: a carri's copper sideboards from which the black paint is wearing off or has been stripped off to simulate wear

GLOSSARY

strumpet: prostitute

sweet Mary: Mary, mother of Jesus

sweets: candy

switch: wig

Talia, Talian: The Torian universe's version of Italy, Italians

teaheart: heart-shaped infuser

tealass: a girl or woman who sells hot tea and cakes in a café or from a street cart

teller: fortune-teller

tenner: ten-pound note

Tillers: a secret society comprising important political, business, and social figures; enemies of the Reapers

timepiece: watch

tinnery: a factory where fresh fish and other perishables are processed and canned in tin containers

tint: a paper-copy image printed from an ambrotype glass plate; makeup used to redden cheeks and lips

tinter: device used to imprint images on ambrotype glass plates

tintest: a professional ambrotype plate developer and tint maker

to let: available for rent

GLOSSARY

tonners: members of high society

Toriana: short name for Provincial Union of Victoriana, the alternate-history name for the United States

tosser: a drunk

trade: business

trolling: looking for work

trunch: a wooden baton carried by beaters

tubes: a system of pneumatic pipes that deliver goods and food across the city

tunneler: an underground city worker who polices the subsurface tunnels and keeps the city's tube in operation

understair: belowground level of building; cellar or basement

unjammer: a mechanical snakelike device used to unblock tubes

uptoppers: above street level

vermage: a mage who specializes in magical extermination of rodents and other vermin

vicar: priest of the Torianglican Church

waders: thigh-high protective rubber boots

waister: a wide cummerbund-type belt made of fabric

that females wear around their waists to cover the joining of skirts and bodices

warders: magic practitioners who create protective charms and spells to protect people, possessions, and property

wardling: an object used as a protective charm

warren: a tunneler's assigned work area

watershed: raincoat

Welshires: people from Wales

whitecart: horse-drawn conveyance used to transport the wounded to hospital or the mentally disturbed to asylum

wichcart: a street cart that sells sandwiches

willowbark: herbal remedy for headaches and hangovers (equivalent to aspirin)

winge: slang for an older, grouchy person

Yard, the: short name for New Scotland Yard

zoopraxiscope: a device that uses images on glass disks as the first form of stop-motion projection